M000277135

What Makes Some Men Evil?

This is not just another book about serial killers. *Destined for Murder* addresses the question, "why did did they do it?" Was it an aberration in their personalities or was it "written in the stars"? Read the personal stories of Jeffrey Dahmer, Ed Gein, and five other madmen. Is it possible that they each had an astrological "blueprint" for murder? Had their birth charts been cast in childhood, could they have been directed toward different paths in life?

The book is arranged for engrossing reading. In the first part of each chapter, master story-teller Sandra Harrisson Young weaves the tale of each killer: his childhood and family, the murders he committed, and his eventual capture. The second half of each chapter is handed over to professional astrologer Edna Rowland, who follows the pivotal points in the killer's life as they're actually happening—and discovers whether or not these pivotal points were astrologically preordained.

Their findings will astound you.

About the Authors

Sandra Harrisson Young has had a life-long interest in what makes some people evil, and others with similar backgrounds good. Her interest in true crime is counterbalanced with a love of romance. She has found that the two interests are not really so very different for both concern the study of people, their emotions, their character, and their behavior. In true crime, she explores the evil that men do while in romance novels she explores the good of which they are capable. She has written twenty-seven romance novels under the pen name of Brittany Young; of these, twenty-five have been translated into nearly thirty languages and sold in more than 100 countries.

Edna Rowland is an author and astrologer, with astrological articles published in many periodicals including *The Astrological Review, CAO Times, Dell's Horoscope Magazine,* and *American Astrology.* Her astrological interests focus on research in the areas of prenatal and conception charts, life/death subjects, and new methods of chart rectification. Edna also enjoys genealogical research and is the author of *How to Obtain Your Birth Certificate.* She is the 1990 winner of the annual PAI Award for her outstanding contribution to the art and science of astrology.

To Write to the Authors

If you wish to contact the authors, please write to them in care of Llewellyn Worldwide, and we will forward your request. The authors and the publisher appreciate hearing from you and learning of your enjoyment of this book. Llewellyn Worldwide cannot guarantee that every letter written to the authors can be answered, but all will be forwarded. Please write to:

Sandra Harrisson Young / Edna Rowland
c/o Llewellyn Worldwide
P.O. Box 64383-K832, St. Paul, MN 55164-0383, U.S.A.

Please enclose a self-addressed, stamped envelope or $1.00 to cover costs.
If outside the U.S.A., enclose international postal reply coupon.

Free Catalog from Llewellyn

For more than 90 years Llewellyn has brought its readers knowledge in the fields of metaphysics and human potential. Learn about the newest books in spiritual guidance, natural healing, astrology, occult philosophy, and more. Enjoy book reviews, new age articles, a calendar of events, plus current advertised products and services. To get your free copy of *Llewellyn's New Worlds of Mind and Spirit,* send your name and address to:

Llewellyn's New Worlds of Mind and Spirit
P.O. Box 64383-K832, St. Paul, MN 55164-0383, U.S.A.

Destined for Murder

Profiles of Six Serial Killers

With Astrological Commentary

Sandra Harrisson Young

Edna Rowland

1995
Llewellyn Publications
St. Paul, Minnesota

FIRST EDITION
First Printing, 1995

Cover design: Tom Grewe
Book design and layout: Susan Van Sant
Book editing: Margaret Sullivan and Susan Van Sant

Photo Credits:
   p. xii, Ed Gein; p. 26, Jeffrey Dahmer; p. 58, Kenneth Bianchi;
      p. 92, Albert DeSalvo; p. 122, John Wayne Gacy—all © AP/Wide
      World Photos, 50 Rockefeller Plaza, NY, NY 10020.
   p. 150, Dennis Nilsen—photo by Tony Crossley, © Camera Press/Retna
      Ltd., 18 E. 17th St., NY, NY 10003.

Astrology charts generated using *Io Edition* by Time Cycles Research, 27 Dimmock Road, Waterford, CT 06385.

Library of Congress Cataloging-in-Publication Data
Young, Sandra Harrisson
      Destined for murder : profiles of six serial killers with astrological
      commentary / by Sandra Harrisson Young and Edna L. Rowland.
            p.   cm.
      Includes bibliographical references.
      ISBN 1-56718-832-X (trade pbk.)
            1. Serial murderers—Biography.   2. Astrology.   I. Rowland, Edna.
      II. Title.
      HV6245.Y68   1995
      364.1'523'0922—dc20   95-17513
                                                                                    CIP

Printed in the United States of America.

Llewellyn Publications
A Division of Llewellyn Worldwide, Ltd.
P.O. 64383, St. Paul, MN 55164-0383

Acknowledgements

This book was a long time in the making, and a lot of people helped along the way. I'd like to thank literary agent Robin Kaigh for her many hours of invaluable assistance in creating an interesting and original format. I'd also like to thank astrologer Jan Warren Allen for her initial contributions; Connie Pannozo for her patient research and record gathering; and the true crime writers who created paths for others to follow. I'd particularly like to thank my husband, Fred, for his support and encouragement during the months of research when his normally gentle wife was up to her neck in murderers. Last, but not least, I'd like to thank Llewellyn for recognizing an interesting concept and seeing it through to publication.

Sandra Harrisson Young

I'd like to thank Llewellyn's Acquisitions Editor, Nancy Mostad, for her support and inspiring encouragement; also editors Susan Van Sant and Maggie Sullivan for their help in editing and their suggestions for making this book the best that it could be. My husband, John, has been supportive, as always.

Edna L. Rowland

Other Books by the Authors

Sandra Harrisson Young

The following novels were published by Sandra Harrisson Young using the pen name Brittany Young:

Arranged Marriage, Silhouette Books, 1982.
A Separate Happiness, Silhouette Books, 1984.
No Special Consideration, Silhouette Books, 1984.
The Karas Cup, Silhouette Books, 1985.
An Honorable Man, Silhouette Books, 1985.
A Deeper Meaning, Silhouette Books, 1985.
No Ordinary Man, Silhouette Books, 1985.
To Catch a Thief, Silhouette Books, 1986.
Gallagher's Lady, Silhouette Books, 1986.
All or Nothing, Silhouette Books, 1987.
Far from Over, Silhouette Books, 1987.
A Matter of Honor, Silhouette Books, 1988.
Worth the Risk, Silhouette Books, 1988.
The Kiss of a Stranger, Silhouette Books, 1988.
A Man Called Travers, Silhouette Books, 1989.
The White Rose, Silhouette Books, 1989.
A Woman in Love, Silhouette Books, 1989.
Silent Night, Silhouette Books, 1989.
The Ambassador's Daughter, Silhouette Books, 1990.
The Seduction of Anna, Silhouette Books, 1990.
The House by the Lake, Silhouette Books, 1990.
One Man's Destiny, Silhouette Books, 1991.
Lady in Distress, Silhouette Books, 1991.
A Holiday to Remember, Silhouette Books, 1992.
Dangerous Men and Adventurous Women, Univ. of Penn. Press, 1992.
Jenni Finds a Father, Silhouette Books, 1995.

Forthcoming:
Brave Heart, Silhouette Books, 1995.
Mistaken Bride, Silhouette Books, 1996.

Silhouette books are routinely translated into thirty languages and sold in more than 100 countries.

Edna L. Rowland

How to Obtain Your Birth Certificate: With Ready-to-Use Forms, American Federation of Astrologers, Inc., 1990.

Forthcoming:
True Crime Astrology: Case Histories of Famous Homicides and Suicides.

Table of Contents

Preface

– Sandra Harrisson Young

T HIS ISN'T JUST ANOTHER BOOK ABOUT

serial killers. This is a book that asks the question, "Why did they

do it?" More than that, this is a book that attempts to answer that

question. Ed Gein. John Wayne Gacy. Jeffrey Dahmer. Dennis Nilsen.

Albert DeSalvo. Angelo Buono and Kenneth Bianchi. They've had their

bodies probed by medical doctors and their minds picked apart by psychiatrists.

Writers have analyzed their childhoods and connected every trauma they ever experienced to their later becoming serial killers.

A lot of people endure similar childhoods and trauma in their lives without becoming murderers. What made these individuals so horribly different? Could it have simply been their destinies to become serial killers? Was it "written in the stars?"

Perhaps.

Putting this book together has been a fascinating excercise, with one author, myself, knowing little to nothing about astrology but a lot about serial killers, and the other author, Edna Rowland, living a life grounded in astrology with a peripheral interest in serial killers. Neither of us could predict what we'd find when we started this search. The results, as you will see, have been interesting.

The book is arranged for easy reading. In the first part of each chapter you'll learn about the killers, their childhoods, the murders they committed, and their eventual capture. In the second you'll follow the pivotal points in their lives and discover whether or not these pivotal points were astrologically preordained.

Of course, if the only thing required to predict behavior was a study of the stars, all we'd have to do to weed out future serial killers would be to create astrological charts for everyone as soon as they were born. Unfortunately, it doesn't work that way. There are other people with the same birthdates as John Wayne Gacy and Jeffrey Dahmer. They may even have had similarly troubled childhoods. So why didn't they become serial killers as well? Because at astrologically pivotal moments in their lives, they made different choices.

This book, however, isn't about the people who chose different paths. It's about seven killers who followed their astrological blueprints for murder.

Sandra Harrisson Young

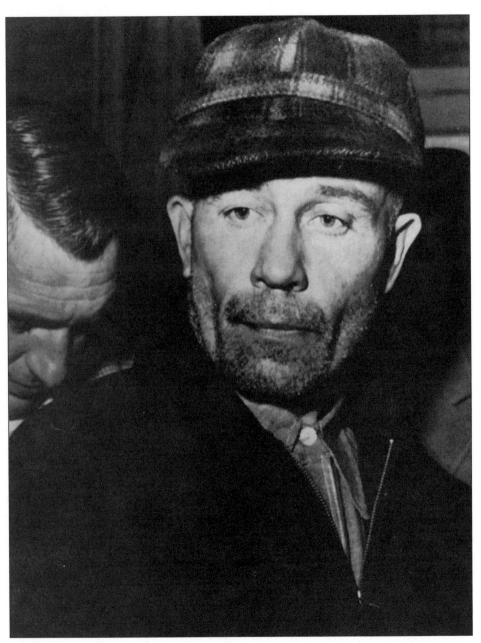

AP/Wide World Photos

Chapter One

The Cannibal Grave-Robber

Ed Gein—His Story

— Sandra Harrisson Young

MOONLIGHT PIERCED THE INKY BLACK-
ness of the November night and reflected off the crusty surface of
snow blanketing the yard of an isolated Wisconsin farmhouse. The
sheriff and police captain stepped cautiously forward. They knew no one
was in the farmhouse. Its owner, Ed Gein, had been arrested a short time

earlier. But that didn't stop them from being nervous. The place was scary. There was no other word for it. It was hard to believe someone actually lived here.

The important thing, though, was to find Mrs. Worden, the missing middle-aged owner of Worden's Hardware and Implement Shop in Plainfield. The only clue to her disappearance was that Ed Gein was the last person known to have been with her.

The two officers, the beams from their flashlights dancing eerily over the dilapidated old house, walked around trying to open different doors. None of them budged.

Except one.

The door to the summer kitchen creaked open. Both officers licked dry, nervous lips and gingerly stepped inside. The beams from their flashlights cut quickly around the cold room. The place was filthy and full of junk. One of the men spotted a door leading to the main house and signaled his partner to follow him through.

As the other officer moved to join him, he bumped into something. Turning slightly, he aimed his flashlight at it.

Tilting his head to one side, a frown creasing his brow, the man passed his beam over what was hanging there. It could have been a side of beef. Or, more likely, a dressed-out deer. After all, this was the first day of deer-hunting season.

He moved the beam of light from top to bottom. There was no head. And as suddenly as that, the officer knew what he was looking at. It wasn't an animal at all.

It was what was left of Bernice Worden.

Ed's parents, George and Augusta Gein, married on December 4, 1899, in La Crosse, Wisconsin. By all accounts (Augusta's included), it was a match made in hell.

Augusta and George couldn't have been more different. Augusta had come from a large German family that lived to work. Her parents were strict in the way they raised their children and held very definite opinions on what was right and what was wrong. It hadn't been a particularly affectionate household, but everyone knew his or her place and held to it. The Lutheran religion was the centerpiece of their family life; a religion that Augusta would adhere to with almost fanatic devotion as she got older, whether it was in an organized church, or on her own when no Lutheran church was available in her community.

Augusta was a very large woman physically, and not at all pretty, with heavy, homely features. She was also a very determined woman who had no difficulty at all imposing her will on others. In Augusta's world, there were no shades of gray; only black and white—but mostly black. She, of course, decided what was black and what was white.

And then there was George, her husband.

Poor George.

When he was only three years old, his mother, father, and older sister were all killed in a freak flood. From that time forward he was raised by his maternal grandparents on their farm in Coon Valley, Wisconsin. Little is known about his early life, but several sources agree that by the time George met the strong-willed Augusta (five years his junior), he was drinking far too much and constantly between jobs. He just couldn't hold onto any kind of employment. He wasn't particularly good at anything and this, frankly, took a toll on his ego. If he initially drank out of habit, he at some point undoubtedly drank to dull the pain of constant failure. In any case, George appeared to have pretty much given up his fight for life long before marrying Augusta—and one can only imagine why he would have selected Augusta for his bride in the first place. By all accounts George was quite a striking man, tall and lean, making up in physical appearance what he lacked in strength of character.

After the marriage, Augusta grew more determined than ever, more self-righteous and unforgiving of faults in others. She grew stronger, as though feeding off George's weakness, haranguing her husband into nothingness day after interminable day. Predictably, George grew weaker, drank more and more, and withdrew further into himself.

Augusta had clearly begun to loathe her husband soon after the honeymoon. Her nagging became so constant and so increasingly vitriolic that George eventually stopped speaking altogether. Fury rose in him over the years with no outlet. He held it inside for so long that it finally burst in him like a faulty dam one night while his wife was verbally laying into him. George beat Augusta. He beat her until she fell on her knees and screamed for his death. After the first episode, it happened with some regularity. Perhaps it was the only time he felt some of his masculinity return to him—he had the power for a change.

What a terrible tragedy for the two of them, and for the children forced to watch. With this kind of rapport, the horror of their sex life can hardly be imagined. Aside from that, Augusta considered sex, even between married people, a vile and disgusting thing. But she wanted a child, and doing the dirty deed was the only way to accomplish this; as a result of Augusta lying there and staring rigidly at the ceiling while George relieved himself inside her, their first child, Henry, was born in 1902. Their second and most infamous child, Edward Theodore, was born on August 27, 1906.

Augusta was bitterly disappointed. She'd desperately wanted a girl. She'd prayed for a girl. How could she have ended up with yet another boy? It wasn't fair—not after what she'd had to subject herself to in order to become pregnant.

But it was, indeed, a boy, and her last child. She wasn't about to go through any of that again. So Augusta decided she'd have to do the best she could with the hand dealt her. Her relationship with her first son had already grown distant by the time little Edward came along. She'd sort of set Henry on the shelf while she waited for her daughter to be born, and on a shelf he remained for the rest of his life. Little Eddie might not be a girl, but she could raise him like one. She would raise him to be just like herself. It was almost as good as having a girl.

Almost.

But as had happened to her husband and everyone else in Augusta's life, Eddie couldn't live up to her expectations. No matter how hard he tried, he was never good enough. And Augusta never hesitated to let him know it.

Harold Schechter, in his beautifully researched book about the Ed Gein case, *Deviant*, tells the story of an Eddie no older than seven being sent on an errand by his mother.[1] She'd given him some change to buy bread from a nearby bakery. But he'd lost the money, as a child sometimes will. It took him a long time to work up the courage to go back home and face his mother with neither the bread nor the money. He was heartsick and sobbing. Augusta looked down at him, the expression on her coarse-featured face one that told the boy more eloquently than words that his failure, once again, was a deep source of sorrow to her, but expected nonetheless. He was, after all, a boy. "You dreadful child," she said, "only a mother could love you."

The little boy believed her. His mother was everything to him. Unlike his worthless father, she worked hard. She was smart. She never made mistakes. His mother was perfect, and more than anything in the world, Eddie wanted to be worthy of her.

Eddie never had a chance.

In the same book, Schechter mentions what might well have been a pivotal moment in Eddie's young life, a moment that may have profoundly affected his later actions. His parents ran a small meat and grocery store in La Crosse. Behind the store was a small wood shed that had no windows. Eddie wasn't allowed to go inside the shed. But one day, as boys will, he sneaked out to it and looked inside through the door, which had been left open just a little. A dead pig was hanging from a rafter by a chain. His father held the pig still while his mother skillfully disemboweled it. Sensing her son's presence, she turned to look at him, her hands and her leather apron glistening with blood.

It was a scene Eddie remembered even as an old man.

In 1913, when Eddie was seven, the Geins moved to a new home just east of La Crosse. They lived there for only a year before moving to a 195-acre farm in Plainfield, Wisconsin. The farmhouse was a two-story white frame with two bedrooms, a sitting room, and a kitchen on the first floor, and five rooms upstairs. Added to the end of the house was a summer kitchen which could be accessed by a door in the regular kitchen. The property also held a barn, an equipment shed, and a chicken coop. The house had neither indoor plumbing nor electricity.

Augusta was meticulous about her housekeeping. Everything was kept orderly and spotless. Even the smallest messes were intolerable to her. The finest pieces of furniture went into the sitting room—but not necessarily to impress guests. Guests in the Gein home were rare.

Augusta liked her new home. In fact, one of the things she particularly liked about it was that it kept them about as far away from other people as it was possible to get and still remain part of a community. She liked no one and trusted no one. She never had, really, but her hatred of others grew more intense and unreasonable as the years passed— perhaps a sign of her own increasing mental instability. She had faith only in herself and her particular version of God. Since there was no Lutheran church in Plainfield, she kept to her own religion at home. The residents of Plainfield were woefully beneath her high standards, as the absence of a Lutheran church conclusively demonstrated, and she kept as far away from them as she could.

Eddie stopped attending school after the eighth grade, when he was sixteen years old. School wasn't a very pleasant experience for him. His classmates were normal kids who came from normal families. Eddie had always been different, and no matter how hard he tried, he could never quite fit in. Part of the problem was his extreme shyness. Part of the problem was his inability to relate to their very normalness. But the lion's share of the problem was Augusta. Every time Eddie started to make a friend, she'd put an end to it.

There was also the fact that Eddie was, frankly, considered a little weird by his peers. He was rather effeminate—never a popular trait among strapping farm boys. He cried at the drop of a hat and didn't join in normal boy-talk about girls. In fact, he went out of his way to avoid it. He laughed at odd moments—a cackle, really—even when being told of tragedies. It might have been nervousness, or it might have been a sign of his growing insanity, even then. He had a lopsided grin that he wore constantly, as though his face were made that way. He also had a growth of some sort at the edge of his left eyelid that made it droop. Kids being kids, he was teased about it.

For the most part, Eddie was on the outside looking in, and it was perhaps in self-defense that he decided he didn't particularly like what he saw. He didn't care if the kids didn't like him. He didn't like them either. They were wicked. He knew this because his mother told him so. He didn't want to be their friend. The only friend he needed (or had) was his mother. His mother, with her almost pathological hatred of other women—women whose appearance and lack of morals she constantly ranted about, quoting Bible verses over and over again about what vile creatures they were. Augusta continuously warned both of her sons against any kind of involvement with women. They were all bad. All evil.

That kind of psychological bombardment would have been difficult for the strongest mind to withstand. Apparently Henry did make an attempt to struggle against Augusta's beliefs. But Eddie, instead of struggling, bent to his mother's will. Eddie believed everything his mother said. His mother would never lie. His mother was never wrong. His mother was the most wonderful woman who ever lived, and no other woman could ever measure up to her.

Eddie's father died in 1940. Both boys were glad to see him go. For most of their lives he had been more of a burden than a responsible parent, with his uncontrollable drinking and drunken rages.

Even after George's death, things on the farm didn't go well. The soil was sandy and unproductive. No matter how hard Eddie and Henry worked, it was never enough to provide for any extras. Putting food on the table was hard enough, much less managing needed home repairs. The farmhouse began to look its age, with peeling paint and a generally neglected air. Other farmhouses in the area had been updated with electricity and indoor plumbing, but that kind of improvement was beyond the financial means of the Geins.

Eddie and Henry began working more and more outside the farm to earn extra money. Eddie became something of a handyman around Plainfield, doing odd jobs, while Henry ventured further afield and took on tougher, more responsible and demanding jobs.

Eddie and Henry were close. Growing up, all they'd really had besides their mother had been each other. And in his own way, Eddie really admired his older brother. Their only point of contention was Augusta. Where Eddie saw quite clearly his mother's perfection, Henry questioned it. Henry had, perhaps, had some problems with Augusta and doubts about her which he'd internalized for years. Now, at forty, still living at home, single, but out in the world a little more because of his work, Henry voiced his concerns. And Eddie never forgave him.

Then one day, May 16, 1944, Henry Gein died under mysterious circum-stances. As was and still is common practice, Henry and Eddie were burning .

off a field. Whether it had been Henry's idea, as Eddie claimed, or Eddie's idea, as the news accounts claimed, is unclear. What is clear, however, is that the fire started burning out of control. Eddie had begun at one end of the field, Henry at the other. As darkness fell and Eddie couldn't find Henry, Eddie went for help and a search party was formed. Amazingly, when they arrived in darkness at the field, Eddie took the searchers straight to Henry's body, lying face down on the burnt grass.

But Henry hadn't been burned. There were what seemed to be bruises around Henry's head, for which there was no explanation. There was also no explanation how Eddie, who hadn't been able to find his brother earlier, suddenly knew exactly where he was. "Funny how that works," he said later, when asked about it.

It was afterward decided by the coroner that Henry had died from suffocation. It didn't occur to anyone that Henry could have been deliberately murdered.

Not until much later.

Now it was just Eddie and Augusta. Just months after Henry's death, Augusta suffered a stroke. For the first time in Eddie's life, she was completely helpless, unable to walk or even speak clearly. Their roles had suddenly reversed: Eddie was now the care-giver, Augusta his helpless patient. Eddie did everything for her. Helping her was his big chance to show her what he was really made of. She'd have to be proud of him now.

Augusta's recovery was slow, but she did, indeed, recover. Eddie was incredibly relieved. Augusta was all he had, all that meant anything to him. And as she recovered, he waited for a "thank you," or words of praise for his competence and hard work. *Some* kind of acknowledgment.

It never came.

And then, according to Schechter's account, in the winter of 1945 there occurred another pivotal event in Eddie's life.

There were still a few cows on the Gein farm. Straw was needed, so Eddie planned to go to a neighbor named Smith and buy some. Augusta decided to go along, still not trusting her son to do things on his own.

Smith was an unpleasant man with a bad temper. As Eddie and his mother arrived, they saw him beating a puppy with a stick. The woman with whom he was living was screaming at him to stop, crying and cursing him at the same time. But Smith didn't stop. He hit the puppy until it was dead. Augusta was outraged.

But it wasn't the beating that outraged her. It was the brazen, sinful woman she'd been forced to look at.

A week later Augusta had a second stroke, and this time she didn't recover. She died on December 29, 1945.

Eddie was devastated, and he blamed his mother's death on the woman at Smith's farm—the woman his mother had called a harlot.

When Augusta died, Eddie lost everything that had ever meant anything to him. The obituary was short and terse. To underscore the point that no love had been lost between Augusta and her Plainfield neighbors, none of them came to her funeral.

For the first time in his life, Eddie was completely alone. Now there was no one to witness his already-tenuous grasp on sanity slipping, no one to notice his downward spiral into madness.

Augusta's funeral had cost more money than Eddie had had. He sold off what was left of his livestock to pay for it. He completely stopped working on the farm and it showed. Even when Augusta had been alive, the lack of money had prevented fresh coats of paint and necessary maintenance, but it had been as well-tended as hard work and pride could make it. Now there wasn't even that.

Eddie earned what little money he needed by hiring himself out as a handyman and renting part of the farm to other people. He was a hard worker with surprising physical strength for his small size. But for all that, he remained effeminate. Women felt sorry for him; men made him the butt of their jokes.

The years passed and Eddie's madness deepened. Neighbors still thought he was weird, but then, a lot of people were a little strange. That didn't make them dangerous.

Deer hunting was a large part of life in Plainfield. But Eddie never participated. He told people he couldn't stand the blood. Some of his acquaintances found that odd, considering his taste in true-crime reading, and that his conversation, when he bothered to talk at all, was filled with vivid descriptions of murders and mutilations.

Eddie grew more and more reclusive. He still did the occasional odd job, but mostly he stayed on the farm alone. When he did venture out, it was usually to Mary Hogan's tavern in Pine Grove, about six or seven miles from Plainfield. He would sit there for hours—not drinking much, just watching Mary Hogan. She was a big woman who reminded Eddie of Augusta physically.

But that's where the resemblance ended. Mary was coarse and crude, with a mouth as foul as any man's and a questionable past. She was as "bad" as his mother had been "good." In Eddie's mind, it just wasn't fair that this woman was alive and his dear mother was dead. It wasn't fair at all. Mary was the one who should be dead.

Eddie could take care of that.

On December 8, 1954, a customer walked into Mary's tavern. It was oddly deserted. The cash register was missing. A bullet casing lay on the floor. A pool of blood that looked as though a body had been dragged through it trailed its way out of the tavern and into the parking lot, where it abruptly ended. The logical conclusion was that the body had been loaded into a car. Years went by without any progress in discovering exactly what had happened to Mary Hogan.

On November 16, 1957, the first day of deer season, a man by the name of Frank Worden went to the hardware store run by his mother, Bernice Worden. To his surprise, he found the door locked and his mother missing. Physically, she resembled both Mary Hogan and Augusta Gein in that she was a large woman. She was also a very competent and independent woman, and had run the store by herself since becoming a widow more than twenty-five years earlier.

Frank discovered that the cash register was gone. And there were stains on the floor he recognized instantly as blood. Worden, himself a deputy sheriff, called Sheriff Art Schley. Schley in turn called his chief deputy, Arnie Fritz, and the two men immediately made their way to the hardware store.

Worden was understandably upset, and searched the store for more clues while waiting for the sheriff to arrive. When he found a sales receipt his mother had made out for antifreeze, Ed Gein immediately came into his mind. Just the day before the odd little man had been asking about the price of antifreeze, and generally pestering Mrs. Worden about going out with him. Here was the receipt, in his mother's handwriting, indicating that Eddie had been the last customer in the store to buy anything. As far as Frank was concerned, that clinched it. Eddie, at the very least, had robbed the hardware store; at the very most, he'd somehow harmed his mother.

Other police came in from nearby counties and started searching for Eddie. He was finally found in his car, outside a neighbor's house where he'd just eaten dinner. At that time, he was merely a suspect in the burglary of the hardware store. What they'd soon discover was that he was guilty of much, much more.

When the officers found Bernice Worden's body hanging in the summer kitchen, strung up by her heels, neither could believe what they were seeing. First they threw up. Then they called for help.

As others arrived, they began going through the house, illuminating it with flashlights. They were all involuntarily dragged into Eddie Gein's living nightmare, and would themselves have nightmares about it for the rest of their lives.

This was a house of horrors.

None of them had ever seen anything so filthy. Discarded food, trash, and stacks of old newspapers and magazines filled all the available space.

But that was the least of it.

It was with disbelieving eyes that the investigators looked through the kitchen, their flickering lights picking out sawed-off skulls that had obviously been used as bowls. More skullcaps had been jammed onto Eddie's bedposts—apparently his macabre idea of interior decorating. Cane in the bottoms of some kitchen chairs had been replaced with strips of human flesh.

Anything a person could imagine covered in or made from human skin, the investigators found: jewelry, lampshades, wastebaskets.

His true-crime magazines were filled with stories of Nazi atrocities, and Eddie had devoured every word of them again and again. As is now common knowledge, the Nazis took the skin of their Jewish victims and made the same household items from them that Eddie had. Was this his inspiration?

Some children had told tales after visiting Eddie of shrunken heads in his bedroom. No one had really believed them: now the investigators discovered that the kids hadn't been exaggerating at all.

And still there was more.

A generator was brought in to replace the flashlights. The already-numb investigators discovered that they could still be shocked. One found a shoebox containing nine vulvas. Another found a box with four human noses.

Incredibly and horribly, they found clothing that Eddie had made from the skin of other people: a pair of leggings he could strap onto himself, and a vest made from the skin of a woman's upper body, with the breasts lovingly formed.

The investigators had no way of knowing it at the time, but Eddie hadn't just worn these things as clothes. He'd used them as his second skin. Had he covered his skin with the skin of women until he "became" a woman, too ... a woman like his mother? Or was his reason for wearing the skin because it was the only way he could get close to a woman?

Who can read the mind of a madman?

And then there were the masks. Imagine, if you will, the faces peering eyelessly at you from his walls—faces peeled from real women, still recognizable as the people they once were, some with the hair still attached to the scalp, some wearing lipstick.

One of the investigators reached into a bag of gruesome, indescribable human things and pulled something out by the hair. Another mask, well maintained.

It was what was left of Mary Hogan—found at last, three years after she'd disappeared.

Bernice Worden's still-warm head was found in another sack between some soiled mattresses. They later found other parts of her scattered around the house; her internal organs wrapped in newspaper, and her heart in a plastic bag in the kitchen.

At the time of his arrest, Eddie Gein was fifty-one years old. He said nothing for more than thirty hours, and when he did break his silence, it was to say that he was in a daze and couldn't remember exactly how Bernice Worden had been killed. He remembered putting her body into the store's delivery truck, driving the truck into the woods, walking back to town for his own car, driving his car into the woods, and then transferring Mrs. Worden's body from the truck to his car. He remembered driving to his farm, taking the body from his car and hanging it by the heels. But more than that, he couldn't recall.

When asked if he had killed other women, Eddie said no.

When asked where all the other body parts had come from, his answer shocked the world.

Graveyards.

He admitted to having dug up at least nine graves from three separate cemeteries and removing from the corpses what he'd wanted before reburying them. Many were women he'd known, whose obituaries he'd read in the newspaper. He claimed that he went into a daze before each grave-robbing expedition. It was as though he had no control over his actions. Prayer, he said, sometimes snapped him out of it. He also claimed that he hadn't robbed any graves since 1954.

Interestingly, that was the year of his first known murder—of Mary Hogan. This raises an intriguing question: had Eddie given up robbing graves because he'd discovered he preferred to kill his victims himself? Was the thrill gone from grave-robbing?

The number of his victims, both from the grave and murdered by himself, was difficult to calculate because of the vast number of body parts found around his house. It was believed to be fifteen; that number was arrived at by counting ten masks, Bernice Worden's head, and four noses that didn't go with any of the masks.

Rumors flew. Some claimed that Bernice Worden's heart had been in a pan on Eddie's stove. (It hadn't.) Investigators on the scene and those who interviewed Eddie said he denied any form of cannibalism, and they believed him. After all he'd admitted to, there would be no reason for him to deny that.

Every unsolved murder or disappearance in Plainfield, Eddie's former home of La Crosse, and even Chicago, was suddenly attributed to him, but thorough investigations completely exonerated him. In three specific disappearances—those of two girls and one boy—he was cleared by virtue of a lie detector test.

What further surprised investigators was that despite what they knew of him—despite the kind of monster they had expected to confront when they questioned him—Eddie seemed like such a nice little man. He wore his lopsided grin while unapologetically confessing to the most monstrous crimes against humanity and almost unbelievable personal perversions. He seemed remarkably unaware of the seriousness of what he'd done.

For those who remained skeptical of Eddie's claims about grave-robbing, and thought he'd taken his grisly trophies from his own freshly-killed bodies, investigators started opening graves Eddie claimed to have desecrated. From the very first one, Eleanor Adams', it became clear that Eddie hadn't been lying. The casket was there; Mrs. Adams was not.

Next they opened the grave of Mrs. Mabel Everson. A few scattered bones lay on top of the casket. Eddie had been there, too.

The investigators quit digging graves after that.

Eddie was given a second battery of lie detector tests in the Madison Crime Laboratory, and was again cleared of any complicity in the unexplained disappearances previously mentioned.

And then, on November 29, yet another discovery was made. At some neighbors' suggestion, investigators had begun digging at a specific spot on Gein's land. There they unearthed a nearly complete skeleton. Because the skull found with it was larger than the ones found in the house, it was at first believed to belong to a man. They found a gold-capped molar attached to a skull. A missing local man named Ray Burgess had had a gold-capped molar. Rumors flew that the man's car had been found on Gein's farm, but that wasn't true.

If it had been Burgess, then how had Eddie passed the lie detector test? In fact, according to the attorney general at that time, Eddie claimed the bones and gold-capped molar had belonged to yet another cadaver he had taken from a cemetery. It was later proven he had told the truth, and that the remains were indeed those of a woman.

After undergoing serious medical and psychological testing, Eddie Gein was determined to be suffering from schizophrenia, and was committed to Central State Hospital on January 6, 1958.

On March 30, there was to be an auction of things at the Gein farmhouse, such as household furnishings and farming equipment. On March 20, the place burned down.

By November of 1968, Eddie was deemed sane enough to stand trial for the murder of Bernice Worden. After a week of trial, he was found guilty of murder in the first degree. Later the same day, though, in the second part of his trial, he was found not guilty by reason of insanity, and was returned to Central State Hospital for the Criminally Insane.

In 1974, Eddie petitioned the courts for release, saying he'd been cured. The petition was heard and rejected, and Eddie was once again sent back to Central State.

In 1978, Eddie was moved to the Mendota Mental Health Institute in Madison.

On July 26, 1984, Edward Gein died in the geriatric ward at Mendota from respiratory failure. He was senile and suffering from cancer at the time. In the middle of the night, so that there would be no witnesses, he was buried in an unmarked grave in the Plainfield cemetery—appropriately enough, beside his mother.

DESTINED FOR MURDER

Important Dates in the Life of Ed Gein

January 4, 1902: Ed's brother, Henry Gein, was born in La Crosse, Wisconsin.

August 27, 1906: Ed Gein was born to George and Augusta Gein at 11:30 p.m. (CST) in La Crosse (according to Lois Rodden's *Astro Data V*).

1909: Ed's father became proprietor of a small grocery and meat store.

1911: Ed's mother took over proprietorship of the store from his father.

1913: The Gein family moved to a farm forty miles east of La Crosse.

1914: The Gein family made a final move to an isolated farm in Plainfield, Wisconsin. As the boys grew into teenagers, Mrs. Gein kept them working on the farm and away from women.

April 1, 1940: Ed's father died.

May 16, 1944: Ed's brother, Henry, was found dead in a mysterious fire. Ed was present, but no charges were filed against him.

Early 1945: Ed's mother suffered a stroke and Ed nursed her. She recovered within a few months.

December 29, 1945: Ed's mother had a second stroke and died, leaving Ed alone on the family farm.

1947–1952: Ed robbed graves, sealed off his mother's room and studied books on female anatomy.

December 8, 1954: Tavern owner Mary Hogan disappeared from her Pine Grove, Wisconsin tavern after a visit from Ed.

November 16, 1957: Hardware store owner Bernice Worden disappeared from her store. Her body was found in Ed's home, and Ed was arrested for her murder.

November 23, 1957: Ed was transferred from the local jail to Central State Hospital for the Criminally Insane for testing.

January 6, 1958: Ed was declared insane and returned to Central State Hospital indefinitely.

March 20, 1958: Local citizens burned down the Gein farmhouse.

March 30, 1958: An auction of the Geins' farm and personal property was held.

January 22, 1968: Preliminary proceedings began to determine whether Ed was sane enough to stand trial for Bernice Worden's murder.

November 7, 1968: Ed's trial began.

November 14, 1968: Ed was found guilty of first degree murder in the shooting death of Bernice Worden. He was returned to Central State Hospital for the Criminally Insane.

February 1974: Ed filed a petition with the Waushara County Clerk of Courts claiming competence and requesting release from the hospital.

June 27, 1974: Ed's petition was rejected in court. He was returned to Central State Hospital the next day.

1978: Ed was transferred to Mendota Mental Health Institute in Madison, Wisconsin.

July 26, 1984: Ed Gein died of respiratory failure in the Mendota Mental Health Institute geriatric ward.

July 27, 1984: Ed was buried in an unmarked grave beside his mother.

Astrological Blueprint for Ed Gein

—Edna L. Rowland

According to Lois Rodden's Astro Data V, Edward Theodore Gein was born at 11:30 p.m. (CST) on August 27, 1906, in La Crosse, Wisconsin.[2] The first thing we notice about Gein's natal birth chart is that his Sun resides in 04° Virgo in the 4th house, so his Sun sign ruler is Mercury. The Sun and Mercury are in mutual reception. Since the 21st degree of Gemini rises, Mercury also rules Gein's Ascendant. Mercury at 15°59' Leo resides in his 3rd house. On August 19, 1906, just eight days before his birth, there was a solar eclipse at 26°07' Leo; the eclipse falls opposite his Midheaven and conjunct his Sun/Mars, Sun/Mercury, and Venus/Jupiter midpoints.

When we look at his birth chart, we see that Pluto at 23° Gemini is almost exactly conjunct his Ascendant. Pluto rising perfectly describes his isolated, loner type of personality. Nearly all planets falling below the chart's horizon (with the exception of Saturn and Uranus) further reinforces this subjective, reclusive tendency. Mars and Pluto, the two most violent planets, are both angular in Ed's natal chart and aspecting all four angles. Mars sextile Pluto and the Ascendant (the self), lies near his 4th house cusp, and opposes his Midheaven.

Venus makes a soft aspect, a trine to Pluto, but is in a homicidal or dangerous degree: 18° Libra. Pluto, the planet of intense, inner compulsions, heavily aspected and afflicted, rules his 6th house of health, indicating that this man was subject to irrational obsessions and phobias over which he exercised little control.

The 4th and 8th house rulers (both of which houses govern death) are in opposition, afflicting the parental angles (the 4th and 10th house cusps). The Sun opposing Saturn indicates a preoccu-

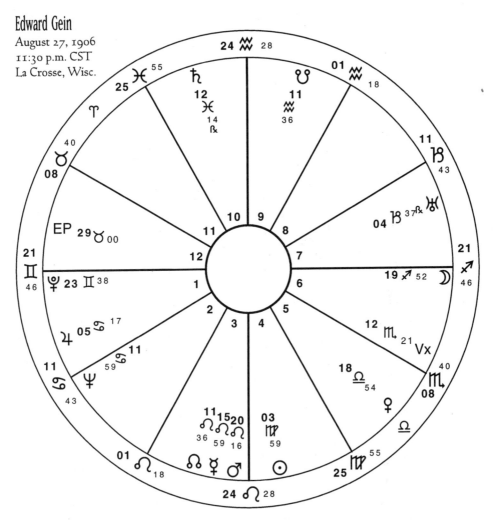

Birth chart for Ed Gein

pation with death and possible abnormal reactions to it. Since the 8th house also rules sexual orientation or adjustment, we see that he was frustrated in regard to women and deprived (Saturn) of normal heterosexual attachments to the opposite sex. While his mother lived, he found satisfaction in serving her needs, as indicated by his natal Moon in the 6th house of service. After her death, he was literally lost, without any stable foundation or direction.

The Moon, the most aspected planet in Gein's birth chart, is in mutual reception with Jupiter; it is just past the first quarter phase, increasing in light, and occupies the 6th house of service to others in his chart. His natal Moon

	☉	☽	☿	♀	♂	♃	♄	♅	♆	♇	MC	AS	IC	DS	☊
☉		26 ♎ 56	24 ♌ 59	26 ♍ 27	27 ♌ 08	04 ♌ 38	08 ♊ 07	04 ♏ 18	07 ♌ 59	28 ♋ 48	29 ♏ 14	27 ♋ 53	29 ♌ 14	27 ♎ 53	22 ♌ 48
☽	105 53		17 ♎ 56	19 ♏ 23	20 ♎ 04	27 ♍ 35	01 ♒ 03	27 ♐ 15	00 ♎ 56	21 ♍ 45	22 ♑ 10	20 ♍ 49	22 ♎ 10	20 ♐ 49	15 ♎ 44
☿	017 59	123 △ 53		17 ♍ 27	18 ♌ 08	25 ♋ 38	29 ♉ 07	25 ♎ 18	28 ♋ 59	19 ♋ 48	20 ♉ 14	18 ♋ 53	20 ♌ 14	18 ♎ 53	13 ♌ 48
♀	044 ∠ 55	060 ✱ 58	062 ✱ 55		19 ♍ 35	27 ♌ 05	00 ♑ 34	26 ♏ 45	00 ♍ 27	21 ♌ 16	21 ♐ 41	20 ♌ 20	21 ♍ 41	20 ♏ 20	15 ♍ 15
♂	013 42	119 △ 35	004 ☌ 17	058 ✱ 37		27 ♋ 47	01 ♊ 15	27 ♎ 27	01 ♌ 08	21 ♋ 57	22 ♉ 22	21 ♋ 01	22 ♌ 22	21 ♎ 01	15 ♌ 56
♃	058 ✱ 42	164 35	040 42	103 37	044 ∠ 59		08 ♉ 45	04 ♎ 57	08 ♋ 38	29 ♊ 27	29 ♈ 53	28 ♊ 31	29 ♋ 53	28 ♍ 31	23 ♋ 27
♄	171 ☍ 45	082 □ 21	153 45	143 19	158 02	113 △ 02		08 ♒ 25	12 ♉ 06	02 ♉ 56	03 ♓ 21	02 ♉ 00	03 ♊ 21	02 ♒ 00	26 ♉ 55
♅	120 △ 37	014 44	138 37	075 42	134 ⚼ 20	179 ☍ 20	067 37		08 ♎ 18	29 ♓ 07	29 ♑ 33	28 ♓ 11	29 ♎ 33	28 ♐ 11	23 ♎ 07
♆	052 00	157 53	034 00	096 □ 55	038 17	006 ☌ 42	119 △ 44	172 ☍ 37		02 ♋ 48	03 ♉ 14	01 ♋ 52	03 ♌ 14	01 ♎ 52	26 ♋ 48
♇	070 Q 21	176 ☍ 14	052 21	115 △ 16	056 ✱ 38	011 39	101 23	169 00	018 21		24 ♈ 03	22 ♊ 42	24 ♋ 03	22 ♍ 42	17 ♋ 37
MC	170 ☍ 29	064 ✱ 36	171 ☍ 30	125 △ 34	175 ☍ 47	130 48	017 45	049 51	137 30	119 △ 09		23 ♈ 07	24 ♏ 28	23 ♑ 07	18 ♉ 02
AS	072 Q 13	178 ☍ 06	054 13	117 △ 08	058 ✱ 30	013 30	099 31	167 09	020 12	001 ☌ 51	117 △ 17		23 ♋ 07	21 ♍ 46	16 ♋ 41
IC	009 ☌ 30	115 △ 23	008 ☌ 29	054 25	004 ☌ 12	049 11	162 14	130 08	042 29	060 ✱ 50	180 ☍ 00	062 ✱ 42		23 ♎ 07	18 ♌ 02
DS	107 46	001 ☌ 53	125 △ 46	062 ✱ 51	121 △ 29	166 29	080 28	012 50	159 47	178 ☍ 08	062 ✱ 42	180 ☍ 00	117 △ 17		16 ♎ 41
☊	022 22	128 △ 15	004 ☌ 22	067 17	008 ☌ 39	036 19	149 ⚻ 22	143 00	029 ⚺ 37	047 58	167 08	049 50	012 51	130 09	

Midpoints and Aspects for Ed Gein

(which represents the mother) in the sign of Sagittarius, opposite Pluto and the Ascendant, describes the critical, possessive, fanatically religious mother who dominated his life. Even after her death, he was psychologically, if not physically, obsessed with and dominated by this strong mother figure, as represented by Moon square Saturn (indicating codependency) in his chart.

A Mutable grand square between the Moon, Saturn, Pluto, and the Sun in or near the angles completes his planetary pattern, indicating that critical adjustments would be required of him to test his survival skills. His chart ruler, Mercury, in the inflexible fixed sign of Leo, conjunct Mars and inconjunct Saturn, apparently made those adjustments difficult for him. His prior conditioning and childhood environment were stern and rigid, leaving little room for compromise. His emotional development was stunted and short-circuited by sympathy for his mother, and further negated by his constant withdrawal, shyness (Saturn square Pluto), and lack of social skills (Jupiter opposite Uranus).

Ed's father, an abusive alcoholic denoted by Saturn in the 10th house, trine Neptune and inconjunct the Nodes, was of no help to him, so he turned toward his over-protective, dominating mother for guidance. Neither parent seemed capable of fulfilling his need for love and affection, as illustrated by his natal Sun opposite Saturn (representing an indifferent father) and Moon square Saturn (unmet needs on the maternal side).

Venus—the desire for love—is sextile Gein's natal Moon and in favorable trine to his Ascendant and Midheaven, so he adored his mother despite her stern, self-righteous attitude. He also feared her judgment (Venus conjunct his Moon/Mars midpoint), however, and rarely brought anyone home with him, even school friends.

Mercury conjunct Mars in Leo and the Moon's Nodes in Ed's 3rd house of siblings aptly describes his older brother, Henry, who died in a fire under rather unusual circumstances. His brother's death may or may not have been the accident it appeared, but their relationship had been close, as denoted by Mercury conjunct the North Node in his 3rd house. For years, Ed's overbearing and possessive mother had kept both sons together at home, occupied with farm chores, and discouraged any normal interests they may have had in the opposite sex.

By 1945, Ed had experienced the loss of his entire family, and resigned himself to living alone on his dilapidated farm. With no one to help him there, he hired himself out as a handyman (Sun in the sign of service, Virgo, opposite Saturn in the 10th house of work and career) in order to earn a meager living.

Virgo is a bachelor sign, and Ed never married. His fear of rejection was probably too strong for him to approach a woman socially; this is suggested by Jupiter, his 7th house ruler, opposing separative Uranus, while Venus semisquares Uranus in his 7th house of partnerships.

Nevertheless, natal Moon (representing the females in his life) trine Mars and opposite Pluto indicates a lot of repressed anger and aggressive sexual urges toward women. It seems significant that all his victims were female.

Mars closely sextile Pluto and the Ascendant (the self), and sesqui-quadrate Uranus, only increases the probability that those urges would be expressed violently. Mars rules gunshot wounds, and both of the women he murdered had been killed by a gun before their bodies were mutilated and butchered.

It is now known that this apparently harmless "mamma's boy" murdered at least two women, and during the night robbed many graves and plundered as many as fifteen female bodies.

After his capture, the local townspeople burned down Gein's Wisconsin farmhouse, which they believed still contained "souvenirs" of his nocturnal grave-robbings. Mars in the fire sign Leo, near the cusp of his 4th house (which rules the home or residence), aptly depicts this belated act of revenge (Mars sextile Pluto) by the locals.

Declared a hopeless schizophrenic, Ed Gein died in an insane asylum at age seventy-seven.

Important Dates as Illustrated by Secondary Progressions and Transits to Ed Gein's Natal Chart

When Ed was eight years old, the progressed Sun (his 4th house ruler) was approaching a sextile to his natal Neptune. At this time, the Gein family moved to an isolated farm in Plainfield, Wisconsin. Both progressed Mars and Mercury at 25° Leo had moved to a conjunction with his 4th house cusp (ruling home and/or change of residence).

On April 1, 1940, when Ed was thirty-three years old, his father died. At his father's death, progressed Mars at 11° Virgo was approaching an opposition aspect to Saturn (representing the father) in his 10th house. The progressed Ascendant at 18° Cancer was making a square aspect to natal Venus and inconjunct his natal Moon; the progressed Moon at 16° Pisces was in the 10th house (which rules the father in a male chart) inconjunct natal Mercury. Progressed Sun at 06° Libra squared Jupiter and semisquared Mars.

Four years later, on May 16, 1944, Ed's brother, Henry, was found dead in a fire under mysterious circumstances. On this date transiting Sun at 25° Taurus squared Ed's Midheaven and 4th house cusp; transiting Jupiter at 18° Leo in the 3rd house of siblings was conjunct natal Mars and the Mercury/Mars midpoint at 18°08' Leo. Ed's progressed Sun (the 4th house ruler of endings) at 10° Libra squared the 8th house cusp of death, and sextiled his North Node in the 3rd house. Progressed Mercury (which rules brothers and sisters) was conjunct natal Venus. The progressed Moon at 08° Taurus on the cusp of Ed's 12th house of secrets was exactly semisquare natal Pluto. Ed's secondary progressed Midheaven at 01° Aries was sesquiquadrate natal Mercury in the 3rd house, and his progressed Ascendant at 21° Cancer was exactly conjunct his Mars/Pluto midpoint of murder. However, no charges were filed against Ed, despite rumors and suspicions of foul play.

In the early part of 1945, Ed's mother suffered two strokes which led to her death on December 29, 1945. At this time, transiting Saturn was conjunct Ed's progressed Ascendant at 23° Cancer, a depressing aspect. Transiting Uranus at 14° Gemini (representing a severed relationship with an important female in his life) was opposite his natal Moon. In a male chart, the 4th house and its ruler represent the mother; in this case, the ruling planet, the Sun, occupied the 4th house at birth. At age thirty-eight, progressed Sun at 12° Libra was exactly square Neptune and inconjunct Saturn, his 8th house ruler of death. Progressed Moon in his 12th house of sorrows at 27° Taurus was semisquare Neptune. Age thirty-eight-and-a-half symbolizes the mid-point in his actual life cycle (a point of crisis), since he was seventy-seven years of age at his death.

When transiting Uranus in Gemini finally reached the conjunction with his natal Ascendant in 1947, Ed began to lose his grip on reality. In an attempt to preserve her memory intact, Ed sealed off his mother's room in the house. During the day he performed manual labor, and picked up extra money baby-sitting for friends and neighbors. But at night he dug up and robbed recent graves, skinned corpses, and became obsessed with the study of female anatomy. He created his own environment by crafting genital organs and vital pieces of skin into decorative household objects and surrounding himself with them. By this time, progressed Midheaven at 04° Aries had moved to the square of natal Uranus and Jupiter, and was making an inconjunct (readjustment) aspect to his natal Sun as well. This inconjunct aspect denotes conflicting energies that are often difficult to integrate, because it brings together two incompatible signs. Unfortunately, Ed's pitiful attempts to adjust to life without the support of his family seemed doomed to fail.

His natal Midheaven at 24° Aquarius is in an alcoholic degree, and so are the natal Moon's Nodes. With natal Neptune afflicting his 4th and 10th house cusps, he finally turned to alcohol to drown his sorrows, just as his father had done. This desperate measure didn't work, either.

The murders began on December 8, 1954, when Mary Hogan disappeared from her tavern shortly after Ed's visit. On this date Ed's progressed Midheaven had reached 11° Aries in square aspect to Neptune (mysterious disappearances), and the progressed Moon at 18° Virgo was square his natal Moon and conjunct his Venus/Mars midpoint. Progressed Venus at 04° Sagittarius was exactly square his natal Sun. His progressed Ascendant at 29° Cancer was sextile his Equatorial Ascendant in the 12th house. Transiting Pluto at 26° Leo was now retrograding back and forth over his natal 4th house cusp, which governs the end of life. Pluto opposed his Midheaven and was conjunct his Mars. Pluto (ruling intense inner compulsions, of both the highest and lowest kinds) was also exactly conjunct the prenatal eclipse at 26°07' Leo, activating several of his natal midpoints, including the Sun/Mars (aggressive impulses) midpoint.

No one yet suspected him. It wasn't until November 16, 1957, when he murdered Bernice Worden and her body was found in his home, that he was arrested. On the date of this second murder, his progressed Ascendant had moved into a new sign, 01° Leo, square his progressed Moon at 01° Scorpio; his progressed Midheaven at 14° Aries trined his natal Mercury. When progressed Mars (violence) reached 22° Virgo in exact square aspect to his natal Ascendant and Pluto, outside forces (the police) intervened in order to bring his violence under control.

The transits for Worden's murder and Ed's subsequent arrest are very potent and graphic. Transiting Sun at 23° Scorpio squared the angles of his natal chart and was conjunct his Mars/Midheaven midpoint. Venus opposed natal Neptune, Saturn opposed his natal Moon, Uranus was conjunct his North Node, and Mars and Neptune at 03–04° Scorpio were conjunct his progressed Moon. At the time of his capture, transiting Pluto at 02° Virgo was approaching a conjunction with his natal Sun in the 4th house of endings. One week later, on November 23, 1957, he was committed indefinitely to the Central State Hospital for the Criminally Insane.

After a trial and his conviction on November 14, 1968, Ed was found guilty of first degree murder in the shooting death of Bernice Worden. His luck ran out, as transiting Pluto squared his Ascendant, and he was returned to the Central State Hospital for the Criminally Insane.

Five years later, in 1974, Ed filed a petition claiming his competency. Although he had been a model patient and obeyed orders, the authorities did not believe he could survive outside a rigidly structured environment such as the hospital, so his petition was denied. This was probably a wise decision, since Venus, his 12th house ruler of hospitals and institutions, is fairly well-aspected compared to the rest of his chart.

On July 26, 1984, Ed Gein died in the Mendota Mental Health Institute geriatric ward, of cancer and immediate respiratory failure. Upon his death, his progressed Midheaven at 11° Taurus exactly squared his Moon's Nodes and opposed his natal Vertex; his progressed Ascendant at 20° Leo was exactly conjunct his natal Mars near the 4th house cusp, which governs the end of life.

AP/Wide World Photos

Chapter Two

The Milwaukee Wolf Man

Jeffrey Dahmer—His Story

—Sandra Harrisson Young

J EFFREY DAHMER WAS EIGHTEEN YEARS

old when he murdered his first human being. He'd been killing

animals for years and chemically stripping the skin from their bones.

Their tiny skeletons littered the woods behind the Dahmer home in

Bath, Ohio. Shattered skeletal bits and pieces of nineteen-year-old Steven

Hicks joined the remains of the animals in June of 1978, and there they remained undetected until the summer of 1991.

Jeffrey Dahmer was born in Milwaukee, Wisconsin, on May 21, 1960, to Joyce and Lionel Dahmer. No one, least of all his parents, could have imagined the horror they were unleashing on the world in the form of their firstborn child; no one could have imagined that this one child would, during his lifetime, devastate the families of seventeen other children.

Lionel Dahmer was still in college when Jeffrey was born. After graduating from Marquette University with a master's degree, Lionel continued his education at Iowa State University, graduating in 1966 with a doctorate in analytical chemistry. A second son, David, was born the same year in Doylestown, Ohio, where Lionel had gotten a job. In 1967, just before Jeffrey's eighth birthday, the family settled in Bath, Ohio.

It was the last home they'd share as a family, and a turning point in Jeff's young life.

No one can ever know for certain what goes on behind the closed doors of someone else's home—or how the experiences of a childhood will play themselves out in adult life. For Jeffrey, who didn't make friends easily in the first place (either because of a crippling shyness, or, perhaps worse, a personality that simply didn't attract other children), moving was a difficult and painful experience. Compounding the problems of this particular move was its timing. School was already out for the summer, so the option of meeting other kids on a common ground didn't exist. Since Jeff wasn't the type of child who would (or could) simply go out into his new neighborhood and make friends, and since his brother was really too little to be a playmate, that left just Jeff. He would play for hours by himself in the woods behind his home, his imagination his only companion.

Or was it? Later in Jeffrey's life, when he was facing some serious legal trouble, Lionel Dahmer told Jeffrey's probation officer that it was around this time that Jeffrey was sexually molested by a neighborhood boy. An incident like this would go a long way to explain some of Jeff's later problems, but Jeff denied that it ever happened.

When he finally did begin school in Bath, Jeff remained a loner, unable or unwilling to make connections with other children. He had a fascination with death that his peers had a hard time relating to. At ten, Jeff was already killing animals and experimenting with various chemicals to discover the most effective method of stripping the meat from their bones—an odd hobby, to say the least, for a little boy. When he was finished with his little rodents and chickens, he would scatter their remains in the woods.

As Jeffrey grew older he began to crave acceptance by his peers, but it seems the harder he tried to win them over, the more firmly and cruelly they rejected him. Certainly his antics caught the attention of other teenagers, and even amazed and amused them, but he was just so weird that no one really wanted him for a friend. Jeff's idea of a fun afternoon was to go to the local mall and pretend to be mentally handicapped as he crashed and careened his way through the shoppers, knocking them off balance and scattering their purchases. Of course his classmates laughed; they couldn't believe he'd done it! But laughing at Jeff wasn't the same as accepting him. He was always on the outside looking in, yearning to be liked, to be part of the group—and then acting as though it didn't bother him when he was rejected over and over again.

Of all the pranks Jeff pulled in high school—and there was a long list of them—one of the most telling was when he placed himself in the middle of a group of honors students having their portrait taken for the school yearbook. The yearbook editor, not at all amused since Jeff was nowhere near having the necessary grade point, inked him out of the picture. If a picture can indeed be worth a thousand words, this one certainly is. It's a portrait of Jeff's life. The invisible man. In the group, yet not *part* of the group.

According to some of Jeff's classmates, even though the other kids' behavior toward him could be cruel in the extreme, he never fought back. He helplessly accepted their rejection and took to heart their judgment of him as worthless. But at the beginning of his high school years, Jeff discovered that drinking alcohol dulled his pain. It became his constant companion.

Jeff's senior year in high school was perhaps his worst. That was the year his family, as he'd known it, disintegrated. The verbal fighting between his parents was bitter and vicious. Lionel was the one who filed for divorce first, but Joyce came right back at him. There are several mentions of Joyce's mental condition in the divorce file—in one instance her "extensive mental illness" is brought up—but no specifics with regard to the type of mental illness from which she was suffering at the time are included, nor are any about how it might have impacted Jeff. Angry words flew through the house with no regard for who else had heard them once they'd reached their intended targets. Jeffrey began drinking more and more to shut it all out. Joyce wanted custody of David, Lionel wanted custody of David—but no one talked about wanting Jeff.

Joyce ended up with David, who was twelve at the time. And Jeff, rejected once again, found himself on the outside looking in. Lionel moved out of the house, but didn't give up the fight for David. This went on for four years, until David decided on his own to live with his father.

Jeffrey quietly watched. He'd turned eighteen just before the divorce was granted and was considered by law to be an adult, which is why there were no custody battles over him. To Jeff, though, it must have looked as if no one wanted him. And as for being an adult, he sure didn't feel like one. Inside his man's body was a frightened child, a rejected misfit with a serious drinking problem.

And he was angry. Angry at the kids who'd rejected him, angry at his parents for not seeming to care, and angry at his own helplessness.

And then, one day, he met Steven Hicks. It was June 18, 1978. Lionel no longer lived at the house. Joyce and David had gone to visit relatives in Wisconsin, leaving Jeffrey alone in the house.

Alone and lonely.

Jeffrey went looking for company. He found Steven Hicks hitchhiking home after having enjoyed the day with friends. It was his father's birthday, and Steven wanted to get home to celebrate with his family before meeting up with his friends again.

Jeff was a nice enough looking guy, and about the same age as Steven. Steven would have had no reason to be suspicious when Jeff offered him a ride and invited him to his house to listen to music and drink some beer. They got along just fine. Jeff liked Steven very much and told police years later that there was no sex involved. For a little while, Jeff had a friend.

But then Steven said he was going to leave. The poor young man couldn't possibly have known what an emotional storm his simple decision was setting off. Jeff didn't want Steven to leave, and wasn't about to let him. No one was ever going to leave Jeff again.

With all the force he could muster, Jeffrey hit Steven in the head with a barbell and then choked him until he was sure he was dead. He dragged the boy's body to the crawl space under the house and methodically dismembered him. Then he put the parts into plastic trash bags and left them in the crawl space.

That didn't work out because of the smell, so a few days later Jeff tried to bury the body. He could only manage a shallow grave, though, because the soil was so hard. But still he wasn't satisfied. He had to do a better job of getting rid of the evidence so that there would be no chance of discovery. Determined to take care of it once and for all, Jeff again dug up Steven's body, peeled the flesh away and smashed the bare bones with a sledgehammer. Turning around and around in circles, he threw Steven's bones into the woods, a handful here and a handful there, joining the other little skeletons, until it was no longer recognizable as a human being. No one but Jeffrey knew that Steven had been there. No one but Jeffrey knew he had died there. And whenever Jeffrey wanted to be with Steven again, all he had to do was go into the woods: Steven was all around him.

In July of that year, Jeffrey's mother and brother left the house in Bath, Ohio, for good and moved to Wisconsin. Jeffrey was left behind with no money and a broken refrigerator. He had promised his mother he wouldn't tell his father, but Lionel found out when he came to visit in August. His father and the woman he was later to marry, Shari, moved into the house and stayed there with him until Jeff left for college at Ohio State University.

Jeff just wasn't a student. He lasted for all of one quarter at the university, and spent most of that brief time drinking. He was in a constant state of hazy drunkenness, both in class and out. By December, not long after his father's December 24th marriage to Shari, Jeff was in the army, courtesy of his father. It was the action of a desperate man trying to help his son. The army had straightened lots of young men out and given some purpose to their lives: he thought it just might work out that way for Jeff.

Even in the army Jeff drank. His weekends were spent either with bought women in town, or in bed drunk and listening to music. The soldiers he lived with tended to leave him alone when he was drunk. Jeff would lose his ability to think rationally and try to start fights he had no hope of winning. He would reel emotionally out of control, filled with hatred and anger and a bleak emptiness the other young men couldn't understand and didn't really care to. It was easier and safer to just stay out of his way. So even in what would normally be the close comradeship of barracksmates, Jeff was alone, his own behavior forcing the others to reject him.

Jeff began his army training with the intention of becoming a military policeman, but couldn't make it through the tough training. Instead, he was transferred to Fort Sam Houston and completed his training there as a medical specialist. It provided him with knowledge and skills he'd find a handy use for later in his life.

As soon as he finished training at Fort Sam Houston, he was transferred to Baumholder, West Germany, the headquarters company in the Sixty-eighth Armored's Second Battalion, not far from Frankfurt.

Jeff made it into his second year of service, but was beginning to prove very unreliable. He drank too often and too much, and his temper was a frightening thing to behold when he'd been drinking. He began missing duty days, and it got to the point where the men he worked with no longer trusted him. He was offered alcohol dependency counseling, but wouldn't have anything to do with it. That was it, as far as the army was concerned. They'd tried to turn him into something and had failed. Jeff was outprocessed at Fort Jackson, South Carolina, on March 26, 1981.

The first place Jeff went after leaving the army was Florida, where he drifted, drank, and occasionally worked. From there he joined his father and stepmother at their new home in Granger Township, Ohio, but that didn't work out for him either. It was the drinking—always the drinking. On October 7, 1981, he managed to get himself arrested at a motel in Bath, Ohio, charged with disorderly conduct, resisting arrest, and carrying an open container of liquor. Lionel and Shari had tried, but there was a limit to their patience. Nothing they did seemed to help. Maybe his grandmother could do something with him, they thought.

And so Jeff traveled to West Allis, Wisconsin, to live with his grandmother.

Jeffrey loved his grandmother. She was a source of unconditional love and stability for him, and when he was with her he was truly a different person. He tried to please her by helping with household chores and working in the yard. He did well for a time, even getting a job drawing blood at Milwaukee Blood Plasma, Inc. He was laid off in 1982, however, and it was a short trip from there to his arrest for exposing himself.

He didn't find steady work again until more than two years later, when he was hired by the Ambrosia Chocolate Company in Milwaukee, Wisconsin, to mix chocolate. He worked the night shift, from 11:00 p.m. until 7:30 a.m., and was happy to do it.

It was also about this time that Jeffrey began to admit to himself that he was gay—although there is some question about whether he was truly homosexual or simply preferred the lifestyle. It was easy for him and suited his personality. Commitment? As a gay man in the 1980s, he could have sex without commitment. There was no need for him to make any kind of emotional connection with his partners the way he might have had to do if he'd bedded women.

Jeff started going to the Club Bath Milwaukee, where he would whip up various potions, convince men to drink them, and watch their reactions—looking, apparently, for the perfect brew to put the men under his control. Jeff did this over and over again, without anyone the wiser, until one poor fellow ended up in the hospital. Jeff wasn't arrested, but he wasn't allowed back into the Club Bath.

On September 8, 1986, he found himself in very serious trouble for the first time in his life. Two boys, both twelve at the time (who later agreed to be interviewed on television about their run-in with Jeffrey Dahmer), spotted him on the bank of the Kinnickinnic River with his trousers and underwear pulled down, masturbating in full awareness that the boys were watching him. The boys called the police and Jeffrey was arrested for lewd and lascivious behavior, which was later reduced to disorderly conduct. Jeff was given a suspended one-year sentence and ordered to undergo counseling.

On September 15, 1987, Jeffrey murdered Steven W. Tuomi, a short-order cook who had moved to Milwaukee from Ontonagon, Michigan. He went into the West Allis apartment and disappeared from the face of the earth.

To get rid of Steven Tuomi's body, Jeffrey used a vat of acid to melt away the flesh, and then tossed everything out with the trash.

Jeffrey's next victim was a Native American boy he killed in January of 1988. The boy was only fourteen years old when he met his death in Jeffrey's grandmother's West Allis basement.

On March 20, 1988, Jeffrey was released from probation after having satisfied all the conditions required of his disorderly conduct charge. Just four days later, on March 24, he killed again. His victim, Richard Guerrero, was going to visit a friend, but never made it.

On September 25, 1988, Jeffrey's grandmother made him leave her home. It distressed her to do it. She had no idea of the horrible things Jeff had done under her roof, but he was no longer trying to conform his behavior to her expectations and she just didn't want him living with her any longer.

Jeff moved out. His new home at the Oxford Apartments, 924 North Twenty-fifth Street, in a seedy Milwaukee neighborhood with a high crime rate, became his new killing field. In fact, the day after Jeffrey moved into his new apartment, he enticed a thirteen-year-old Laotian boy to enter it by offering the child fifty dollars to pose for pictures. Once in the apartment, Jeffrey fixed the child one of his knockout drinks. As the boy grew weak and dizzy, Jeffrey fondled his genitals. Somehow, disoriented though he was, the boy managed to escape. His family immediately notified the police, and once again Jeffrey was arrested. This time he was charged with second-degree sexual assault and enticing a child for immoral purposes. Just a week later, released on bail, he was back on the streets.

While waiting for his trial, Jeffrey murdered Anthony Sears, a nice, good-looking young man working as manager of a Baker's Square restaurant. Anthony had thoughts of becoming a model and enjoyed having his picture taken. On the evening of March 25, 1989, he met Jeffrey quite by chance at a local gay bar called LaCage. Anthony was with a friend, so when Jeffrey and Anthony decided to leave for their late-night tryst, Jeffrey had the friend drive them to West Allis and drop them off on a corner not far from Jeff's grand-mother's house, rather than at his apartment.

Once again, Jeff took a victim to his unsuspecting grandmother's home—where the two men had sex before Jeffrey drugged Anthony with one of his special drinks. Jeffrey strangled Anthony, then performed his usual ritual of chopping up the body. This time, though, he boiled Anthony's decapitated head until the flesh fell away, painted it gray, and took it back to his apartment to display as a knick-knack.

On May 23, 1989, there was a sentencing hearing that followed Jeff's trial for molestation. The assistant District Attorney asked that Jeff be sent to jail for a minimum of five years, with a lengthy probation to follow. She apparently sensed the danger in him that others hadn't. At the same hearing Jeff's father told the judge that Jeff needed professional treatment, not prison. His attorney, Gerald Boyle, also asked for a lengthy probation period, but no time in prison. But it was Jeffrey who clinched the matter. He put on quite a show, admitting to everything, including needing help and a willingness to work through his problems if given the chance. He understood his audience and knew exactly what they wanted—and needed—to hear.

The judge was between a rock and a hard place. He knew the weaknesses of the Wisconsin prison system: there were no treatment programs for people with Jeff's problems. In the end Jeff was found guilty of second-degree sexual assault and enticing a child for immoral purposes. He was sentenced to three years in prison, which was reduced to one year on a work-release program to be followed by five years of probation and alcohol abuse treatment.

DESTINED FOR MURDER

Jeffrey ended up at the Community Correctional Center in downtown Milwaukee. He made it to work every night and back to his cell every morning.

As his son's one-year sentence came to a close, Lionel Dahmer realized he didn't like what he was seeing. The whole point of Jeff serving a lenient sentence had been to get him help for his drinking, and Lionel hadn't seen that happening. He wrote to the judge who had sentenced his son, to voice his concerns and explain that Jeff hadn't attended any alcohol treatment program at all. He said he was worried about what might happen to Jeff if he didn't get treatment before being released because, as far as he could see, alcohol was at the root of all Jeff's problems.

Unfortunately, nothing was done. The letter was too little, too late. Just a day after it was written, Jeff was back on the Milwaukee streets.

On June 11, 1990, Jeff saw his probation officer. On June 14, twenty-eight-year-old Eddie Smith disappeared. He had gone out clubbing in the gay bars and, quite simply, hadn't come home. When Dahmer was later captured, there was no evidence implicating him in Eddie's death, but he recognized Eddie's picture as someone he'd killed. Strangely, Eddie's sister, Caroline, told a talk show audience that she'd received a phone call the April following Eddie's disappearance. A voice at the other end had said, "Don't bother looking for your brother." She asked why not and the voice said, "Because he's dead." Caroline asked how he knew that. The caller said, "Because I killed him," then hung up. Jeffrey Dahmer admitted later to having made that call, and many others, to the families of his victims.

On July 8, 1990, Jeff picked up a fifteen-year-old boy. He offered the child money to pose for some pictures. When the boy agreed, Jeff brought him to his apartment and did, indeed, take pictures. At one point, though, he hit the boy over the head with a rubber mallet and tried to choke him. In the midst of their struggle Jeff, amazingly, decided to let him live and agreed to let him go. He even went so far as to call a taxi for the boy after getting him to agree not to call the police or tell anyone about the incident.

But the boy did tell. He gave Jeffrey's description to the police investigating the incident, as well as his address, but nothing was done. Jeff was never even contacted.

On July 9, Jeffrey had an appointment with his probation officer. Six days later, he murdered Ricky Beeks, thirty-three. Following his usual method of operation, Jeffrey picked Ricky up in a bar, took him home, and fixed him a drugged drink. He then strangled him, stripped him, and had oral sex with the dead body. After dismembering Ricky's corpse, he kept and painted the skull.

On September 3 of the same year, Ernest Miller, visiting from Chicago, met Jeffrey Dahmer in front of a bookstore. According to Jeffrey, he offered Ernest, a promising dancer, money. When Ernest went back to Jeff's apartment the two men had sex. Afterwards, Jeff drugged Ernest and slit his throat, took pictures, dismembered the body, and put the biceps in his freezer to eat later. He then removed the flesh from the skull and painted it. But this time he added a new twist: he kept Ernest's skeleton.

Jeff had yet another meeting with his probation officer on September 24. It was around this date that he murdered David Thomas. According to police, Jeff wasn't sexually attracted to David, so there was no physical relationship between the men, but Jeff killed him anyway, after slipping David one of his knockout drinks. Jeff was apparently afraid David would report him to the police when he woke, so he murdered him to avoid the problem. As with the others, Jeffrey dismembered the body, taking pictures as he worked. Unlike the other times, Jeff didn't keep any mementos of this victim around his apartment. David Thomas disappeared as completely from the face of the earth as if he had never existed.

After David, Jeffrey didn't kill again for nearly five months. He continued meeting with his probation officer on schedule and maintained contact with his grandmother (although this was almost entirely through the old woman's own efforts). Jeff was also mugged several times during these five months and installed a security system in his apartment.

During the 1990 Thanksgiving and Christmas holidays, Jeffrey spent time at his grandmother's home in West Allis, along with his father, stepmother, and his brother, David. His real mother, Joyce, had moved to California; Jeff hadn't had any contact with her for more than five years.

On February 18, 1991, Jeffrey skipped the scheduled meeting with his probation officer and instead invited nineteen-year-old Curtis Straughter to his apartment for sex. Naturally he offered Curtis one of his special drinks. After the two men had oral sex and the drink was taking effect, Jeffrey strangled Curtis. Afterwards, he dismembered the young man, taking pictures while he worked. He added Curtis' skull to his macabre collection.

Jeff's mother called him from California on March 25, 1991. After five years of no contact at all, she was suddenly there for him, understanding of his homosexuality because of her work with AIDS patients, and accepting of him for what he was. It was after this call that Jeffrey began his final murderous rampage.

His eleventh victim was Errol Lindsey, a nineteen-year-old singer in the choir of a Baptist church. On April 7, Errol left his mother's home and ran into Jeffrey Dahmer. Jeff, following his usual pattern, talked Errol into returning to his apartment, drugged and strangled the young man, had oral sex with the body, dismembered it, and, once again, saved the skull.

Then came Tony Anthony Hughes, a deaf-mute who met his fate on May 24 when he agreed to pose for photographs. There was the drink, the death, dismemberment, and the saved skull. But apparently this dismemberment didn't happen immediately. Jeff left Tony's body lying in the bedroom until he had time to get to it.

Konerak Sinthasomphone was Jeff's thirteenth victim. He was just fourteen years old at the time of his death. Konerak was wandering around the Grand Avenue Mall in downtown Milwaukee when he was spotted by Jeffrey Dahmer, who apparently didn't recognize him as the brother of the Laotian boy he'd been convicted of molesting. Jeff offered the child money to pose for pictures and Konerak accepted. At the apartment, Jeff took some pictures of him in his underwear, gave him a drink loaded with a sleeping potion, and waited until the child was unconscious before performing oral sex on him. When he was done with that Jeff wanted a drink, but discovered he was out of beer. He felt safe leaving his apartment for a few minutes to buy some because Konerak was insensible.

It turned out, though, that Konerak wasn't as deeply drugged as Jeffrey had thought. As he returned from the store, he spotted the naked boy wandering down the street with two girls who were trying to help him. Jeff reached the boy and attempted to hustle him away, but two police cars and a fire engine pulled up before he could make his escape. He put on his calm, sane face: the same one that had fooled people for most of his life. Jeff's explanation to the officers was that Konerak was his lover, and that after drinking too much, the two had argued. He told them that the same thing had happened before.

The three officers went back to the apartment with Jeffrey and Konerak, Jeffrey feeding them his line all the way. Inside, Konerak sat quietly on the couch. What the officers didn't know was that on the other side of the bedroom door lay the body of Tony Anthony Hughes. Jeffrey had completely convinced them that everything was fine.

How could policemen who had seen Jeffrey that briefly be any wiser than the people who had dealt with him for years? How could they have been expected to see through Jeffrey's facade of sanity when his own probation officer hadn't? When his own family hadn't? The officers bore the added burden of having to avoid giving even the slightest impression of prejudice against the two men because of their homosexuality. Nothing in Jeffrey's behavior had suggested a serial murderer was standing before them. In their efforts to be tolerant of a different lifestyle—a lifestyle they didn't fully understand—the officers had perhaps gone too far; but hindsight is always 20-20.

The policemen left, told the dispatcher the situation had been settled and that they were going to "delouse" themselves—not, perhaps, the wisest thing they might have said, and later used against them to show their insensitivity. As they were filing their report, Jeff strangled Konerak. He then had oral sex with the child's dead body, took pictures, and cut up not just Konerak's body, but Tony Anthony Hughes' as well, and saved both their skulls.

Victim number fourteen was Matt Turner. He met Jeffrey at a Gay Pride parade in Chicago and joined him on the busride back to Milwaukee. Matt met the same fate as the others as soon as he downed the drink Jeff had prepared for him. He was strangled and dismembered. Jeff set Matt's decapitated head in his refrigerator.

On July 5, Jeff was back in Chicago, picking up Jeremiah Weinberger and bringing him via Greyhound back to his apartment in Milwaukee. The two men spent Saturday together having oral sex, but when Sunday came around and Jeremiah wanted to leave, Jeffrey went into action. There was the drink, the strangling, the pictures, and the cutting. Jeremiah's head, too, went into Jeff's freezer.

The apartment had become glutted with body parts. Neighbors were complaining about the stench wafting from Jeff's quarters. Jeff apologized and blamed it on bad meat in a broken refrigerator. Clearly, something needed to be done. Accordingly, Jeff bought a fifty-seven-gallon barrel of hydrochloric acid, set it up in his apartment and began filling it with body parts, waiting patiently for the acid to eat away the flesh from the bones before adding more human remains.

Oliver Lacy, twenty-three, became Jeffrey's sixteenth victim. Following the usual scenario, he went to Jeff's apartment to pick up some easy money posing for pictures. He and Jeff gave each other body rubs, and then Jeff gave Oliver a drink. A few minutes later, Jeff strangled Oliver and had sex with his dead body. Oliver's head was put into a box and joined the others in Jeff's refrigerator, and his heart was cut out and stored in the refrigerator for a later meal.

Jeff was out of control. His lust for blood had completely overtaken him, and he started showing up for work late or not at all. His appearance was also becoming more and more unkempt and dirty. The chocolate factory fired him, but Jeff was so lost to reality at this point that even when his probation officer offered to help him get his job back, Jeff didn't bother to try.

Into this mess walked Joseph Bradehoft. The Minnesota man, married with three children, was job hunting. He fell for Jeff's line, went with him to his apartment, had sex, drank Jeff's usual potion, and was strangled by his new friend. His head joined the others in the freezer and the rest of him went into the acid vat. Joseph would be Jeff's last victim.

Jeffrey met his denouement in the person of Tracy Edwards, a loser wanted by police in Mississippi for sexual battery of a thirteen-year-old girl. Tracy was hanging out at the Grand Avenue Mall in Milwaukee with a group of buddies when they ran into Jeff. A decision was made, according to Tracy in various talk show appearances after the fact, that he and Jeff would buy some beer and join the others later at Jeff's apartment. Jeff, of course, gave the other men the wrong address. When Jeff and Tracy arrived at the apartment and Tracy had a chance to look around, he noticed—it would have been impossible not to—pictures of mutilated male torsos on the walls. Amazingly, he wasn't at all alarmed, but calmly drank a beer and waited for his friends to show up.

And waited. And waited. When the beer was gone, Jeff fixed him one of his knockout drinks, expecting him to fall unconscious. When Tracy didn't, but instead talked of leaving, Jeff suddenly snuck up behind him and hand-cuffed one of his wrists. Alarmed at last, Tracy struggled and prevented Jeff from cuffing his other wrist. He stopped, however, at the sight of the butcher knife that Jeff was holding to Tracy's heart. All Tracy could do was play for time and try not to agitate his captor.

If Jeff said jump, Tracy did. When Jeff wanted to go to the bedroom, Tracy did so without complaint. And it was in the bedroom, where he saw Jeff's graphic pictures of dismembered bodies, that Tracy finally figured out what his fate was supposed to be.

Terrified, he was forced to watch *The Exorcist* with Jeff. Jeff grew calm and confident that he was in control. So confident, in fact, that he allowed Tracy to make several trips to the bathroom. And each time, Tracy said, he looked for ways to escape. There were so many locks on the front door! It was impossible to know which ones to turn to secure his freedom. If he made a run for it and was wrong, he would be a dead man.

More than four hours ticked by. Suddenly Jeff decided it was time to act. He made Tracy lie on the floor and told him he was going to cut his heart out. But first he wanted to take some pictures. When Jeff turned his head to get the camera, Tracy slammed his fist into Jeff's face. Then he smashed his foot into Jeff's stomach, doubling him over with pain.

Edwards raced through the living room to the door and miraculously hit the magic lock to his freedom on the first try. Just moments later he was outside and racing down the street of one of the toughest neighborhoods in Milwaukee, the handcuffs dangling from his wrist. He spotted a police car and ran toward it, happy for once in his life to see the men in blue. As the words spilled from his lips, the policemen could hardly believe what they were hearing. They went with him to Jeff's apartment and knocked. Jeff answered, his mask of sanity firmly in place, bearing absolutely no resemblance to the madman Tracy had hysterically described. In fact, Jeff remained calm until he was ordered to get the key to the handcuffs Tracy was wearing. That was when he grew obstreperous, in an effort to keep the policemen out of his apartment. In a minute, it was Jeffrey in handcuffs.

With Jeff under control, the policemen had a chance to look around. To their shock and horror, they saw the pictures and the blood. They saw Jeff's tools of death and the severed heads in the refrigerator. The smell coming from the acid vat in the bedroom nearly overwhelmed them. Within minutes other officers, evidence technicians, and every other imaginable official party were on the scene, along with reporters and neighbors, all curious about what was going on in apartment 213. It was impossible to work there without some kind of breathing apparatus, so bad was the smell.

How was it that the neighbors, who had complained so often to Jeff and each other about that smell, had never reported it to police? How could they have heard Jeff's power tools grinding bone at all hours of the night and not grown suspicious about what he was doing? How was it, as a community, that no one had noticed these men disappearing? Seventeen of them!

Investigators at the scene were left to deal with the horrifying aftermath of Jeffrey's rampage and the task of identifying the victims and notifying the families.

Bail for Jeff was set at one million dollars just days after his arrest. Not long after that Jeff began detailing his crimes to the police, helping them to piece the evidence together. Not everyone believed that he was being completely honest, however, and as the rumors flew and more and more states came to him with questions about other crimes, he issued a statement through Gerald Boyle, his attorney: "I have told the police everything I have done relative to these homicides. I have not committed any such crimes anywhere in the world other than this state, except I have admitted an incident in Ohio. I have not committed any homicide in any foreign country or in any other state. I have been totally cooperative and would have admitted other crimes if I did them. I did not. Hopefully this will serve to put rumors to rest."

Officers in Bath, Ohio, were finally able to solve the mystery of the missing Steven Hicks when Jeffrey casually identified his photograph. On July 30, 1991, evidence-gatherers began the long and exhausting search of the grounds of the Dahmers' former Bath residence for human bones. They found them. Identifying the tiny fragments was another matter, however; even the Smithsonian Museum got involved.

In January 1992 Jeff was sentenced to fifteen consecutive life sentences after a jury found him sane. Jeff was beaten to death in 1994 by a fellow prison inmate. His ashes were divided into two equal portions and given to his parents.

So many questions still remain. Did some early event in Jeff's life cause him to commit these crimes? These days, more children than not come from broken homes with unstable parents and manage to grow into fine, emotionally healthy adults. Was it some inherent weakness in Jeffrey's makeup that turned his thoughts—and later his actions—in such bizarre directions? His childhood experiments with forest creatures should have signaled a problem to anyone paying attention.

How did he select his victims, most of whom (except for Steven Hicks) were men of color? Most of whom were also gay? It's thought by some that Jeff selected victims he perceived as being inferior to himself. Easy marks. He could play the white bigshot. He hated his homosexuality; by killing gay men, he may have felt he was killing that part of himself. And having sex with their corpses may have been to ensure that there was no chance of rejection. This reasoning makes sense in all but Steven Hicks' case. With Steven, Jeff seemed to simply want to keep the boy with him. Everyone else in his life had left him, and when Steven tried to—Steven, who was trusting and likeable and everything Jeff wasn't—Jeff just decided to take control and "keep" him.

These are all interesting theories about why Jeff might have done what he did. But perhaps the answers lie in another realm entirely. Could it have been Jeff's destiny from the moment of his birth to become a serial killer? Was he born with a blueprint for murder?

Important Dates in the Life of Jeffrey Dahmer

May 21, 1960: Jeffrey Dahmer was born to Joyce and Lionel Dahmer in Milwaukee, Wisconsin, at 4:34 p.m. (CDT), according to Lois Rodden's *Astro Data V: Profiles of Crime*.

December 18, 1966: David Dahmer, Jeffrey's brother, was born.

May 17, 1968: The Dahmer family moved to Bath Township, Ohio.

June 18, 1978: Jeff committed his first murder, of a nineteen-year-old hitchhiker named Steven Hicks. (This murder was not detected until Dahmer confessed thirteen years later.)

July 24, 1978: Joyce and Lionel Dahmer's final divorce decree was granted.

August 1978: Jeffrey's mother took his younger brother, David, away, leaving Jeff alone in the Bath house with no money for food or necessities. His father found him and attempted to enroll Jeff in college in Columbus, Ohio.

December 24, 1978: Lionel Dahmer remarried.

December 28, 1978: Jeff dropped out of college at age eighteen and signed up for army duty.

January 12, 1979: Jeff began army duty at Fort McClellan in Alabama.

June 22, 1979: Jeff completed his training as a medical specialist.

July 1979: Jeff was sent to Baumholder, West Germany, where he spent the next two years.

March 26, 1981: Jeff was discharged from the army because of his alcoholism and refusal to take part in a substance abuse program. He drifted to south Florida.

October 7, 1981: Jeff was arrested in Bath, Ohio, for disorderly conduct, and at his father's suggestion went to stay with his grandmother in West Allis, Wisconsin.

January 14, 1985: Jeff found a job as a mixer at Ambrosia chocolate factory in Milwaukee.

September 8, 1986: Jeff was arrested on charges of lewd behavior (urinating in public).

March 10, 1987: Jeff was convicted on reduced charges of disorderly conduct.

September 15, 1987: Jeff murdered Steven W. Tuomi, his second victim, and began a random spree of murders of young men which lasted until his arrest in July of 1991. (Unbeknownst to his grandmother, he used the basement of her house to hide some of his crimes and dismember his victims.)

September 25, 1988: Jeff moved out of his elderly grandmother's home at her request, and into the Oxford apartment building at 924 North 25th Street in Milwaukee. The murders began again, in apartment 213.

September 26, 1988: Jeff was arrested for second degree sexual assault and enticing a child for immoral purposes.

May 23, 1989: Jeff was sentenced to five years of probation.

July 8, 1990: Jeff attacked a fifteen-year-old boy and let him go. Police didn't follow through on the boy's report.

September 24, 1990: David Thomas was reported missing by his family. (He was later learned to have been murdered by Jeff.)

March 25, 1991: Jeff's mother, Joyce, called him after five years without contact.

July 15, 1991: Jeff was fired from the job he had held for six years at the chocolate factory.

July 22, 1991: Jeff was captured and charged with murder. He confessed to seventeen murders, including an earlier one police hadn't known about— that of Steven Hicks.

January 1992: Jeff was sentenced to fifteen consecutive life sentences after a jury found him sane.

November 28, 1994: Jeff was murdered by a fellow prison inmate.

Jeffrey Dahmer's Victims

June 18, 1978: Steven Hicks, a nineteen-year-old hitchhiker, murdered in Bath, Ohio, and buried in the Dahmers' backyard.

September 15, 1987: Steven W. Tuomi, a twenty-year-old from Michigan, murdered.

January 1988: James E. Doxtator, a fourteen-year-old Native American, murdered at Jeffrey's grandmother's house in West Allis.

March 24, 1988: Richard Guerrero, murdered in the basement apartment of the house in West Allis.

March 25, 1989: Anthony Sears, murdered at the house in West Allis.

June 14, 1990: Eddie Smith, murdered in Jeffrey's Milwaukee apartment.

July 15, 1990: Ricky Beeks, murdered.

September 3, 1990: Ernest Miller, murdered.

September 24, 1990: David Thomas reported missing, and later found to have been Jeff's murder victim.

February 18, 1991: Curtis Straughter, murdered.

April 7, 1991: Errol Lindsey, murdered.

May 24, 1991: Tony Anthony Hughes, a deaf-mute, murdered.

May 27, 1991: Konerak Sinthasomphone, a fourteen-year-old Laotian immigrant, murdered.

June 30, 1991: Matt Turner, a twenty-year-old, murdered.

July 5, 1991: Jeremiah Weinberger, a twenty-three-year-old Jeff met at a bar, murdered.

July 15, 1991: Oliver Lacy, murdered.

July 19, 1991: Joseph Bradhoft, murdered.

Astrological Blueprint for Jeffrey Dahmer

—Edna L. Rowland

Serial murderers are a statistical anomaly that occur only once in every five million members of the total population. According to the FBI's National Center for Analysis of Violent Crime, there are as many as fifty serial killers in America today. They walk among us and we seldom notice. Isn't that a frightening thought?

	☉	☽	☿	♀	♂	♃	♄	♅	♆	♇	MC	AS	IC	DS	☊
☉		10 ♉ 21	03 ♊ 24	26 ♉ 29	04 ♉ 25	16 ♓ 27	24 ♓ 22	09 ♋ 02	18 ♌ 58	17 ♋ 12	27 ♊ 02	10 ♌ 07	27 ♓ 02	10 ♉ 07	26 ♋ 33
☽	040 53		12 ♉ 58	06 ♉ 03	13 ♈ 59	26 ♒ 00	03 ♓ 56	18 ♊ 35	28 ♑ 31	26 ♊ 45	06 ♊ 35	19 ♋ 41	06 ♓ 35	19 ♈ 41	06 ♋ 06
☿	005 ☌ 13	046 ∠ 06		29 ♉ 06	07 ♉ 02	19 ♓ 03	26 ♓ 59	11 ♋ 38	21 ♌ 35	19 ♋ 48	29 ♊ 38	12 ♌ 44	29 ♓ 38	12 ♉ 44	29 ♋ 10
♀	008 ☌ 36	032 ⊻ 16	013 49		00 ♉ 07	12 ♓ 08	20 ♓ 04	04 ♋ 43	14 ♌ 40	12 ♋ 53	22 ♊ 44	05 ♌ 49	22 ♓ 44	05 ♉ 49	22 ♋ 15
♂	052 45	011 ☌ 51	057 ✶ 58	044 ∠ 08		20 ♒ 04	28 ♒ 00	12 ♊ 39	22 ♑ 35	20 ♊ 49	00 ♊ 39	13 ♑ 45	00 ♓ 39	13 ♈ 45	00 ♋ 11
♃	148 ⚻ 42	107 48	153 55	140 05	095 □ 56		10 ♑ 01	24 ♎ 41	04 ♐ 37	02 ♏ 51	12 ♎ 41	25 ♏ 46	12 ♑ 41	25 ♒ 46	12 ♏ 12
♄	132 ⚼ 50	091 □ 57	138 03	124 △ 13	080 05	015 51		02 ♏ 36	12 ♐ 33	10 ♏ 46	20 ♎ 37	03 ♐ 42	20 ♑ 37	03 ♓ 42	20 ♏ 08
♅	076 28	117 △ 21	071 Q 14	085 □ 04	129 13	134 ⚼ 49	150 ⚻ 41		27 ♍ 12	25 ♌ 26	05 ♌ 16	18 ♍ 21	05 ♏ 16	18 ♊ 21	04 ♍ 47
♆	156 20	162 46	151 ⚻ 07	164 57	150 ⚻ 54	054 57	070 48	079 52		05 ♎ 22	15 ♍ 12	28 ♎ 18	15 ♐ 12	28 ♑ 18	14 ♎ 43
♇	092 □ 47	133 ⚼ 41	087 □ 34	101 24	145 32	118 △ 30	134 ⚼ 21	016 19	063 ✶ 32		13 ♌ 26	26 ♍ 31	13 ♏ 26	26 ♊ 31	12 ♍ 57
MC	052 28	093 □ 21	047 15	061 ✶ 05	105 13	158 49	174 ☍ 40	023 59	103 52	040 19		06 ♍ 21	23 ♎ 16	06 ♊ 21	22 ♌ 47
AS	138 39	179 ☍ 32	133 ⚼ 25	147 15	168 35	072 Q 38	088 □ 30	062 ✶ 11	017 41	045 ∠ 51	086 □ 10		06 ♐ 21	19 ♋ 27	05 ♎ 53
IC	127 △ 31	086 □ 38	132 44	118 △ 54	074 46	021 10	005 ☌ 19	156 00	076 07	139 40	180 ☍ 00	093 □ 49		06 ♓ 21	22 ♏ 47
DS	041 20	000 ☌ 27	046 ∠ 34	032 44	011 24	107 21	091 □ 29	117 △ 48	162 18	134 ⚼ 08	093 □ 49	180 ☍ 00	086 □ 10		05 ♋ 53
☊	111 △ 30	152 ⚻ 24	106 17	120 △ 07	164 15	099 47	115 △ 38	035 02	044 ∠ 49	018 43	059 ✶ 02	027 08	120 △ 57	152 51	

Midpoints and Aspects for Jeffrey Dahmer

According to Lois Rodden's *Profiles of Crimes*, serial killer Jeffrey Lionel Dahmer was born on May 21, 1960, in Milwaukee, Wisconsin.[1] The birth certificate states that birth occurred at 4:34 p.m. (CDT).

If this time is accurate, Dahmer's Sun is at 00° Gemini, on the Taurus/Gemini cusp, in the dual sign of the Twins. The 19th degree of Libra—a dangerous homicidal degree—rises on his Ascendant, and the Ascendant ruler, Venus, resides in his 8th house at 22° Taurus. Although the birth chart is besieged with adverse configurations, the Venus-ruled Ascendant bestows a pleasing appearance and good looks. His Moon, Mars, and Saturn occupy Gauquelin plus sectors.

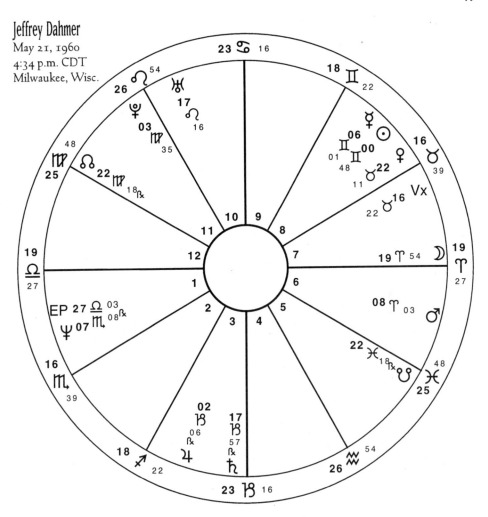

Birth chart for Jeffrey Dahmer

The Moon, which rules subjective feelings and early childhood conditioning, is exactly conjunct the Descendant at 19° Aries, indicating a strong need for emotional balance and control. He belongs to the Balsamic Moon type, since he was born about three days before the New Moon. Anciently, the Moon in Aries refers to the wolf—the most murderous of animals with the exception of mankind.

The Sun generally rules individuality, identity, ego, and self-esteem, but in a male chart it signifies the living body and energy level as well. Dahmer's natal Sun resides in 00° Gemini in the 8th house, so this is a daytime birth.

The Sun's position in a house connected with sexual identity and death and its lack of any favorable aspects indicate an inherent, inborn lack of physical vigor and vitality. The Sun only makes three aspects: a neutral conjunction to Mercury (its dispositor), an unfavorable inconjunct aspect to Jupiter, and a close square to Pluto.

In traditional astrology, Mars represents sexual activity, masculine energy, and assertiveness, but when misdirected or adversely aspected—as it is here—it can be a violent planet. At "home" in its own sign of Aries, this planet might have had a counteracting influence on the de-energizing effect of the natal Sun's weak position, but Mars doesn't aspect the Ascendant and makes only one favorable aspect, a sextile to Mercury.

The ruler of Dahmer's 7th house of partnerships, Mars, is located in his 6th house. Pisces occupies the cusp of his 6th house, which rules health and diet problems. Mars here makes a weak inconjunct aspect to the 6th house ruler (Neptune) and the separating Mars/Jupiter square signifies misdirected or dissipated energy. Unlike John Wayne Gacy—a pedophile serial killer who married twice—Dahmer never married, and reportedly showed little interest in the opposite sex.

Dahmer's early obsession with chemistry is depicted in the chart by Neptune in Scorpio; by age ten he was already beginning to experiment with acid (Mars) to melt the bones of animals. He kept skulls of chipmunks, squirrels, and other small animals in a backyard shed. Dahmer was given the gift of a chemistry set while in elementary school, and used it to satisfy his preoccupation with torture and death.

Many serial killers display signs of cruelty to animals and/or insects at an early age, so this should be considered a danger signal when it occurs, especially if part of a pattern of negative or violent behavior. Dahmer's father claims that his son was molested by a boy in his neighborhood when he was eight, but Jeffrey denied this, or repressed this traumatic memory. With Saturn trine his 8th house cusp and square his Ascendant, he may indeed have repressed this memory. At the time, his progressed Midheaven was sextile his natal Sun in his 8th house (sexual identity).

Although Dahmer managed to complete high school, heroic attempts by his father to offer his son a college education seemed doomed to fail. With Saturn in his 3rd house of schooling, exactly inconjunct Uranus, and Jupiter, his 3rd house ruler, square Mars, Dahmer just didn't have the self-discipline (Saturn) needed to apply himself, although he wanted to please his father. By the time he entered college, his drinking problem had already become acute, and he frequently skipped classes.

Neptune retrograde at 07° Scorpio is in an alcoholic degree, and this planet, which rules alcohol and drugs, is inconjunct (an unfavorable health aspect) Mars in Dahmer's 6th house.[2] When arrested in 1991, Dahmer was known to have all the symptoms of untreated and prolonged alcoholism. At age eighteen, after only one semester of college, he dropped out to join the army as a medic, but was discharged two years later because of substance abuse and his inability (or refusal) to cope with the problem.

Pluto, the higher octave of Mars, rules mediumship. Dahmer's Neptune/Pluto midpoint at 5°22' Libra is opposed by Mars. According to Reinhold Ebertin's *The Combination of Stellar Influences*, the interpretation for this planetary picture, or tree, is as follows: "A lack of energy, the misfortune to be used as a tool for other people's interests, a lack of resistance or stamina. The tendency to succumb to external powers, the state of being utilized as a medium."[3] In other words, possession. It's interesting that Dahmer's favorite videotape (which he forced some victims to watch) was *The Exorcist*—a popular movie about a child supposedly possessed by demons.[4]

On March 27, 1960, just two months before Dahmer's birth, a solar eclipse occurred at 06°39' Aries. This prenatal eclipse opposes his Ascendant/North Node and Neptune/Pluto midpoints at 05° Libra, and forms a close conjunction with his natal Mars at 08° Aries. Falling as it does in his 6th house, this prenatal conjunction only serves to emphasize the importance of health problems in his life, as well as the folly of ignoring or neglecting them.

Apparently knowledgeable enough about narcotics to drug all seventeen of his male victims before killing them, Dahmer then used a potent combination of chemicals to dispose of their dismembered bodies. In this way, he successfully concealed the extent of his crimes. Neptune in the 1st house (which rules the outer self or personality) points to the deceptive, sometimes disarming mask he wore to seduce the young men (Mercury) he picked up at gay bars and brought home—as illustrated by natal Mercury inconjunct Neptune. When finally captured, the progressed Moon at 07° Gemini was activating this Mercury/Neptune natal aspect. He had a secret life that he shared only with his victims. But the penalty for knowing Dahmer's secret self was death (Pluto)—Mercury square Pluto.

Although legally declared competent enough to stand trial, this ruling didn't mean Dahmer wasn't suffering from mental illness. (Legal sanity is an issue distinct from legal competence.) Even though he was judged competent to stand trial, physicians who diagnosed him after his arrest and conviction in 1991 believed him to be schizophrenic.

Dahmer's ruling planet, Venus, makes a close trine to the Moon's North Node at 22° Virgo, as well as a trine to Saturn in another Earth sign, Capricorn. The South Node at 22° Pisces is near the fixed star Markab, which is connected with violent death and insanity.[5]

According to Annette Rubin's research into 262 cases of schizophrenics, Pluto in adverse aspect to the natal Sun is often found in charts of this type, and is usually accompanied by Saturn afflictions.

Let's see if these statistics are applicable to Dahmer's chart. At birth, Dahmer's natal Sun closely squares Pluto; Saturn, the other significator, is square the Ascendant, opposite the Midheaven, square the Moon, inconjunct Uranus and sesquiquadrate Pluto. Saturn not only rules Dahmer's 4th house of genetic inheritance, but is within a five-degree orb of conjunction with the 4th house cusp as well. So astrology, in this case, serves to confirm the reported opinions or diagnosis of the medical experts.

In an article published in the summer 1969 issue of *The Astrological Review*, Rubin states: "The concept that the disease pertains to a deficiency in the chromosomal structure and is transmitted through genetic inheritance is strengthened by the presence of an afflicted Saturn in 147 charts." Her research also suggests that Sun/Pluto adverse aspects indicate a paranoid type of schizophrenia.[6]

Let's take another quick look at Dahmer's birth chart. If we count the Ascendant degree as one point, his chart displays a Cardinal T-square pattern composed of the Ascendant, Moon, and Saturn. Pluto adversely aspects all of these Cardinal angles. Saturn, the focal planet, squares the Moon, which represents the mother who abandoned Jeff. His Moon/Saturn midpoint at 03°56' Virgo is exactly conjunct Pluto. According to Ebertin, this planetary picture can be described as follows: "The necessity to rely upon oneself only, the inclination or necessity to rise in life by using force and to go one's way alone. Organic suffering in conjunction with strong feelings or depression. The separation from the wife or the mother."[7]

In natal astrology, Saturn and its ruling sign, Capricorn, are standard astrological symbols for the father. This planet, at home in 17° Capricorn, makes a harmonious trine aspect to Dahmer's ruler, Venus, indicating a favorable relationship with the parent of the same sex, his father.

In a male chart, the 10th house and its occupants usually denote the father. Saturn exactly inconjunct Uranus in Dahmer's 10th house shows that it would probably take another major crisis (Uranus) to bring his father to his side again. Jeff's father, Lionel, is appropriately represented in the natal chart by an elevated Uranus in the Lion's sign, Leo. Lionel Dahmer had been emotionally and financially supportive of his thirty-one-year-old son ever since Jeffrey's arrest, even offering to pay for his defense attorney. With Dahmer's 10th house ruler—the Moon—in the public 7th house trine Uranus, his father evidently didn't recognize his son's predicament or the extent of his illness until it was made public by the news media at the time of his unexpected arrest on July 22, 1991. (Since then, Dahmer was tried and convicted for first degree intentional homicide.)

Important Dates as Illustrated by Secondary Progressions and Transits to Jeffrey Dahmer's Natal Chart

On December 18, 1966, when the progressed Sun reached 07° Gemini, conjunct Dahmer's natal Mercury—natural ruler of siblings—his brother, David, was born. Two years later, when Dahmer's 4th house ruler, Saturn, activated his natal Cardinal T-square, the family moved to a new home in

Bath, Ohio. At that time, transiting Saturn at 20° Aries opposed his Ascendant, squared his natal Saturn, and was conjunct his natal Moon.

His parents' bitter divorce broke the family apart in the summer of 1978. Soon after the divorce, Jeff's distraught mother moved out of the family home in Ohio and went to another state, taking his younger brother, David, to live with relatives. While his parents fought over David's custody, Dahmer felt left out, neglected and, apparently, angry. Jeffrey, who had just turned eighteen, was left behind and told to look out for himself. During this upsetting interval he committed his first murder. Steven Hicks, a nineteen-year-old hitchhiker, became the victim of Jeff's loneliness and anger. But this murder wasn't discovered until Dahmer was arrested and confessed to it thirteen years later.

On the date of this murder, June 18, 1978, transiting Pluto at 13° Libra directly opposed his Moon/Mars midpoint at 13° Aries. Transiting Mars at 02° Virgo was exactly conjunct his natal Pluto! (Mars and Pluto are the two most potentially violent planets in the zodiac.) Progressed Sun at 18° Gemini was sextile Jeff's natal Uranus and trine his Ascendant. Progressed Mars at 21° Aries had recently crossed his chart's Descendant, and was just separating from a conjunction with his Moon, probably denoting the mounting anger he felt toward his mother. His progressed Ascendant at 03° Scorpio was exactly sextile natal Pluto, while his progressed Midheaven had moved to 10° Leo square his Sun/Moon midpoint.

A few months later his father remarried on December 24, 1978, and in an attempt to make amends, offered his son a home. Evidently, though, it was too late to mend "broken fences." Dahmer's progressed Moon at 17° Sagittarius was rapidly approaching an exact opposition to the progressed Sun at 18° Gemini—this is a progressed Full Moon, which usually marks a turning-point or time of personal crisis. At the same time, transiting Pluto at 18° Libra was conjunct his Libra Ascendant and about to cross the natal horizon. Transiting Neptune at 18° Sagittarius conjunct his progressed Moon and opposite progressed Sun didn't help a bit since it clouded his judgement, making him prone to escapist solutions such as alcohol and drugs.

With transiting Uranus in 19° Scorpio square his natal Uranus, it was actually a prime time for him to show some independence (Uranus) and break out of the family cocoon. He couldn't conceal the anger and adolescent rebelliousness (Uranus) he felt towards his family, but at the same time was also actually confused and bewildered. He chose the wrong path; murder was no solution. (Thirteen years later, when transiting Pluto reached 17° Scorpio on July 22, 1991, squaring his Uranus, he was captured and arrested, and lost his freedom forever.)

A second chance came on December 28, 1978, when Jeffrey joined the army, but he blew that, too. In June of 1979 he completed his training as a medical specialist and spent two years in Germany, but on March 26, 1981, he was outprocessed after refusal to take part in an alcoholism treatment program. At the time of his discharge (after which the rampage of murders resumed), his progressed Sun at 20° Gemini was conjunct his Mars/Pluto midpoint—the midpoint of murder, according to Ebertin. Transiting Pluto (retrograde) at 23° Libra was exactly square the Midheaven and traveling through the 1st house. The progressed Moon at 22° Capricorn was conjunct another angle—his 4th house cusp—opposed his Midheaven (which governs reputation), and squared transiting Pluto.

During March of 1981, his growing health problems were emphasized by a transiting Jupiter/Saturn conjunction at 05–06° Libra in his 12th house of hospitalization and illness, exactly conjunct his Neptune/Pluto midpoint in opposition to his natal Mars. At the same time, Mars was making a return to its natal sign position in Aries, creating a double impact between the configurations in his 6th and 12th houses. On March 26, the date of his discharge, the Sun and Venus were also in transit between 02–05° Aries in Dahmer's 6th house of health, and aspecting his natal Mars.

These aspects confirm what we already know—Jeffrey Dahmer was in desperate need of help for his substance abuse problems. It's unfortunate that he didn't accept it when it was offered him. On October 7, 1981, he was arrested for disorderly conduct. As a result, his father encouraged him to live with his grandmother in West Allis, Wisconsin. This didn't work either, although he began steady employment at a Milwaukee chocolate factory on January 14, 1985. At that time, his progressed Midheaven had moved to 16° Leo, conjunct his natal Uranus. The progressed Ascendant was at 08° Scorpio conjunct natal Neptune, so denying his alcoholism was not the answer. Or did he use alcohol to mask the dark side of his personality—his sexual perversion?

The following year, on September 8, 1986, when his progressed Midheaven was at 18° Leo (still in conjunction with natal Uranus) and his progressed Moon was at 08° Aries exactly conjunct his natal Mars, he was arrested again, this time for lewd and lascivious behavior.

A week later, on September 15, 1987, he murdered Steven Tuomi, his second victim. On this date, transiting Pluto at 08° Scorpio was conjunct his progressed Ascendant at 09° Scorpio and conjunct natal Neptune. He was twenty-seven years old in 1987, so his progressed Moon at 21° Aries had just completed its twenty-seven-year return cycle to its natal sign position. (During this twenty-seven-year cycle, the aspects to the natal Moon will be repeated by the progressed Moon.) The progressed Moon squared progressed Mercury, his Sun sign ruler, at 21° Cancer. An Aries Moon conjunct his natal Descendant would seek reassurance from others. Their emotions could explode quickly, and as suddenly die down (Aries/fire=Moon/emotions=Descendant/house cusp of "others").

When arrested in Milwaukee on July 22, 1991, Dahmer confessed to seventeen murders, including the first one in Ohio. He was finally caught and captured when one of his would-be victims, Tracy Edwards, escaped from Dahmer's apartment and immediately alerted police.

Major configurations for his arrest on July 22 include: progressed Midheaven at 23° Leo squaring his ruling planet (Venus), and progressed Ascendant at 12° Scorpio semisquare progressed Jupiter. Transiting Pluto at 17° Scorpio makes an exact square to his Uranus and conjuncts his natal Vertex. Transiting

Saturn (which rules endings) is at 03° Aquarius, exactly inconjunct natal Pluto. Transiting Mars at 03° Virgo is exactly conjunct natal Pluto, and Venus, Dahmer's ruler, at 05° Virgo, is just two degrees past a conjunction with his Pluto. Neptune, in transit at 15° Capricorn, is conjunct natal Saturn, and transiting Jupiter conjuncts Uranus.

Since there is no death penalty in either Ohio or Wisconsin, where the murders were committed, Dahmer could not be executed. But he was sentenced to serve consecutive prison terms and spend the rest of his life behind bars, as indicated by the progressed Moon's position at 07° Gemini conjunct his natal Mercury (ruler of his 12th house of prisons and other places of confinement) at the time of his capture on July 22, 1991.

However, the 12th house also rules karma, as well as prisons, and on the morning of November 28, 1994, Dahmer was murdered by another inmate at the Columbia Correctional Institution in Portage, Wisconsin. After serving two years of his sixteen consecutive life sentences, Dahmer died on the way to the hospital from brain trauma and extensive skull fractures. It is reported that he was attacked while cleaning a recreational area and was found in a pool of blood in the prison bathroom.

His progressed Moon at 17° Cancer was almost exactly in opposition to his natal Saturn (planet of karma and ruler of his 4th house of endings) on the date of his death. At the same time transiting Mars (a potentially violent planet) was conjunct his progressed Midheaven at 26° Leo, and also inconjunct transiting Uranus at 23° Capricorn exactly on the cusp of his 4th house.

His progressed Sun/Venus conjunction at 3-4° Cancer was activating the midpoint of his progressed Mars/Pluto (murder midpoint) at 3°51' Cancer, and his progressed Ascendant at 15° Scorpio was opposite his 8th house cusp (death) so his time had come.

Kenneth Bianchi

Chapter Three

The Hillside Stranglers

Angelo Buono and Kenneth Bianchi—Their Stories

—Sandra Harrisson Young

THE DETECTIVE STOOD IN THE LOS

Angeles morgue and looked at the two bodies lying side by side on

separate tables. Physically, the women were quite different, one tiny—

almost childlike—and the other husky and full-figured. But it wasn't their physical differences that made his blood run cold. It was the similarity of the ligature marks around their wrists, ankles, and throats.

The bodies of the two women had been found on different days and in different locations, but it was the detective's gut feeling that they had been killed by the same man—or men. He was convinced there were two of them. It was the way the bodies had been carried, not dragged, to the spots where they were later found.

Serial killers.

The detective's instincts were proven all too horribly correct as the body count mounted. Between October of 1977 and February of 1978, ten bodies were found, all linked by detectives to the same pair of killers.

The citizens of Los Angeles were terrified. The girls murdered could have been anyone. The victims included a student, a waitress, a would-be actress, a runaway, and a prostitute, among others. One young woman had been boldly abducted as she parked in front of her own home. Had her parents been looking out their window, they would have seen it happen. Another had vanished from her apartment. No one felt safe.

Indeed, no one *was* safe.

When Angelo Buono started murdering women in Los Angeles in 1977, he was forty-four years old. There was nothing handsome about him in a traditional sense. He resembled a buzzard, with his overly large head, arms, and hands. "Buzzard" was, in fact, an affectionate nickname used for him by his family.

Angelo had a small house which he kept in immaculate condition. It was one of the few residences left on a street that had been taken over by small businesses and fast food restaurants. In a garage attached to the house by an aluminum awning that prevented neighbors from watching his comings and goings was Angelo's Trim Shop, where he skillfully reupholstered automobile seats. He was rumored to have worked on cars belonging to the likes of Frank Sinatra, such was the quality of his work. He raised rabbits, had a dog and a small tank of fish. To the casual observer, everything would have seemed normal.

The thing about Angelo, though, was that he hated women. As far as he was concerned, they were good for only one thing, which was allowing him to do with their bodies whatever he wanted, whenever he wanted. That included his daughter, as well as his sons' girlfriends. (It has even been suggested he violated some of his sons.)

No one knows what triggered this hatred, but it started early. His parents divorced when he was fourteen years old. He was raised by his mother, who was said to have offered sexual favors to men as payment for household repairs. Angelo claimed that she had sometimes taken him along on her "dates" and made him wait outside while she spent time with various men. By the time he was fourteen, he was referring to his mother in the most vulgar and degrading sexual terms.

Angelo fathered seven sons and one daughter with three women. He left the mother of the first child before the birth, had their marriage annulled by the Catholic Church and married another woman, with whom he fathered his next five children. This wife finally left him after seven years of marriage, when she could no longer endure the beatings and rapes at Angelo's hands. He began a live-in relationship with yet another woman in 1965. She already had two of her own children and bore Angelo two more.

All during this time, Angelo piled up arrests and jail time, but not for any serious offenses until his arrest for auto theft in 1968. Even then, though, the sentence was light: three years of probation with fifteen weekends to be served in the county jail.

In 1971, after listening to complaints from her fourteen-year-old daughter that Angelo was touching her too much, his live-in girlfriend packed up her four children and moved to Florida—despite death threats from Angelo.

It was 1975 when Angelo opened his car upholstery shop on East Colorado Street. When word got out that he was there, women—young women—swarmed over the place, all but bumping into each other going in and coming out. He was forty years old and kept girlfriends as young as thirteen. He was crude and had no interest in any kind of relationship with

DESTINED FOR MURDER

any of them other than sex on demand, yet they kept coming back for more. It only served to fuel his disrespect and treatment of the girls as objects. Why should he respect them? The worse he treated them, the more they wanted him.

Angelo had no conscience, but he might never have resorted to murder as a way to pass a dull evening if he hadn't hooked up with his younger cousin, Kenneth Bianchi.

Ken, twenty-six and good-looking in a plastic, California kind of way—although he'd just arrived from New York—was the original born loser. He had quite a high opinion of himself and his pseudo-intellect, and elaborate dreams about the way he wanted to live. The problem, though, was that he was lazy. He wanted everything handed to him. People *owed* him. He wanted to be a psychologist, but rather than working toward a degree, he fraudulently obtained copies of other people's degrees and inserted his own name.

Bianchi was a magnificent liar, a skill he had honed from the time he was just five years old. He could spin remarkable tales out of air and convince people of the truth of what he was saying by appearing absolutely sincere.

Ken was the son of a prostitute who had given him up at birth. He was adopted by Angelo Buono's aunt when he was only three months old. His otherwise-childless adoptive mother was obsessed with Kenny. In her eyes he could do no wrong. When troubles at school cropped up, they were never his fault. There was always someone else to blame.

He was a constant problem as a child, with his lying and temper tantrums. His worried mother was advised to get Kenny psychological counseling, but she didn't. At one point she was even told to get counseling herself, but by then it was too little, too late.

The adult Kenny couldn't separate fact from fiction any better than the child Kenny could. He married at eighteen, but divorced shortly thereafter. He needed more than one woman at a time, yet demanded fidelity from all of them. He could be as sleazy as he wanted, but expected an impossible perfection of his women—and was always disappointed in them.

Another flaw in Kenny's character was his refusal to take responsibility for his own actions. If he failed at something, it was someone else's fault. If someone didn't like him, there was something wrong with *them*, not him.

In addition to his interest in psychology, Ken was interested in law enforcement—but couldn't get past the psychological screening to become a policeman. The closest he came was working as a security guard in a department store, and even then managed to pervert his performance into a shoplifting extravaganza.

In 1976, his relationships in the east falling apart and his unrealistic plans for the future coming to nothing, Ken blamed it all on New York and decided to move to California, where he felt his talents might be better appreciated. Since he didn't know anyone there, his cousin, Angelo, agreed to put Ken up temporarily until he found his feet.

Predictably, Los Angeles was a repeat of New York. Even with his phony psychology degrees papering the walls of an office he'd rented, he couldn't drum up enough business to keep himself in perms. But there were women. Lots of women. He was swimming in them while he stayed at Angelo's house—not just his own, but Angelo's, and Angelo's sons' girlfriends.

Although Ken didn't have much success at earning a living, he was able to drive around, in a 1972 Cadillac given to him by his mother. For the most part, he lived off the generosity of his girlfriends. Life, for Ken, was one big scam.

The chemistry between the two cousins was dangerous. There's a good chance that neither would have killed separately; together, they proved a lethal combination.

The first murder wasn't really intentional. Angelo and Ken had toyed with pimping. It seemed like an easy way to earn extra money—so easy, in fact, that they decided to become serious pimps. To do that, they needed contacts. Yolanda Washington was a prostitute who had the misfortune of being present when one of her co-workers sold a trick list to Angelo and Ken: 175 names at a dollar per name. It was supposed to be a list of men who wanted call girls to come to their homes. It turned out to be a list of men who wanted to come to the girls, making it virtually worthless to Angelo and Ken.

They had been scammed and they didn't like it. They went looking for the prostitute who had sold them the list, but she was nowhere to be found.

They did, however, find Yolanda, on a corner plying her trade. Buono, driving Bianchi's Cadillac, dropped Bianchi off and approached her alone. She got into the car and the two of them had sex. With Yolanda still in the car, Buono went back for Bianchi. Ken climbed into the backseat with Yolanda, who sensed that something was wrong and began screaming. The cousins handcuffed her and continued driving. Bianchi, not wanting to be left out of the fun, raped Yolanda and, on an impulse, began to strangle her. Yolanda didn't die easily or well, but she did die. Bianchi stripped off her clothes and stole her turquoise ring. The cousins then dumped her body near the entrance to Forest Lawn Cemetery.

They had murdered their first victim and found it remarkably easy. There was no guilt. On the contrary, it whetted their appetite for more. Less than two weeks later, on Halloween Eve, they went looking for another victim.

Judy Miller was a skinny child of fifteen who had already been a prostitute for over a year when the cousins spotted her standing in the parking lot of a diner looking for business. Following pretty much the same plan they had executed with Yolanda, Buono dropped Bianchi off and approached the girl alone. She got into the car. Buono turned the car around and picked up his cousin, who flashed a phony police badge, handcuffed her, and claimed that they were arresting her. Though little Judy didn't know it, she was as good as dead already.

The cousins drove to Buono's house and walked her inside, under the protective cover of the metal awning. Angelo went to his shop and returned with tape, rope, and some foam seat stuffing to put over her eyes. They took turns raping the terrified girl, all the while telling her that if she cooperated she wouldn't get hurt. As they got ready to kill her, they tightly bound her ankles, made sure the homemade blindfold of foam stuffing and tape was in place, and put a plastic bag over her head, tying it off with a rope around her thin neck. The girl desperately tried to get air. The bag inflated and deflated with each frantic breath, but it was hopeless. She was dead within minutes.

They then removed all evidence of the night's work from her body: handcuffs, tape, foam, ropes, and bag. They put everything, including all her clothes and belongings, into a trash bag and tossed it in a dumpster. Then they put Judy into the trunk of the Cadillac and drove to Alta Terrace Drive, where they left her body on a lawn in plain view. Buono had chosen the dump site. It was near the home of a fourteen-year-old girl whose parents had objected to her seeing Angelo.

Police found Judy Miller's body on Halloween morning, though they had no way of knowing who she was at the time. The man who owned the property had spotted the body early in the morning and called the police. In an effort to provide what little dignity he could to the dead girl, and to prevent anyone else from having to see her, he'd covered her with a blanket he'd retrieved from some toys and stuffed animals. Not at all happy about this tampering with the crime scene, but understanding the man's feelings, the police removed the blanket and looked at the body.

Judy's tiny body told the story of her death. There were bruises at her slender throat where the rope had choked the life out of her; there were marks on her ankles and wrists indicating that she'd been bound. And there was a puff of some unidentified foamy material on the girl's right eyelid. It could have been cotton. It could have been anything. And unfortunately, it could also have come from anywhere—even the blanket the citizen had used to cover her. It was removed for analysis. No one at that time had any idea what a pivotal piece of evidence this would prove to be when the murderers were at last arrested.

Buono and Bianchi couldn't believe how easy it was to kill people and get away with it. There wasn't even any mention of the murders in the newspapers. Ken was frankly disappointed about the lack of publicity, but it also made him feel invincible. In fact, he and Angelo were so emboldened that they decided to set their sights on victims other than prostitutes. Los Angeles was full of beautiful women there for the taking. From now on, they were going to be more selective about whom they killed.

For their next victim they selected Lissa Kastin, a twenty-one-year-old waitress they spotted as she drove home from work. They used the police scam, approaching her car with a badge as soon as she'd parked, and telling her she was a suspect in a robbery. They handcuffed her and drove her to a "satellite police station" which was, in fact, Angelo's home.

Once there, neither man found her to his liking sexually. So as not to waste the evening entirely, they took particular pains with her murder. With a rope around her neck, Buono brought Lissa to the brink of death time and time again. Bianchi said later that he thought it might have taken an hour for her to die, but he wasn't really sure. It was Bianchi, not wanting to miss out on the fun, who took over for Buono and finally killed her. Lissa's post-mortem fate was the same as the two who had gone before her: all her belongings were placed in a dumpster and her body was left in a drainage ditch near the Chevy Chase Country Club.

Neither man was satisfied with the night's work. They'd moved too fast. Had they taken the time to look closely at Lissa, they never would have abducted her. Next time would be different. Next time they'd find a woman who was "choice."

That woman turned out to be Jane King, a beautiful, long-legged aspiring actress and Scientology follower. When the cousins spotted her sitting on a bench waiting for a bus after an acting class, they couldn't believe their luck. This time it was Bianchi who approached the would-be victim on foot, pretending to wait for a bus also, striking up a conversation with her and conning her with his charm.

Buono pretended to come upon them accidentally. Bianchi, acting surprised and pleased to see him, suggested to Jane that perhaps his cousin, an L.A.P.D. Reservist like himself, would give them a ride.

Jane fell for it.

The cousins really enjoyed Jane. She was by far the prettiest of their victims. They took their time with her. Instead of tossing a coin to see who went first as they had with the others, Angelo simply announced that she was his. Bianchi had to settle for going second.

Jane's beauty didn't save her from suffering the same fate as the others. As they had done with Lissa Kastin, they cut Jane's air supply off by tightening a rope around her neck, then loosening it and tightening it again. It was two weeks before her body was found, in some bushes off the Golden State Freeway.

Buono and Bianchi's next two victims were abducted, raped and murdered together. They were Dolores Cepeda, twelve, and her best friend, Sonja Johnson, fourteen. The cousins picked them up as they got off a bus, flashing their badges and claiming to be police officers. The girls, who thought they were being arrested for shoplifting at the mall they'd just left, went with the men. When they reached Angelo's house they were raped and murdered. Their bodies were dumped in a place Angelo called the "cowpatch" because of the stench of rotting garbage left by litterers. (He had brought girls there for sex when he was young.)

Their next victim, Kristina Weckler, was selected by Bianchi. She lived in an apartment complex where Bianchi had once lived, and had rejected his advances with the comment that he reminded her of "a sleazy used-car salesman." Bianchi knocked on her apartment door and told her that he was now an L.A.P.D. Reservist. While on his rounds, he said, he'd noticed that her car had been in an accident. When Kristina went with him to check on the damage, she was abducted by the cousins and, like the others, taken to Angelo's house, where she was raped.

Kristina's murder, however, didn't follow along the normal lines. She was brutally tortured with injections of Windex that sent her into convulsions. When those didn't kill her, they placed a gas pipe from a disconnected stove at her neck, covered it and her head with a plastic bag, and tied it all up with rope. While Bianchi worked the rope, Buono worked the gas, turning it on and off until she was finally dead.

Kristina's body was dumped on Ranons Way in Eagle Rock, where she was found the next day.

Eighteen-year-old Lauren Wagner was next. The cousins followed her as she drove to the home she shared with her parents, and boldly abducted her at gunpoint, again flashing their badges—but unaware that this time there was a witness. Despite her desperate efforts to make the men believe she was not only willing but looking forward to having sex with them in an attempt to save her life, they raped and then killed her. With this murder they added a new dimension to their torture by trying to electrocute her. Though they managed to burn her with the live wires taped to her hands, Lauren didn't die. The men ended up having to strangle her. Her body was dumped near the Pasadena Freeway.

Angelo and Ken were getting bored with their routine. For a change of pace, they located a vacant apartment and arranged to have a call girl meet them there. Seventeen-year-old Kimberly Diane Martin was nearly their undoing. Instead of going quietly into the night, she screamed at the top of her lungs and disturbed people in neighboring apartments. The cousins eventually managed to subdue her. Then they raped, murdered, and disposed of her body as they had the others.

It was nearly two months before they struck again, and when they did it was close to home. Cindy Hudspeth, a waitress at a restaurant Angelo frequented, had brought her Datsun to the trim shop for Angelo to work on. As luck would have it, Ken was there. Both men liked what they saw, lured Cindy into the house where so many had died before her, and then raped and murdered her. Their method of disposal was unique this time: the cousins caravaned to the dump site, Bianchi driving Cindy's car with her body in the trunk, and Buono in the Cadillac. They pushed the car over a cliff (where it was found the next day), got into the Cadillac and took off.

Bianchi was making Angelo nervous. The younger man had a big mouth and took far too many chances. At one point during their murder spree, Bianchi went on a citizens' ride along with a patrol unit of the Los Angeles Police Department, and even asked to see the dump sites for the victims of the murderer now being referred to as the Hillside Strangler.

A perfect opportunity arose to get Bianchi out of Los Angeles. His live-in girlfriend had just delivered his baby and promptly decided to leave Bianchi and Los Angeles to be near her parents in Bellingham, Washington. Angelo strongly encouraged Bianchi to join her. Bianchi missed his girlfriend and child, but didn't want to leave Angelo. They had a history together. They shared secrets. Angelo ordered Bianchi out of Los Angeles, though, and Bianchi resentfully left.

That might have been the end of it. The cousins might never have been caught if not for Bianchi's stupidity. He got a job at Whatcom Security and quickly rose in the ranks. Again he began using his position to steal things from the very businesses and homes he was supposed to protect.

But stealing wasn't enough. He missed the killing. And he wanted to prove to Buono that he was smart enough to pull off a murder on his own.

He called a college girl he'd met while working security at a department store and offered her and her roommate each an easy hundred dollars to watch the home of a vacationing family for two hours while the alarm system in their house was repaired.

Karen Mandic and Diane Wilder arrived at seven o'clock that evening, both prepared to stay two hours. (Karen had arranged to be away from her station at the department store until nine o'clock.)

By nine o'clock Karen and her friend were dead.

It was a messy business for Bianchi. It was the first time he'd done anything like that alone, and the experience left him exhausted and unable to rape either girl. He lugged their bodies to Karen's car, piled them in on top of each other and drove the car to a residential cul-de-sac, where it was found the next day.

Everything pointed to Bianchi. Despite his request that the girls not tell anyone about the housesitting job, Karen had called a friend (who happened to be a campus cop) to share the news of her good fortune. She had not only mentioned Bianchi's name, but left a note at her apartment with his name and phone number on it.

Nothing had prepared Bianchi for getting caught. It'd never occurred to him that his name could come up—and yet when it did, he managed a convincing lie about his whereabouts during the time of the murders. The problem was, though the lie was slick, if the police checked it out they'd discover that in fact he had no alibi. The day after he was first questioned, he went to the police station and tried to straighten things out by telling them that he had really lied, but was now going to tell them the truth.

It didn't wash. The Bellingham police force might have been small, but they knew what they were doing. As the investigation proceeded, a detective who had kept abreast of the news of the Hillside Strangler in Los Angeles began to put two and two together. Bianchi was from Los Angeles. He'd left L.A. three months ago, when the killings there had stopped. He'd arrived in Bellingham and suddenly there were two new strangling victims. Coincidence?

When he called the L.A.P.D. to check Bianchi out, it was discovered that one of Bianchi's old addresses just happened to be the same as a Strangler victim's. A search of Bianchi's possessions unearthed the turquoise ring that had belonged to Yolanda Washington, the first Hillside Strangling victim. More coincidences?

The L.A.P.D. sent their investigating detectives to Bellingham to talk to Bianchi. Suddenly they were confronted with a man who claimed to have an alter ego named Steve who had committed the murders—with Angelo Buono.

Bingo. It was the first confirmation of the detectives' suspicion that there were two Hillside Stranglers. They promptly sent men to watch Buono.

Bianchi, in his typical, blame-shifting fashion, had really come up with a unique excuse this time. He hadn't killed anyone; his alter ego, Steve, had done it. Kenny would never do anything like that—and had no memory of committing the murders.

With his years of reading in psychology, Bianchi was able to pull off yet another scam on the psychiatrists who examined him. Two of them were absolutely convinced they were dealing with a man who had multiple personalities. Two others were convinced he was insane and prepared to testify to it. The Los Angeles detectives couldn't believe it. There was actually a chance that the guy who had admitted to the murders in Los Angeles and Seattle might get off with a plea of insanity.

But one doctor didn't believe Bianchi. He viewed some of Ken's sessions with other doctors and came to the conclusion that they had been planting ideas into his head about how he should behave if he had multiple personalities with the questions they'd asked. He also didn't believe that Ken had truly been hypnotized in the sessions where he was supposed to be in a deep hypnotic state induced by the psychiatrists.

To test both theories, this lone doctor "suggested" to Bianchi that it was unusual for true multiple personalities to have only one other identity. Ken immediately concocted another personality, thrilling the other psychiatrists. The doctor then "hypnotized" Bianchi, and when he appeared to be in a deep trance, introduced him to someone who wasn't in the room. Ken appeared to shake the invisible man's hand. People in true hypnotic states never, ever attempt any kind of physical contact with imaginary people.

With his plan to plead insanity destroyed, Ken decided to plea bargain. He would plead guilty to some of the crimes in both California and Washington without threat of receiving the death penalty. He was also expected to testify against Angelo Buono.

He plead guilty to the murders of Karen Mandic and Diane Wilder, and was then escorted by Los Angeles detectives to California, where he plead guilty to five Hillside Stranglings.

Detectives were finally able to arrest Angelo. The problem was that the only real evidence against him was the word of his cousin. Bianchi promptly "went into his little nut bag" (as Angelo later so aptly put it to a fellow inmate) and feigned insanity, apparently believing that now that he had his plea-bargained deal he could do anything he wanted, up to and including getting Angelo off the hook by being an unreliable witness.

It didn't work.

Ken hadn't given up on attempting to prove his innocence, either. He thought that if there was another murder in Bellingham just like the ones he had committed, the police would be convinced they'd arrested the wrong man. To that end he enlisted the help of an emotionally unstable twenty-three-year-old woman who flew from Los Angeles to Bellingham and attempted to murder a pregnant woman. Happily, she didn't succeed, and was herself caught and sent to prison.

The preliminary hearings alone for Angelo Buono lasted ten months. The trial dragged on for nearly two years, at that time the longest trial in Los Angeles criminal history. One of the key pieces of evidence was the little piece of fluff from Judy Miller's eyelid, which had been so carefully preserved by the police. It matched upholstery foam found in Buono's trim shop. He was found guilty of murder in all the deaths except that of Yolanda Washington. Though the judge would have liked to have sentenced Angelo to death, the jury decided on life in prison without parole.

As for Ken Bianchi, because he *had* been such an unreliable witness, the judge determined that he had effectively nullified the plea agreement that would have allowed him to spend part of his sentence in a cushy California prison, and returned Bianchi to Washington to serve time at Walla Walla, one of the toughest prisons in the country.

He has already come up for parole twice.

Important Dates in the Lives of the Hillside Stranglers

Kenneth Bianchi

May 22, 1951: Kenneth Alessio Bianchi was born at 2:55 p.m. (EDT) in Rochester, New York. His biological mother gave him up at birth.

August 1951: Ken was adopted from a foster home by an Italian-Catholic family named Bianchi. Jenny

Buono's sister, Frances S. Bianchi, was the adoptive mother and Nicholas Bianchi, a foundry worker, the adoptive father.

Childhood to 1959: Ken suffered from a urination problem and other illnesses and allergies which interfered with his school attendance and caused trouble with classmates.

1964: Ken's adoptive father died of a heart attack. Ken was thirteen years old.

1968: At age eighteen, Ken married Brenda Beck. The marriage was annulled after a few months.

January 1976: Ken moved to Glendale, California, and stayed with his older cousin, Angelo Buono.

January 1, 1977: Ken met Kelli Boyd, who would become his long-time girlfriend, at a New Year's Eve party. They began living together.

October 17, 1977: Ken and Angelo murdered Yoland Washington, beginning a series of at least ten murders of females ranging in age from twelve to twenty-eight.

February 1978: Kelli Boyd delivered Ken's son, Ryan.

January 1979: At Angelo's insistence, Ken moved to Bellingham, Washington, to be with Kelli and Ryan.

January 11, 1979: Ken murdered two young Bellingham college students, Karen Mandic and Diane Wilder, after offering them a house-sitting job. He was arrested for double murder the next day.

October 23, 1979: In Los Angeles, Ken plead guilty to five counts of murder.

November 1983: Ken was sentenced to life imprisonment.

January 9, 1984: Ken was sent back to Washington to serve out his life-imprisonment sentence at Walla Walla.

Angelo Buono

October 5, 1934: Angelo Buono was born at 4:09 a.m. (EST) in Rochester, New York. His parents, Angelo Buono, Sr. and Jenny Sciolino Buono, divorced. Both later married other people.

1950: At age sixteen, Angelo quit high school.

December 1951: Angelo got into trouble with the law and was placed in a California reform school for boys.

July 2, 1955: At age twenty, Angelo married a sixteen-year-year-old girl named Geraldine Y. Vinal. They had a son, Michael Lee, on January 10, 1956, but were divorced shortly thereafter.

April 15, 1957: Angelo married for the second time, in a Roman Catholic ceremony. His bride was the seventeen-year-old Mary Catherine Castillo, by whom he had five children.

May 13, 1963: Mary Catherine filed for divorce, claiming extreme cruelty and abuse that had endangered her life. The divorce became final in 1964.

1965: Angelo began living with Nanette Capina, a twenty-five-year-old who had two children of her own. He fathered two sons by her between 1967 and 1969.

March 1968: Angelo was arrested for auto theft and sentenced to three years of probation.

1975: Angelo moved to 703 East Colorado Street in Glendale, California. He ran an auto upholstery shop in the back garage.

January 1976: Angelo's younger cousin, Kenneth Bianchi, arrived from the east coast to live with him until he could find a job.

October 17, 1977: The cousins killed their first victim, Yolanda Washington, whose naked body was found raped and strangled in Griffith Park.

October 17, 1977–February 17, 1978: The two men murdered ten young women. Victims were raped, sodomized, tortured, and either beaten to death or strangled.

January 1978: Angelo's mother died of cancer.

March 29, 1978: Angelo was married for the last time, to a twenty-one-year-old Chinese student from Hong Kong named Tai-Fun Fanny Leung.

October 19, 1979: Angelo Buono was arrested and charged with ten counts of premeditated murder.

November 14, 1983: Buono was sentenced to life in prison without parole after a long trial in which Kenneth Bianchi testified against him.

Kenneth Bianchi and Angelo Buono's Victims

October 17, 1977: Yolanda Washington, a prostitute whose body was found in Griffith Park.

October 31, 1977: Judy Miller, a fifteen-year-old prostitute, raped and strangled.

November 9, 1977: Jane King, a beautiful aspiring actress, tortured, raped, and strangled. Her body was found on November 23, 1977, in some bushes off the Golden State Freeway.

date unavailable: Lissa Kastin, a twenty-one-year-old waitress, tortured, raped, and strangled. Her body was found in a drainage ditch near the Chevy Chase Country Club on November 6, 1977.

date unavailable: Dolores Cepeda, twelve, and her best friend, Sonja Johnson, fourteen. They were raped and murdered, and their bodies dumped in a place Angelo called the "cowpatch" because of the stench of garbage left by litterers. Their bodies were found on November 20, 1977.

date unavailable: Kristina Weckler, who had previously rejected Bianchi's advances. She was tortured with injections of Windex, raped, and strangled. Her body was dumped on Ranons Way in Eagle Rock, and was found on November 20, 1977.

date unavailable: Eighteen-year-old Lauren Wagner, tortured with electrocution, raped, and strangled. Her body was dumped near the Pasadena Freeway.

date unavailable: Seventeen-year-old Kimberly Diane Martin.

date unavailable: Cindy Hudspeth, a waitress at a restaurant Angelo frequented.

January 11, 1979: Karen Mandic and Diane Wilder, murdered by Bianchi in Bellingham, Washington.

Astrological Blueprint for the Hillside Stranglers

–Edna L. Rowland

In the 1970s, Kenny Bianchi and his cousin, Angelo Buono, Jr., raped, strangled, and mutilated at least ten young women in California. They abandoned their victims' bodies on the hillsides of Los Angeles. But it wasn't until Bianchi, the younger cousin, left Los Angeles and killed two coeds in Bellingham, Washington, that the men were caught and convicted. The case finally broke on January 13, 1979.

According to Lois Rodden's *Astro Data V*, Kenneth Bianchi was born on May 22, 1951, at 2:55 p.m. (EDT) in Rochester, New York, to a prostitute who gave him up at birth.[1] An Italian-Catholic Rochester family named Bianchi adopted the three-month-old boy from a foster home, so his birth records were not readily available. Although the date has been confirmed, the time is speculative.

Is a fetus affected by psychological trauma its mother experiences during pregnancy and childbirth? If so, then Kenny was traumatized from the start. Although a full-term baby, his was a breech birth, so the labor was difficult. Astrologically, breech birth is often associated with Sun in Pisces or Virgo/Pisces on the angles, since Pisces rules the feet. In this case, Kenny's natal Ascendant is 26°41' Virgo, and the prenatal eclipse, ten weeks before his birth, falls in Pisces as well. (The significance of these factors will be explained later in the chapter.)

Given up at birth by his unwed fourteen-year-old mother, the child was not given the benefit of a mother's care or nurturing during the vital first three months of his life. This is confirmed by the natal Saturn (deprivation) at 25° Virgo, almost exactly on the Ascendant (the self), and in square to the natal Moon (the mother) at 22° Sagittarius.

The natal Moon was still in Full Moon phase (actually just one day after the Full Moon), and decreasing in light. Bianchi's retrograde Saturn in Virgo also closely squares the parental cusps (4th and 10th house cusps at 26°

	☉	☽	☿	♀	♂	♃	♄	♅	♆	♇	MC	AS	IC	DS	☊
☉		11 ♓ 53	18 ♉ 17	22 ♊ 02	00 ♊ 50	03 ♉ 40	28 ♋ 13	19 ♊ 06	08 ♌ 59	09 ♋ 12	13 ♊ 28	28 ♋ 46	13 ♓ 28	28 ♈ 46	23 ♈ 20
☽	157 56		29 ♒ 18	03 ♎ 04	11 ♓ 52	14 ♒ 41	09 ♏ 14	00 ♎ 08	20 ♏ 00	20 ♎ 13	24 ♍ 30	09 ♏ 48	24 ♐ 30	09 ♒ 48	04 ♒ 22
☿	025 10	132 ⚼ 46		09 ♊ 27	18 ♉ 15	21 ♈ 05	15 ♋ 37	06 ♊ 31	26 ♋ 24	26 ♊ 37	00 ♊ 53	16 ♋ 11	00 ♓ 53	16 ♈ 11	10 ♈ 45
♀	042 ∠ 20	159 42	067 31		22 ♊ 00	24 ♉ 50	19 ♌ 23	10 ♋ 17	00 ♍ 09	00 ♌ 22	04 ♋ 38	19 ♌ 57	04 ♎ 38	19 ♉ 57	14 ♉ 30
♂	000 ☌ 03	157 53	025 06	042 24		03 ♉ 38	28 ♋ 11	19 ♊ 05	08 ♌ 57	09 ♋ 10	13 ♊ 26	28 ♋ 44	13 ♓ 26	28 ♈ 44	23 ♈ 18
♃	054 ⚹ 23	103 32	029 ⚺ 13	096 □ 44	054 20		01 ♋ 01	21 ♉ 55	11 ♑ 47	12 ♊ 00	16 ♉ 16	01 ♋ 34	16 ♒ 16	01 ♈ 34	26 ♓ 08
♄	114 △ 41	087 □ 21	139 51	072 Q 20	114 △ 45	169 05		16 ♌ 27	06 ♎ 20	06 ♍ 33	10 ♌ 49	26 ♍ 07	10 ♏ 49	26 ♊ 07	20 ♐ 41
♅	036 29	165 33	061 ⚹ 39	005 ☌ 51	036 33	090 □ 53	078 12		27 ♌ 13	27 ♋ 26	01 ♋ 43	17 ♌ 01	01 ♎ 43	17 ♉ 01	11 ♉ 35
♆	136 ⚼ 14	065 ⚹ 49	161 24	093 □ 53	136 ⚼ 17	169 22	021 32	099 44		17 ♍ 19	21 ♌ 35	06 ♎ 53	21 ♏ 35	06 ♑ 53	01 ♑ 27
♇	076 40	125 △ 23	101 50	034 19	076 43	131 03	038 01	040 10	059 ⚹ 34		21 ♋ 48	07 ♍ 06	21 ♎ 48	07 ♊ 06	01 ♊ 40
MC	025 12	176 ☍ 50	050 22	017 08	025 15	079 36	089 □ 29	011 17	111 01	051 27		11 ♌ 22	26 ♍ 04	11 ♉ 22	05 ♉ 56
AS	115 △ 49	086 □ 14	140 59	073 28	115 △ 52	170 ☍ 12	001 ☌ 07	079 19	020 25	039 08	090 □ 36		11 ♏ 22	26 ♐ 41	21 ♐ 14
IC	154 47	003 ☌ 09	129 37	162 51	154 44	100 23	090 □ 30	168 42	068 58	128 32	180 ☍ 00	089 □ 23		11 ♒ 22	05 ♒ 56
DS	064 ⚹ 10	093 □ 45	039 00	106 31	064 07	009 ☌ 47	178 ☍ 52	100 40	159 34	140 51	089 □ 23	180 ☍ 00	090 □ 36		21 ♓ 14
☊	075 03	082 □ 53	049 53	117 △ 24	074 59	020 39	170 ☍ 14	111 33	148 ⚻ 42	151 ⚻ 43	100 15	169 07	079 44	010 52	

Midpoints and Aspects for Kenneth Bianchi

Gemini/Sagittarius). The signs Cancer and Capricorn are intercepted on these parental cusps, so the Moon and Saturn are co-rulers of the 4th and 10th houses, along with Jupiter and Mercury. Jupiter, the 4th house ruler (representing the mother in a male chart), squares Bianchi's Venus/Uranus conjunction in the 10th house. Uranus often indicates adoption, especially when it occupies either the 4th or 10th house. Unable to have or adopt any other children, Kenny was raised as his adoptive parents' only child. Although devoted to him, they were also reportedly possessive and overprotective. When he was adopted in August of 1951, the Moon had moved three degrees, to exactly square his natal Ascendant and conjoin his 4th house cusp.

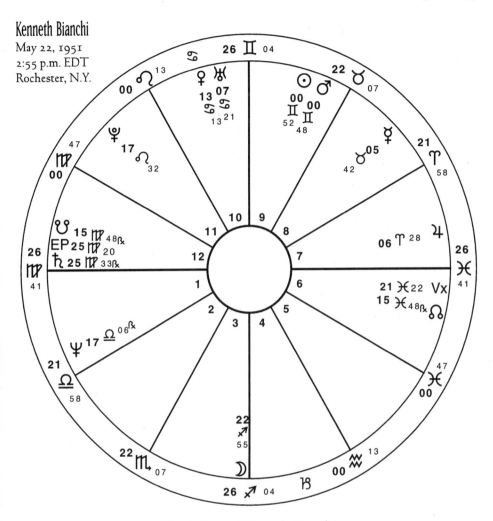

Kenneth Bianchi
May 22, 1951
2:55 p.m. EDT
Rochester, N.Y.

Natal chart of Kenneth Bianchi

On March 7, 1951, there was a solar eclipse at 16°29' Pisces, almost exactly conjunct Bianchi's natal North Node at 15° Pisces in his 6th house of health. The eclipse trined Venus but was inconjunct his 6th house ruler, Neptune, indicating the health problems that he developed as a child (and eventually outgrew).

Bianchi's natal Sun at 00° Gemini is exactly conjunct natal Mars at 00° Gemini, denoting a hot-blooded nature with a potential for violence if energy is misdirected. Since his Sun sign, Gemini, is also Mercury-ruled, he is a double Mercury type. Natal Mercury resides in his 8th house at 05° Taurus.

Natal Neptune, at 17° Libra (near the homicidal degree of 18° Libra), occupies his 1st house.

As a child, Bianchi developed a long-standing problem (Neptune square Venus) of wetting his pants which lasted throughout his elementary years (until 1959) and interfered with his school attendance. The other children teased him about it unmercifully. His Venus/Neptune midpoint falls exactly on the cusp of his 12th house (illness). His adoptive mother took him to doctors when the condition became progressively worse, and at one time he was diagnosed as having petit mal seizures, making him prone to falls. He also developed asthma.

The child was hard to handle, misbehaved, and became a chronic liar. For six years he attended a private Catholic elementary school where it was hoped he would be properly disciplined. But nothing seemed to help.

Then, when Kenny was thirteen years old, his adoptive father suffered an unexpected heart attack and died. By this time, Kenny's progressed Midheaven had moved to 09° Cancer and was at the midpoint of a Venus/Uranus conjunction in his 10th house (representing the father). His mother then had to go to work in order to support herself and her son.

At age eighteen, when his progressed Midheaven had reached a conjunction with his natal Venus, Kenny married Brenda Beck, a nurse. This marriage lasted only a few months. (In referring to his divorce, Bianchi preferred to call it an "annulment.") During his lifetime, the only long-term, lasting female attachment Kenny had was with a young woman named Kelli Boyd, with whom he fathered a son. Their relationship abruptly ended after Bianchi was convicted of murder and sentenced to life imprisonment in November of 1983.

According to Rodden's *Astro Data V*, Bianchi's older cousin, Angelo Buono, Jr., was born on October 5, 1934, at 4:09 a.m. (EST) in Rochester, New York.[2] Mercury is the natural zodiac ruler for the sign of the Twins, Gemini. Although not related by blood, the cousins share the same birthplace and are also related by zodiac

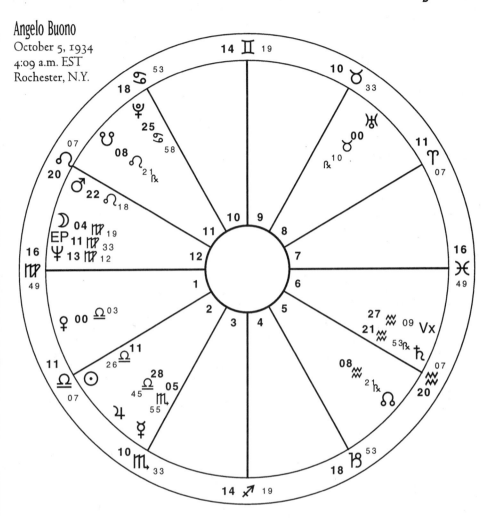

Angelo Buono
October 5, 1934
4:09 a.m. EST
Rochester, N.Y.

Natal chart of Angelo Buono

rulerships, since they both have Mercury-ruled Virgo ascendants. Sharing natal Ascendants, these zodiacal twins also share similar house rulerships.[3]

Angelo has a 16° Virgo Ascendant, with Neptune at 13° Virgo within a three-degree orb of conjunction to his Ascendant. His natal Moon is at 04° Virgo, and the Sun occupies 11° Libra. He was born just two days before the New Moon—the exact opposite Sun/Moon phase of Kenneth Bianchi's, who was born the day after the Full Moon. Angelo's Ascendant ruler, Mercury, at 05° Scorpio in his 2nd house, exactly opposes his cousin's Ascendant ruler at 05° Taurus!

	☉	☽	☿	♀	♂	♃	♄	♅	♆	♇	MC	AS	IC	DS	☊
☉		22 ♍ 53	23 ♎ 41	05 ♎ 44	16 ♍ 52	20 ♎ 05	16 ♐ 39	20 ♋ 48	27 ♍ 19	03 ♍ 42	12 ♌ 52	29 ♍ 07	12 ♏ 52	29 ♐ 07	09 ♐ 53
☽	037 06		05 ♎ 07	17 ♍ 11	28 ♌ 19	01 ♎ 32	28 ♏ 06	02 ♋ 15	08 ♍ 45	15 ♌ 09	24 ♋ 19	10 ♍ 34	24 ♎ 19	10 ♊ 34	21 ♏ 20
☿	024 29	061 ✶ 36		17 ♎ 59	29 ♍ 07	02 ♏ 20	28 ♐ 54	03 ♒ 03	09 ♎ 34	15 ♍ 57	25 ♌ 07	11 ♎ 22	25 ♏ 07	11 ♑ 22	22 ♐ 08
♀	011 ☌ 22	025 43	035 52		11 ♍ 10	14 ♎ 24	10 ♐ 58	15 ♋ 07	21 ♍ 37	28 ♌ 01	07 ♌ 11	23 ♍ 26	07 ♏ 11	23 ♐ 26	04 ♐ 12
♂	049 07	012 01	073 37	037 45		25 ♍ 31	22 ♏ 05	26 ♊ 14	02 ♍ 45	09 ♌ 08	18 ♋ 18	04 ♍ 33	18 ♎ 18	04 ♊ 33	15 ♏ 19
♃	017 19	054 ✶ 25	007 ☌ 10	028 ⚺ 41	066 27		25 ♐ 19	29 ♋ 28	05 ♎ 58	12 ♍ 21	21 ♌ 32	07 ♎ 47	21 ♏ 32	07 ♑ 47	18 ♐ 33
♄	130 26	167 33	105 57	141 49	179 ☍ 34	113 △ 07		26 ♓ 01	02 ♐ 32	08 ♉ 55	18 ♈ 06	04 ♐ 21	18 ♑ 06	04 ♓ 21	15 ♒ 07
♅	161 15	124 △ 08	174 ☍ 14	149 ⚻ 52	112 △ 07	178 ☍ 34	068 17		06 ♋ 41	13 ♊ 04	22 ♉ 15	08 ♋ 30	22 ♒ 15	08 ♈ 30	19 ♓ 16
♆	028 ⚺ 14	008 ☌ 52	052 43	016 51	020 53	045 ∠ 33	158 41	133 ⚼ 01		19 ♌ 35	28 ♋ 45	15 ♍ 00	28 ♎ 45	15 ♊ 00	25 ♏ 46
♇	075 27	038 21	099 57	064 05	026 19	092 □ 46	154 05	085 □ 47	047 13		05 ♋ 08	21 ♌ 24	05 ♎ 08	21 ♉ 24	02 ♉ 09
MC	117 △ 07	080 □ 00	141 36	105 44	067 59	134 ⚼ 26	112 △ 26	044 ∠ 08	088 □ 52	041 39		00 ♌ 34	14 ♍ 19	00 ♉ 34	11 ♈ 20
AS	024 36	012 29	049 06	013 14	024 31	041 55	155 03	136 ⚼ 38	003 ☌ 37	050 51	092 □ 30		00 ♏ 34	16 ♐ 49	27 ♏ 35
IC	062 ✶ 52	099 □ 59	038 23	074 15	112 △ 00	045 ∠ 33	067 33	135 ⚼ 51	091 □ 07	138 20	180 ☍ 00	087 □ 29		00 ♒ 34	11 ♑ 20
DS	155 23	167 30	130 53	166 45	155 28	138 04	024 56	043 ∠ 21	176 ☍ 22	129 08	087 □ 29	180 ☍ 00	092 □ 30		27 ♒ 35
☊	116 △ 55	154 01	092 □ 25	128 17	166 03	099 36	013 31	081 49	145 09	167 36	125 △ 57	141 31	054 02	038 28	

Midpoints and Aspects for Angelo Buono

On August 10, 1934, just two months before Buono's birth, a solar eclipse occurred at 17°02' Leo, in conjunction with his own natal Mars, and exactly conjunct Bianchi's natal Pluto! Bianchi's prenatal eclipse at 16°29' Pisces falls exactly opposite Angelo's Virgo Ascendant.

When these two met, the two most violent planets in the zodiac—Mars and Pluto—came together in conjunction (by chart comparison or synastry). Buono's natal Mars at 22° Leo resides in his 12th house of self-undoing, and Bianchi has Pluto at 17° Leo within a five-degree orb of Buono's natal Mars. An explosive combination, as one person tends to set off the other. In

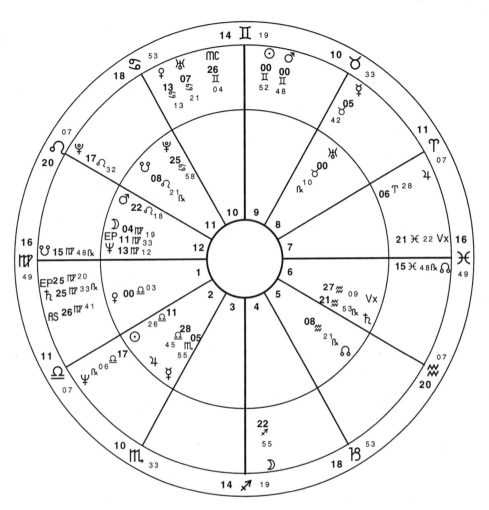

Buono and Bianchi natal chart comparison
(inner chart and cusps, Buono; outer chart, Bianchi)

addition, Buono's natal Pluto exactly sextiles his cousin's Saturn/Ascendant conjunction. Bianchi's South Node (representing a negative energy drain and/or karmic relationships) at 15°48' Virgo is in close unfavorable conjunction with Buono's Virgo Ascendant.

Angelo's childhood wasn't much happier than Kenny's. His parents divorced and his father remarried shortly thereafter, acquiring another family to support. On Angelo's sixteenth birthday, the progressed Full Moon at 11° Aries exactly opposed his natal Sun, marking a major crisis point in his life.

His progressed Ascendant at 00° Libra had reached an exact conjunction with his natal Venus, and was also inconjunct his natal Uranus. (Venus/Uranus aspects often indicate a very unconventional or erratic sex life.) Angelo quit school at sixteen, and soon after began getting into trouble for stealing, when his progressed Midheaven at 00° Cancer reached a sextile to his natal Uranus (representing adolescent rebellion). Around the time of that progressed Full Moon, Buono was also placed in a reformatory, the Paso Robles School for Boys in central California, where he remained for one year.

Always a hard worker and good with his hands (a Virgo trait), he took jobs in small machine shops, where he quickly learned manual skills and picked up his trade. (People with Moon in Virgo are usually willing to begin in subordinate positions and quietly work their ways into better jobs.) In 1975, after working industriously at auto upholstering for several years, he acquired his own business, Angelo's Trim Shop. The shop was behind his house at 703 East Colorado Street in Glendale, California, and was the scene of many of the murders.

Angelo had a close and sympathetic relationship with his mother, Jenny Sciolino Buono, as shown by his wide Moon/Neptune conjunction. His natal Neptune semisquared Jupiter in Libra and Pluto in Cancer (Jupiter square Pluto), spoiling their rapport. He visited her often, however, and always lived nearby.

Angelo's mother died in 1978 from vaginal cancer, when transiting Uranus opposed his natal Uranus (later coming to a conjunction with his Ascendant ruler, Mercury). Angelo was forty-four and experiencing his second adolescence—the classic midlife crisis, triggered by transiting Uranus opposed natal Uranus. In addition, transiting Uranus (indicating imminent separation) left a conjuction with his natal Jupiter a few months previously. That year, his progressed Midheaven at 28° Cancer squared natal Jupiter—the 4th house ruler, representing his mother.

Married and divorced several times, Angelo fathered eight children. His second marriage, to Mary Catherine Castillo on April

15, 1957, ended when she filed for divorce for extreme cruelty on May 13, 1963. The divorce was finalized by 1964. At the time of the marriage, Buono's progressed Venus at 28° Libra was exactly conjunct natal Jupiter, but progressed Mars was in conjunction with his natal Moon. This Moon/Mars progressed conjunction probably set off his repressed anger and hatred towards women, because from then on he began to express these inner feelings more openly and aggressively.

At the time of his divorce from Mary Catherine in 1964, Angelo was thirty years old and his progressed Midheaven at 14° Cancer had reached a sextile aspect to Neptune, his 7th house ruler. His progressed Ascendant at 11° Libra was conjunct his natal Sun. In addition, progressed Uranus at 28° Aries (the planet Uranus representing separation or divorce), now in retrograde motion, was opposing natal Jupiter. All his wives were allegedly beaten, badly treated, and had to fight him in court for even a semblance of child support. A close Mars/Saturn opposition in his birth chart confirms this innate streak of cruelty in his nature—which was rapidly turning into sexual sadism.

Despite his overly-macho manner, Angelo fancied himself a ladies' man (Sun in Libra trine the North Node, with Venus in the 1st house). He preferred, however, to spend his money on himself as indicated by the 2nd house ruler, Venus, in the 1st house. After age forty-three (the halfway point of the Uranus cycle—the classic midlife crisis timer), he decided to indulge his bachelor tastes, forget his prior responsibilities, and live entirely for his own sexual pleasures. He worked hard at his trade, bragged that he never drank, and generally believed he deserved the best. His friends noticed that he was obsessively neat and orderly as behooved his natal Virgo Moon and Ascendant.

The brutal rapes and murders began around 1976, after Angelo took in his younger cousin, Kenny Bianchi, giving him a temporary home at his aunt's request. At first these two attempted to establish a brothel. Looking for money, they set themselves up as pimps at Angelo's home. After two of their acquired prositutes managed to escape their enforced servitude, the cousins' anger erupted. Their mode of operation was to lure young girls with promises of money, a job, a ride, or, if all else failed, intimidation, and then bring them to Angelo's house, where they were brutally raped and then strangled.

Afterward, the men deposited their bodies around the Glendale or Los Angeles hillsides—hence the name "Hillside Stranglers."

The police soon realized that two men were involved because the bodies were apparently being lifted, rather than dragged, to their resting places (the killings had obviously occurred elsewhere). When the police questioned Bianchi for the third time, Angelo grew afraid and bluntly told him to leave town. He knew his cousin had a tendency to talk too much.

Around this time, on March 29, 1978, Angelo remarried. Evidently he didn't want Kenny hanging around the house anymore; according to Bianchi, he threatened to kill him if he didn't leave Los Angeles for good. After some initial reluctance, Bianchi moved to Bellingham, Washington, where his girlfriend, Kelli, and their son were living with her relatives. Neptune (symbolizing a confused state of mind) at 19° Sagittarius was in transit over his natal Moon (which represents females in general). Neptune, his 7th house (marriage) ruler, was bringing partnership problems to his attention, but he obviously preferred to ignore them. Kelli still didn't consider Kenny mature enough to handle a close, permanent relationship. She refused to marry him. Although this time he did manage to get a job, and at least attempted to support his family, Bianchi soon soon became bored with the roles of husband and father. He missed Angelo, and needed some excitement in his life.

Bianchi's job in Washington as a real estate security guard allowed him to offer two young female roommates a housesitting job. On January 11, 1979, he met them at a house, killed them both in the basement, and hid their bodies in the trunk of their car. He was arrested almost immediately afterwards, because one of the girls had had the foresight to leave a note behind with Bianchi's phone number on it, and told a friend where she was going to be that night. When the car was found, Bianchi became the primary suspect.

On the date of these double murders, January 11, 1979, transiting Pluto (death) at 19° Libra (the homicidal degree) was

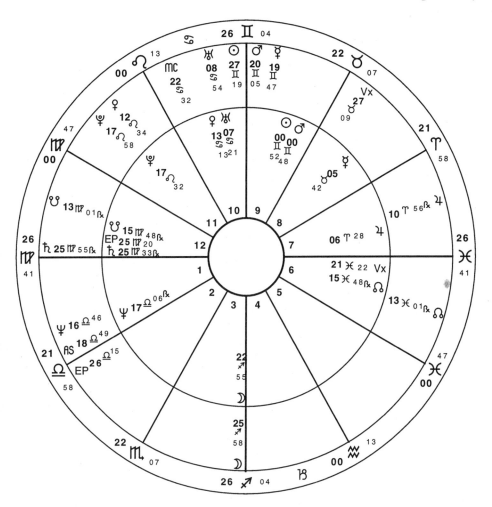

Comparison of Bianchi's natal and progressed charts at time of coed murders in Bellingham, Washington

conjunct Bianchi's natal Neptune and progressed Ascendant; and transiting Uranus at 20° Scorpio was square his natal Pluto. Pluto in the angular houses (in this case, the progressed 1st house/Ascendant conjunction) denotes a strong and ruthless urge toward power and control.

Bianchi's progressions on the day he murdered Karen Mandic and Diane Wilder are even more impressive than his transits. At age twenty-seven, his progressed Sun at 27°19' Gemini had already reached a conjunction with the degree on his Midheaven (26°04' Gemini). His progressed Moon at

25°58' Sagittarius was conjunct his natal 4th house cusp on this date, in square aspect to his natal Saturn, ruler of his 4th house of endings. Together these two progressed planets (or luminaries) were in close opposition and creating a progressed Full Moon, which marks a major turning-point or crisis. The influence was especially strong since they were activating all four angles of his chart. At the same time, his progressed Ascendant at 18° Libra (a homicidal degree) was conjunct his natal Neptune (his 7th house ruler) and the progressed Midheaven at 22° Cancer was inconjunct his natal Moon.

Progressed Mercury, Bianchi's chart ruler, at 19° Gemini was also applying to a conjunction with his 8th house ruler, progressed Mars, at 20° Gemini, and Mercury was trine the progressed Ascendant. Mercury/Mars aspects such as these show impulsive, fast speech, with a tendency toward anger, impatience, and the desire to act first and think later.

Bianchi was soon arrested for the two murders he had committed without Angelo's help in the state of Washington. While in prison, Bianchi tried to fool the court-appointed psychiatrists who examined him into thinking he was a multiple personality. Desperate to find a way out of his dilemma, under hypnosis he invented a third party named Steve to whom he attributed the murders. Not everyone, however, was convinced by Bianchi's apparent sudden loss of memory—it just seemed to be a bit too convenient and selective. Shortly after a psychiatrist caught him in the lie, he agreed to testify against Angelo in the Hillside Murders. Angelo was arrested by Los Angeles police on October 19, 1979, and charged with ten counts of murder.

Many still believe Buono to have been the leader and Bianchi the follower; others, however, think it may not have been that simple. They were partners in crime, but on the surface they seem to have had little else in common. Perhaps an examination of the astrological aspects for the murders these two committed can throw some light on this confusing and tragic relationship.

When Yolanda Washington, their first victim, was murdered on October 17, 1977, the transiting Sun at 23° Libra was conjunct Buono's natal Jupiter. But the violent planet Mars (Buono's 8th house ruler of death and sexual preferences) at 25° Cancer was transiting his 11th house and exactly conjunct his natal Pluto! Mars/Pluto aspects such as these imply buried rage and the type of bestial sexuality that must take by force (rape).

Note the recurrent Mars/Pluto aspects—they reoccur frequently in these men's charts and encourage the violation of society's death and sexual taboos. Transiting Saturn at 27° Leo was conjunct Buono's natal Mars—an aspect often associated with death, cruelty, and/or extremely painful conditions. Neptune, transiting the fourteenth degree of Sagittarius, was crossing (making a conjunction to) Buono's natal 4th house cusp, which symbolizes death and endings. Transiting Pluto at 14° Libra, conjunct Buono's natal Sun, was exactly trine his natal Midheaven degree. (A Sun/Pluto aspect is often present in the charts of rapists and their victims.)

At this time, Buono was forty-three years old. His progressed Midheaven at 27° Cancer was just separating, but still within a one-degree orb of exact conjunction with natal Pluto—the planet ruling compulsions and obsessions. On that fateful day, October 17, 1977, Buono's progressed Mars (Pluto's lower octave), was at 17° Virgo, in conjunction with his natal Ascendant, indicating an inclination to become physically violent.[4]

On the day of Yolanda Washington's rape and murder, Angelo's progressed Sun at 24° Scorpio was trine natal Pluto. Progressed Venus, at 23° Scorpio, was on the midpoint of his natal Mars/Saturn midpoint of death (22° Scorpio). In his book *The Combination of Stellar Influences*, Reinhold Ebertin, a Uranian astrologer, interprets this occupied midpoint as follows: "The inability to love or express love. Loss (death) of female persons."[5] (Due to legal and technical difficulties in obtaining physical evidence, however, Buono and Bianchi were never prosecuted for this first murder.)

On February 17, 1978, when Bianchi and Buono committed their last murder together, Buono's progressed Moon at 11° Aries was on the cusp of his 8th house, exactly opposite his natal Sun in Libra. This was the *second* progressed Full Moon he had experienced. (The first one, mentioned previously, occurred when he was sixteen years old and sent to reform school.)

During February of 1978, progressed Mars (a potentially violent energy) was still within orb of his natal Ascendant (the self).

On October 19, 1979, when Angelo was charged with ten counts of murder, his progressed Moon at 04° Taurus occupied his 8th house and opposed Mercury, his Ascendant ruler. (According to the late British astrologer Charles Carter, a Moon/Mercury hard aspect often denotes a liar.) Note that Buono's progressed Moon was also then applying to a conjunction with Kenny's natal Mercury at 05° Taurus. At this time, Buono was denying any involvement in the murders at all. Meanwhile, however, the authorities had made a deal with Kenneth Bianchi, enabling him to avoid the death penalty if he would agree to testify against his partner in crime.

Some of the women the men had previously held hostage for prostitution also agreed to be witnesses—against both of them. The evidence against them grew overwhelming. By this time Angelo's progressed Mars at 18° Virgo was separating, no longer aspecting his natal Ascendant degree; the violence finally subsided and the murders stopped.

Angelo Buono was sentenced to life in Folsom Prison on November 14, 1983. Kenneth Bianchi ended up in Walla Walla Prison in Washington, where he tried to legally change his name to avoid the stigma of having been one of the Hillside Stranglers— a title he had previously been very proud of.

Chapter Four

The Boston Strangler

Albert DeSalvo—His Story

— Sandra Harrisson Young

I DID IT. I KILLED ALL OF THOSE WOMEN."

It was 1965. George Nassar, a criminal confined to a state mental hospital and awaiting psychological testing before trial on a charge of murder, listened in disbelief to fellow patient and roommate Albert DeSalvo's boast that he was the so-called Boston Strangler. The Strangler had held Boston in a grip of fear for more than two years. His victims had ranged in age from nineteen to eighty-five. Old, young, heavy, thin, pretty, plain—no one was safe. There seemed to be no pattern to his selection of victims, so there was no concrete action the women of the city could take to protect themselves, aside from locking their doors and refusing admittance to anyone they didn't know—and even, sometimes, people they did know.

After the most massive (but unsuccessful) manhunt ever staged by Boston law enforcement, here was the murderer, arrested on unrelated charges of rape, bragging to Nassar that he was the Strangler.

It was June 14, 1962. Anna Slesers, a handsome-looking woman of fifty-five, was getting ready to attend a 7 p.m. memorial service at the Latvian Lutheran Church with her son. She'd already had dinner and was running her bath. The music of Tristan and Isolde, turned up a little loud so it could be heard over the running water, filled the tiny apartment.

When her son, Juris, arrived—perhaps an hour after she'd started her bath—no one answered his knock. The apartment was silent. He knocked again, louder. Still no answer. More annoyed than worried, he went downstairs and paced awhile, then sat on the front stoop. He was doing her a favor by picking her up, and she didn't even have the courtesy to be home.

He waited. Perhaps she was out shopping and had lost track of time. He waited a little longer, then went back upstairs and hammered louder on her door.

Where could she be?

He went back downstairs to wait, but now he was more worried than angry. He returned to the apartment and noisily knocked again. What if she was ill or injured and couldn't get to the door?

He had to get inside, but the janitor wasn't there to let him in. Juris slammed his shoulder against the door. It gave a little. He slammed into it a second time. It burst open, knocking away a chair that had been placed in front of it on the apartment side.

Juris went from the living room to the bedroom. He looked at the drawers that had been pulled out and left open. His mother was such a neat person. She would never have left things in this kind of disarray.

With increasing panic he looked in the bathroom.

His mother was there, lying on the floor, her legs obscenely positioned to shock anyone entering. Her dressing gown was open, exposing her completely. The belt of the gown had been tied tightly around her throat and finished off with an elaborate bow.

It was clear to him that his mother was dead. Juris, numb with shock, turned and walked to the phone to call the police. He hadn't really registered much of the scene in the bathroom, except for the body. He believed his mother had committed suicide, and must have wondered what part he'd played in it. He'd spoken to her the night before. She'd been depressed and lonely. He hadn't really wanted to, but had finally agreed to take her to church.

And now this.

When the police arrived on the scene, suicide was rejected. Clearly the woman had been murdered. What they had was a perfectly nice woman who had been the victim of a home invasion, during which nothing of value appeared to have been stolen.

And she'd been sexually assaulted.

Unbeknownst to the police, they were looking at the first victim of a murderer who would hold the city of Boston in the grip of a terror unlike any it had ever known—a murderer who would eventually come to be known as the Boston Strangler.

Only sixteen days passed before the Strangler struck again. This time it was Nina Nichols, sixty-eight. It'd been a busy Saturday for her. She had always been an active woman, but the past few days had been particularly hectic. It was nearly five o'clock in the afternoon. She was due at her sister's home for dinner around six. She called her sister to confirm that she would be there shortly. During the conversation there was a knock at Nina's door. Her sister could hear it on her end of the line. Nina told her sister she had to answer the door and that she'd call right back.

She never did.

Six o'clock came and went. Nina didn't arrive at her sister's. Six-thirty, seven o'clock and no Nina. Her telephone went unanswered.

When Nina still hadn't shown up by seven-thirty, her sister's husband contacted the janitor of her apartment building to check on her safety.

After determining that Nina's car was still there, the janitor used his passkey to open the door. Horrified astonishment kept him from stepping inside. The apartment had clearly been ransacked. After taking that in, he saw Nina's body, positioned in such a way as to shock anyone entering the apartment. She was clearly dead, her eyes open wide with the horror of what had happened to her. Her legs, like Anna Slesers', had been spread apart by the murderer, and her slip and dressing gown were bunched up around her waist. Two nylon stockings had been used to strangle her, and were neatly knotted under her chin, the ends arranged in a cheerful bow. The janitor slammed the door shut and ran to call the police.

There was nothing in Mrs. Nichols' background to give the detectives any clues as to why she had come to this kind of end. As in the Slesers case, though the apartment had been thoroughly ransacked, valuable and easily-transportable items had been left untouched. Unlike Anna Slesers, though, Nina Nichols hadn't been raped. She had, however, been viciously sexually assaulted.

The detectives were stymied. If burglary wasn't the motive, what was?

In 1962, there were fewer than fifty murders in Boston. These two, with such obvious similarities, telegraphed a problem to the police. Yet there was really nothing they could do; the murderer had left no clues. There was nothing for them to sink their teeth into, no bad guy to chase.

They discussed the murders and waited, with the hope that the murderer was finished but the gut feeling that these two innocent women were merely the tip of an iceberg.

How right they were. To the dismay of the police, another murder was discovered to have occurred on the same day as Nina

Nichols'. The victim was Helen Blake, sixty-five, a nurse. She had been reported missing by concerned neighbors, and was found dead in her bedroom, essentially nude, strangled with a stocking. A brassiere under the stocking had been fashioned into an elaborate bow. Once again, the apartment had been ransacked, yet nothing appeared to have been taken—except, perhaps, two diamond rings that she was known to have worn but were not found either in her apartment or on her person.

The indications were that Helen Blake had been killed several hours before Nina Nichols.

Two murders in one day.

It continued: Ida Irga, age seventy-five, was killed on August 19, 1962. From what police were able to determine afterward, she had let a young man into her apartment to do some work. He changed from a nice young man into a murderer in the blink of an eye, grabbing her around the throat and throwing her to the ground. As with all of his other victims except Nina Nichols, he raped Ida, strangled her with a pillowcase tied neatly into a bow, and then arranged her body obscenely, with her legs spread apart and propped up on chairs.

Jane Sullivan, sixty-seven, was killed on August 20, but her body wasn't found for ten days. Jane was a large woman, and the evidence showed that she had struggled mightily before being subdued and murdered. She was found in her bathroom, on her knees beside the tub with her head in the water. Her body was exposed. She had been strangled with stockings, raped by the murderer, and violated with a broomstick.

Another murder eventually attributed to the Strangler was of Mary Mullen, eighty-five, who died on June 28, 1962. When DeSalvo confessed to this crime she was added to the list of Strangler victims.

So far, if the Strangler had any particular pattern, it seemed that he murdered older, white women who lived alone.

Then came Sophie Clark, age twenty, killed on December 5, 1962. She was young, black, pretty, and lived with two roommates. Sophie had apparently had some sort of premonition about the Strangler. Even though he was known to murder women of a far greater age than her, she was reported by acquaintances to have been terrified of him. The morning of her murder she had said as much to a friend.

Sophie was a cautious young woman. There were two locks on her door and she used them both, whether her roommates were home or not. No one who knew Sophie could believe she had let a stranger into the apartment. It went against everything her friends knew about her.

The way Sophie died was thus reconstructed by police: she had apparently been interrupted in the process of writing a letter to her fiance (it was found on her desk only partially completed). Someone knocked on her door and identified himself to her satisfaction. She let the man in and was immediately struck down. She was then raped and strangled, the familiar signature bow fastened in place. She was found later by her roommates, who were so terrified that they, too, might be marked for death that they never spent another night in the apartment.

The next victim was Patricia Bissette, age twenty-three, who died on December 31, 1962. She was a secretary and very pretty. As he had so many times before, the Strangler apparently talked his way into her apartment, caught her off-guard, raped, and strangled her. This time he constructed his bow from a combination of her stockings and a blouse. It was her boss who found her the next morning and called police.

February 18th was nearly the undoing of another woman who had stayed home from work because of illness. She let someone who claimed to be a workman in, and was attacked for her trouble. Despite her illness, she managed to fight him off and save her life.

Though it wasn't realized at the time, Mary Brown became a Strangler victim on March 9, 1963. This unsuspecting sixty-nine-year-old widow thought, as had so many before her, that she was letting a workman in. The "workman" then bludgeoned her with a pipe, raped and stabbed her repeatedly in the breast with a fork (which was found protruding from her body). The cause of her death was blows to the head, but the intruder had strangled her for good measure. There was no elaborate bow this time, and instead of the body being left vulgarly displayed it had been covered with a sheet.

Beverly Samans, also only twenty-three years old, was murdered on May 6th, 1963, but lay spread-eagle on her bed with her ankles tied to the bedposts until a friend found her on May 9th. She had been raped, stabbed, and strangled. There were similarities to the Strangler's work here, but there were also differences. The police were inclined to believe she'd been killed by the same man, but weren't sure until DeSalvo later confessed.

Evelyn Corbin, age fifty-eight, met her end on September 8. Once again he'd selected a woman who lived alone. No one knew anything had happened to her until she failed to show up for a social engagement. She was found with stockings stretched around her throat, but this time the signature bow had been made with a third stocking tied around her ankle. She'd been left exposed, her legs spread wide.

Joann Graff, yet another twenty-three-year-old, was murdered on November 23 of the same year. Again the Strangler had posed as a workman. She was attacked, raped, and strangled. The bow around her neck was made from stockings and a black leotard.

Mary Sullivan, age nineteen, was killed on January 4, 1964. This appeared, if possible, to have been an even more vicious killing than the previous ones. Mary had been beaten and raped. The bow had once again been made with stockings, and she'd been positioned with her legs stretched far apart. A broomstick was thrust into her vagina, and propped against her foot lay a "Happy New Year" greeting card the killer had found in the apartment.

It was incredibly frustrating for the police. They knew all of the murders tied up with the signature bows had been committed by the same person, but there were no real clues as to the strangler's identity. The victims appeared to have been completely random. There seemed to be no connection between the women and anyone who could have done this to them.

They went over the records of all known sex offenders. Unfortunately, although DeSalvo had been arrested for sexual offenses in the past, his most recent crime had been listed as breaking and entering because he'd been caught with what appeared to be burglary tools.

lbert DeSalvo was born in 1931, in Chelsea, Massachusetts, one of six children. His childhood was a difficult one of tremendous poverty and physical abuse from his father. By the time his mother divorced his father in 1944, Albert had already been arrested for breaking and entering. At seventeen he joined the army, was stationed in Germany, and fell in love with a German girl whom he later married. Also while in Germany, Albert won the U.S. Army European middleweight boxing championship. He was strong for his size and skilled in the art of fighting. The women he later attacked had very little chance of escape.

Back in America, awaiting discharge in 1955, he was accused of molesting a nine-year-old girl. The girl's mother, however, refused to press charges, concerned that her daughter would suffer even more trauma in the process of his conviction. She just wanted to put the incident behind her family.

DeSalvo was left free to strike again, and he did.

Albert craved sex. His poor, beleaguered wife couldn't keep up with his constant demands of intercourse four, five, and six times a day. It infuriated him that she wouldn't have sex with him as often as he wanted, but he still loved her. The problem was, Albert needed an outlet for his excess sexual needs; if his wife wouldn't provide that, he'd get it elsewhere.

He also needed money.

An old hand at burglary, Albert took it up again in 1960. Apparently he wasn't very good, though; within the course of four weeks he was arrested and given suspended sentences for breaking and entering.

That wasn't the worst of it, however. Albert set up a scheme whereby he presented himself to attractive women as a representative for a modeling agency. It was his job, he claimed, to conduct initial interviews with prospective models and take their measurements. Amazingly, many women fell for the story and allowed him access to their homes and their bodies. He carefully measured each woman, touching her intimately. Some he was able to seduce; some drew the line at measurement. Still others called the police to report the man with the measuring tape when other representatives of the bogus modeling agency didn't show up as promised. Because of this ruse, DeSalvo was nicknamed "Measuring Man" by the police.

On March 17, 1960, he was caught running from an attempted burglary. He admitted to being the "Measuring Man" when a tape measure was found on his person, and was charged with attempted breaking and entering, assault and battery, and lewd and lascivious behavior. (He was only found guilty of attempted breaking and entering, for which he served eleven months in prison.)

When DeSalvo was released from prison, his dangerous behavior upped a notch. The relatively mild "Measuring Man" was reborn into "The Green Man."[1] In this guise, Albert did considerably more than fondle his victims; he forcibly tied them up and raped them. His own later estimate of the victim count in Massachusetts and Connecticut was one thousand. When the description given by one of his victims matched that of the "Measuring Man," police arrested DeSalvo in 1965.

It was the beginning of the end for the Boston Strangler's rape and murder spree.

After claiming to hear voices while in police custody, DeSalvo was sent to a prison psychiatric hospital, where he was diagnosed as suicidal and overtly schizophrenic. Because of this diagnosis, he was judged unfit to go to trial and remanded to the custody of the hospital until further notice.

Enter George Nassar.

George was, himself, a clever man and dangerous criminal, being held on a charge of murder at the same psychiatric hospital as DeSalvo. George said that he listened to DeSalvo's claims of sexual prowess and didn't think much of them until DeSalvo one day openly boasted of being the Boston Strangler.

Nassar wasn't exactly a good citizen, but he did report what DeSalvo had told him to his own attorney, F. Lee Bailey.

Did he do it for the $10,000 reward? Was Nassar, in fact, the Strangler and using DeSalvo to take the heat off his own case? No one will ever know. Bailey, however, was intrigued by what his client told him. He spoke to Albert and came away convinced that the man was, indeed, the real Boston Strangler.

The problem he ran into when he tried to convince police Albert DeSalvo was the Boston Strangler was that dozens of confessions to the murders had poured in over the months from unstable people. Why should they have believed Albert over and above the other crazies? Granted, the man knew a lot about the stranglings, but most of the information could have been gleaned from news accounts or even another inmate. For all that Albert knew, there was also a lot he didn't know. In his defense, though, if his own estimate of the number of women he'd raped over the years was correct, his lack of memory with regard to some particulars could easily be attributed to the staggering number of his victims.

Yet he knew other things that only the real Strangler, or someone in extremely close contact with him, could have known. Bailey, in an attempt to keep DeSalvo off the streets of Boston, was unrelenting in his efforts to convince the authorities of his newest client's guilt. He taped his conversations with DeSalvo and played the tapes to the police. No physical or eyewitness evidence linking DeSalvo to any of the crimes could be provided, though. His confessions were all they had.

The police interviewed DeSalvo over a period of nearly seven months and were finally convinced that they had their man. Not only could he tell them the names of the women the police knew to be Strangler victims, but added two more names to the list. He knew where the victims lived, what they'd been wearing when they'd died, the positions their bodies had been placed in, and what their apartments had looked like, right down to the arrangement of the furniture.

It was impossible to know, of course, if these details were from his own memory or if he was only repeating what someone else had told him. There was a chance that in his weakened mental state he confused what he'd heard with what he'd done.

Interestingly, it turned out to be not so much what he said that convinced the authorities, but what he did: DeSalvo used the same unusual bow to tie his shoes that he'd used to decorate his victims. It was also the same gay bow he'd used to fasten the laces of his little daughter's leg braces.

According to F. Lee Bailey in an interview on the television program "American Justice," it was police error that had allowed DeSalvo to escape capture for so long. Official records showed DeSalvo still in prison at the time of the killings, but the records were wrong; in fact, he'd been released a year earlier. When police saw the erroneous information, DeSalvo was completely eliminated as a suspect.

Bailey also claimed that DeSalvo had twice been encountered at the scenes of the Strangler's crimes. Both times he'd pointed out to police the direction in which he claimed the suspect had run, and both times the police gave chase and let DeSalvo go.

Bailey's main goal in his representation of DeSalvo was to save the murderer from execution. Never mind that he'd murdered more than a dozen times without showing any mercy to his victims.

In the same interview, Bailey argued that the key to saving DeSalvo's life had been proving his insanity. DeSalvo had agreed that, if found insane, he would make a formal confession and plead not guilty, in the hope of being sent to a mental institution instead of prison. He was ruled insane, but prosecutors claimed he couldn't make a plea under protection of insanity. Bailey worked around that and arranged for his client to stand trial for the Green Man rapes and not the earlier stranglings. Bailey hoped DeSalvo could then be found legally insane without risking execution for the strangling crimes.

DeSalvo went on trial six months later for the Green Man rapes and plead not guilty by reason of insanity. The jury, however, didn't buy it. After listening to the opinions of several doctors who said DeSalvo was insane, they opted to believe the one doctor who said he was unbalanced but, on the whole, not insane. Perhaps it wasn't so much that they believed the doctor as that they wanted DeSalvo imprisoned for life, and not sent through the revolving door of a mental hospital. One juror even admitted as much after the trial.

DeSalvo was, indeed, found guilty and sentenced to life in prison on January 18, 1968—without ever standing trial for the Boston stranglings, or even making a formal, signed confession for the record.

After only five weeks in prison, DeSalvo escaped. The manhunt was on. The citizens of Boston, after months of breathing easier with the man who had terrorized them behind bars, went back on full alert.

It wasn't necessary. DeSalvo turned himself in after only two days on the run, without having hurt anyone.

He claimed at a press conference that the reason for his escape was to bring attention to his plight. And what was that plight? He claimed that he wanted to be removed from prison and placed in a hospital to get help for his mental disease.

Needless to say, it didn't work. He went straight back to prison.

Once there, he got involved in selling speed to other inmates. The Mafia wanted that market sewed up and warned him off. DeSalvo didn't listen, though, and ended up paying the ultimate price: in 1973, he was stabbed to death in his cell.

No one has ever been charged with his murder.

Important Dates in the Life of Albert DeSalvo

September 3, 1931: Albert Henry DeSalvo was born in Chelsea, Massachusetts, at 11:58 a.m. (EDT) to Charlotte Roberts and Frank DeSalvo.

1944: Albert's mother divorced Frank DeSalvo when Albert was thirteen years old.

September 16, 1948: Albert enlisted in the army. He was seventeen years old.

December 5, 1953: Albert married a German girl named Irmgrad, whom he had met while in the service overseas.

January 15, 1955: Albert committed his first sex offense, molestation of a nine-year-old girl, but the girl's mother dropped charges.

February 15, 1956: Albert was honorably discharged from the army after seven and a half years of service.

1958: Albert and Irmgrad's first child, Judy, was born. She had a crippled leg.

March 17, 1960: Albert was arrested for breaking and entering in Cambridge, Massachusetts, and was sentenced to two years of imprisonment. At this time he confessed to being the "Measuring Man."

April 1962: Albert was released from prison.

June 14, 1962: Albert DeSalvo committed his first murder, of Anna Slesers, a fifty-five-year-old woman living in Boston. She was sexually assaulted and strangled with the cord of her housecoat.

January 4, 1964: DeSalvo committed his last murder, of nineteen-year-old Mary Sullivan, also from Boston.

February 4, 1965: Judge Pecce committed Albert to Bridgewater State Hospital as mentally ill, and ordered him detained there "until further order of the court."

June 30, 1966: Albert's trial began.

February 24, 1967: Albert escaped from Bridgewater with two others, but turned himself in shortly thereafter.

January 18, 1968: Albert was convicted on ten counts of armed robbery, assault, and various sexual crimes. He was sent to Walpole State Prison for life.

November 25, 1973: Albert died from sixteen stab wounds inflicted by an inmate who was never identified.

DESTINED FOR MURDER

Victims Murdered by Albert DeSalvo [2]

June 14, 1962: Anna Slesers, age fifty-five.

*June 28, 1962: Mary Mullen, age eighty-five.

June 30, 1962: Nina Nichols, age sixty-eight.

June 30, 1962: Helen Blake, age sixty-five.

August 19, 1962: Ida Irga, age seventy-five.

August 20, 1962: Jane Sullivan, age sixty-seven.

December 5, 1962: Sophie Clark, age twenty.

*March 9, 1963: Mary Brown, age sixty-nine.

December 31, 1962: Patricia Bissette, age twenty-three.

May 6, 1963: Beverly Samans, age twenty-three.

September 8, 1963: Evelyn Corbin, age fifty-eight.

November 23, 1963: Joann Graff, age twenty-three.

January 4, 1964: Mary Sullivan, age nineteen

*These two victims were not reported by the police, but added by DeSalvo under hypnosis.

Astrological Blueprint for Albert DeSalvo

–Edna L. Rowland

In the 1960s, the Boston Strangler raped, sexually abused, and killed thirteen women within the space of eighteen months—from June 14, 1962, to January 4, 1964. The women he murdered were between the ages of nineteen and eighty-five. Under the advice of his

attorney, F. Lee Bailey, he underwent hypnosis. Although he confessed to thirteen murders, he was never convicted for any of them. Other than his voluntary
confession, made while in a mental institution, there was no physical evidence
against him and there were no witnesses to these crimes.

In 1964, DeSalvo was sent for evaluation to Bridgewater State Hospital, a
mental institution, where psychiatrists found him "potentially suicidal and
quite clearly overtly schizophrenic." On February 4, 1965, Judge Pecce
ordered him to be retained there "until further order of the court."

When questioned, DeSalvo was seemingly open about the facts of his life.
He frankly admitted to having a strong sex drive, but added that he didn't
smoke or drink. At age twenty-two he had married, while in the service in
Germany. His wife, Irmgrad, was from Frankfurt. They had two children, a
boy and a girl (who was crippled). Although his wife feared having another
abnormal child, DeSalvo admitted that he sought intercourse with her three or
four times a day, and when she objected, went elsewhere to fulfill his needs.

In January 1955, De Salvo was charged with his first sex offense, molesting
a nine-year-old girl, but the charges were dropped because the child's mother
feared adverse publicity.

On March 17, 1960, he was charged with breaking and entering, and
while being detained, confessed to being "The Measuring Man." In this role,
he told women they would make good models, offered them nonexistent jobs,
and felt and measured their bodies.[3]

After his release, he began to combine the two offenses—breaking and
entering, and raping women who lived alone. By 1964, he had raped
hundreds of women and earned the title "The Green Man" as well as "The
Measuring Man." By the autumn of 1965 he had murdered thirteen women,
and his crimes were travelling further afield, into Connecticut, New Hamp-
shire, and Rhode Island.

According to Lois Rodden's *Astro Data V*, Albert Henry DeSalvo was born
September 3, 1931, in Chelsea, Massachusetts, at 11:58 a.m. (EDT).[4] The
date is from the birth certificate but the time is speculative. In examining his
birth chart, we see that he has the Sun at 10° Virgo, and his Moon in the 21st
degree of the sensual, Venus-ruled sign Taurus. The majority of his planets are
in Earth signs. The 16th degree of the intensely passionate sign Scorpio is
rising, so Mars and Pluto are his Ascendant co-rulers. His dark hair and eyes,

	☉	☽	☿	♀	♂	♃	♄	♅	♆	♇	MC	AS	IC	DS	☊
☉		15 ♋ 49	11 ♍ 28	09 ♍ 33	00 ♎ 33	25 ♌ 21	13 ♏ 32	29 ♊ 28	07 ♍ 56	15 ♌ 55	04 ♍ 08	13 ♎ 26	04 ♐ 08	13 ♋ 26	22 ♊ 54
☽	108 43		17 ♋ 07	15 ♋ 12	06 ♌ 11	00 ♋ 59	19 ♓ 11	05 ♉ 07	13 ♋ 34	21 ♊ 33	09 ♋ 47	19 ♌ 05	09 ♈ 47	19 ♉ 05	28 ♈ 32
☿	002 ☌ 36	111 △ 19		10 ♍ 51	01 ♎ 51	26 ♌ 39	14 ♏ 50	00 ♋ 46	09 ♍ 14	17 ♌ 13	05 ♍ 26	14 ♎ 44	05 ♐ 26	14 ♋ 44	24 ♊ 12
♀	001 ☌ 13	107 29	003 ☌ 49		29 ♍ 56	24 ♌ 44	12 ♏ 56	28 ♊ 51	07 ♍ 19	15 ♌ 18	03 ♍ 32	12 ♎ 49	03 ♐ 32	12 ♋ 49	22 ♊ 17
♂	040 44	149 ⚻ 27	038 08	041 58		15 ♍ 43	03 ♐ 55	19 ♑ 50	28 ♍ 18	06 ♍ 17	24 ♍ 31	03 ♏ 49	24 ♐ 31	03 ♌ 49	13 ♑ 16
♃	029 ⚺ 39	079 04	032 15	028 ⚺ 25	070 23		28 ♎ 43	14 ♊ 39	23 ♌ 06	01 ♌ 05	19 ♌ 19	28 ♍ 37	19 ♉ 19	28 ♊ 37	08 ♊ 04
♄	126 △ 44	124 △ 32	124 △ 08	127 △ 57	085 □ 59	156 23		02 ♓ 50	11 ♏ 18	19 ♎ 17	07 ♏ 31	16 ♐ 48	07 ♒ 31	16 ♓ 48	26 ♒ 16
♅	141 24	032 ⚺ 40	144 00	140 10	177 ☍ 51	111 45	091 □ 51		27 ♊ 14	05 ♊ 13	23 ♊ 26	02 ♒ 44	23 ♓ 26	02 ♉ 44	12 ♈ 12
♆	004 ☌ 28	104 14	007 ☌ 04	003 ☌ 15	045 ∠ 13	025 10	131 13	136 ⚼ 55		13 ♌ 40	01 ♍ 54	11 ♎ 12	01 ♐ 54	11 ♋ 12	20 ♊ 40
♇	048 30	060 ⚹ 12	051 06	047 17	089 □ 15	018 51	175 ☍ 15	092 □ 53	044 ∠ 02		09 ♌ 53	19 ♍ 11	09 ♉ 53	19 ♊ 11	28 ♉ 39
MC	012 03	096 □ 39	014 39	010 50	052 48	017 35	138 47	129 20	007 ☌ 34	036 27		07 ♎ 24	28 ♏ 07	07 ♋ 24	16 ♊ 52
AS	066 32	175 ☍ 15	063 ⚹ 56	067 45	025 47	096 □ 11	060 ⚹ 12	152 03	071 Q 00	115 △ 02	078 35		07 ♑ 24	16 ♌ 42	26 ♑ 10
IC	167 56	083 □ 20	165 20	169 09	127 △ 11	162 24	041 12	050 39	172 ☍ 25	143 32	180 ☍ 00	101 24		07 ♈ 24	16 ♓ 52
DS	113 △ 27	004 ☌ 44	116 △ 03	112 △ 14	154 12	083 □ 48	119 △ 47	027 56	108 59	064 57	101 24	180 ☍ 00	078 35		26 ♈ 10
☊	154 32	045 ∠ 49	157 08	153 18	164 42	124 △ 53	078 43	013 08	150 ⚻ 03	106 01	142 28	138 55	037 31	041 04	

Midpoints and Aspects for Albert DeSalvo

large prominent nose, and insatiable sex drive fit perfectly with the Scorpio rising sign.

Albert was the third of six children (four boys and two girls) born to Frank DeSalvo and Charlotte Roberts. Charlotte was only fifteen years old when she married Frank, who continually battered and abused her (and later, their children). They lived in a lower-middle-class suburb of Boston but were desperately poor, and usually dependent on welfare. The alcoholic Frank was constantly in and out of jail. He taught his children to shoplift, and completely abandoned the family when Albert was only eight years old. In 1944, when Albert was thirteen, his mother divorced his father. She remarried a year later.

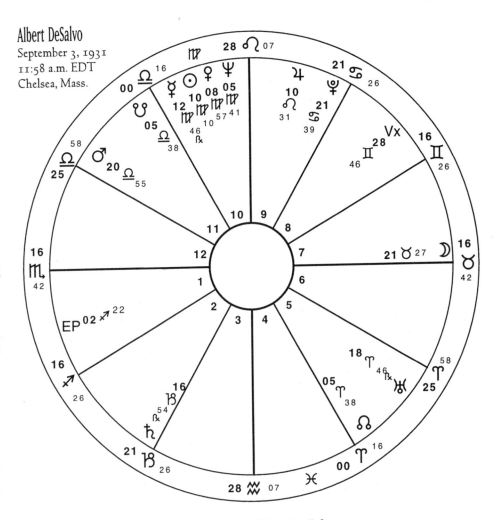

Birth chart for Albert DeSalvo

On September 16, 1948, when Albert was seventeen, he enlisted in the army, where he rose to the level of sergeant. He spent five years in Germany, until he was honorably discharged on February 15, 1956. He married on December 5, 1953.

Astrologically, DeSalvo's insatiable sex drive can probably be attributed to his close natal Cardinal grand square, composed of Saturn, Uranus, Mars, and Pluto, in combination with his Scorpio Ascendant. The co-rulers of his Scorpio Ascendant, Mars, and Pluto, in almost exact square, are part of a four-planet Cardinal grand square pattern which is undoubtedly extremely stressful and active. Whereas a T-square affords some relief from stress, the grand square offers little or no escape from constant tension, since it can be activated by any one of its four angles, and any time a transiting or progressed planet afflicts any one of the four natal planets (Saturn, Mars, Uranus, or Pluto), the other three natal planets are also automatically activated.

DeSalvo's Ascendant at 16° Scorpio, in exact sextile to natal Saturn (discipline and limitations), may have offered some control over these erratic sexual impulses, but the close Mars/Uranus opposition in his chart (part of the Cardinal grand square) urged him to strongly rebel against any restrictions on his liberty of action. Mars opposite or square Uranus often denotes impatience and the potential for sudden, unexpected loss of control over one's impulses and/or sexual desires.

Even by itself, a Mars/Pluto square can be considered a dangerous and violent configuration, but because these two violent planets rule DeSalvo's natal Ascendant (the self), this "hard" aspect becomes doubly important. Many murderers have had this configuration in their charts, including Jack the Ripper, John R. Christie, and Henri Landru.

In *The Combination of Stellar Influences*, astrologer/cosmobiologist Reinhold Ebertin defines the psychological correspondence of the Mars/Pluto midpoint, frequently associated with murder, as: "the attainment of one's own objectives by means of ruthlessness extended to others, brutality, cruelty." DeSalvo's natal Venus at 08° Virgo in the 10th house occupies his Mars/Pluto midpoint at 06° Virgo. Ebertin describes this occupied midpoint (Mars/Pluto= Venus) as follows: "A passionate disposition, assault or rape." His natal Neptune at 05° Virgo conjunct this same Mars/Pluto midpoint is described as follows: "Irreconcilableness or implacability, cunning and deceitfulness, the tendency to cause harm to others secretly and unobtrusively."[5] An apt description of a vicious killer.

The Boston Strangler's natal Midheaven at 28° Leo is within a one-degree orb of Regulus, a fixed star, which rules the point of fame or infamy. This left-handed killer strangled nearly all his victims with either his own bare hands or their stockings. He preyed only on women, mostly single or living alone. His natal Moon at 21° Taurus on the Descendant squares his Leo Midheaven. Taurus is the sign corresponding to the neck and throat. DeSalvo's Moon (representing females) is closely inconjunct natal Mars at 20° Libra, and exactly sextile compulsive Pluto, denoting his obsessive rage directed at the female sex.

Was he acting out memories of past abuses? Many serial killers, most of them male, were mistreated during childhood and had unsatisfactory relationships with their fathers. Half of them reportedly had poor or cold relationships with their mothers as well. In any case, many serial killers grew up without necessary positive male role models during their early formative years.

As a child, Albert often witnessed violent domestic scenes. (His father once knocked most of his mother's teeth out, and Albert tried in vain to stop him by throwing a vase at him.) The fear and psychic scars he suffered from witnessing such violence in the home must have been at least as great as the physical wounds.

Albert's father was born on May 7, 1908, in Boston, Massachusetts. Taking a quick look at Frank DeSalvo's chart (page 113), we note that he had an explosive Mars/Pluto conjunction between 20–23° Gemini, which falls within his son's 8th house, inconjunct Albert's natal Saturn. This Mars/Pluto hard aspect (a square) recurs in Albert's own birth chart, and the vicious cycle of violence is repeated.

We already know that as children Albert and his siblings received many beatings. Albert's natal Moon is conjunct his father's Sun at 16° Taurus, however, and this Sun/Moon conjunction is considered by most astrologers to be a favorable aspect in synastry, denoting sympathetic rapport or understanding. His father's natal Sun is also closely conjunct Albert's Descendant.

What conclusions can we draw from this? Apparently Albert decided to identify with the aggressor, as his later lifestyle reveals an inherent lack of respect for women in general. He demeaned and abused them just as his father had, while at the same time attempting to maintain the facade of a traditional marriage and family.

Let's take a closer look at the parental angles in Albert's horoscope. Since the signs Virgo and Pisces are intercepted in the 4th and 10th houses, we'll use the cusp rulers for the signs Leo and Aquarius instead.

Albert's natal Sun rules his 10th house, which in a male chart represents the father. Albert's Virgo Sun is conjunct Mercury, Venus and Neptune, and these four planets form a stellium in his 10th house; by contrast, the 4th house (representing the mother) is unoccupied. Although the natal Moon, which traditionally rules the mother, is strong and angular in Albert's 7th house, and it receives a supportive trine from Saturn, it's poorly aspected since Uranus, ruler of his 4th house of the mother, is opposite Mars. Albert was always his mother's favorite son; however, this aspect suggests estrangement and separation from the mother both psychologically and physically, due to circumstances beyond one's control. As a result of this Mars/Uranus opposition (as well as hard aspects to the other two Cardinal square planets), their relationship (opposition) could not easily be sustained for any length of time because it quickly became much too stressful and challenging.

In Albert's chart, the other traditional significator of the father, Saturn, at 16° Capricorn is at "home" in its own sign and sextile his Ascendant, but is also part of the stressful Cardinal grand square pattern, where it squares both Uranus and Mars, and opposes Pluto. Is a violent, abusive father better than none at all? Does violence sustained in early childhood have lasting or irreparable effects? Society is just beginning to ask these questions, but hasn't found any definitive answers yet.

DeSalvo's natal Sun in 10° Virgo and his Venus/Neptune conjunction in that sign reveal just how well he managed to deceive (Neptune) so many women (Venus) by posing as a helpful repairman, ready to take care of their broken appliances or other household problems. His sexual lifestyle was also kept secret from his wife, represented by Venus, his 7th house ruler and dispositor of his natal Moon. As soon as he'd gained entrance to his victims' apartments and their backs were turned, he attacked them. He was careful to escape detection by leaving behind no fingerprints. He didn't want to risk going back to prison or losing his children. According to his wife, he was fond of their children and liked to spend time with them (Sun trine Saturn). To his credit, he didn't take his anger out on them.

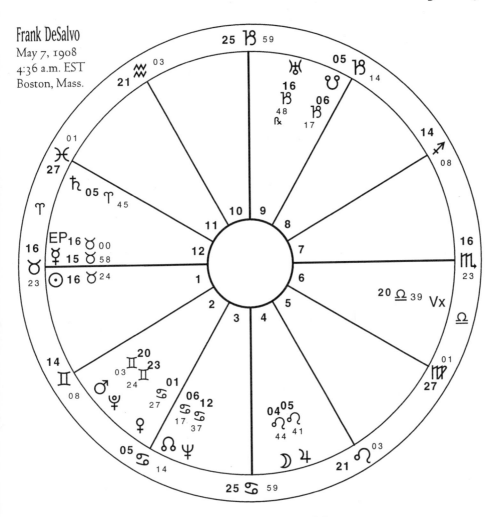

Frank DeSalvo
May 7, 1908
4:36 a.m. EST
Boston, Mass.

Sunrise chart for Frank DeSalvo

Despite his precautions and almost fool-proof modus operandi, he was arrested once again, in Lynn, Massachusetts. None of DeSalvo's family attended his trial on June 30, 1966. On January 18, 1968, he was convicted on ten counts of assault, armed robbery, and various sex crimes. He lost everything that he had worked for—his home and family. His wife refused to bring the children to see him in prison.

DeSalvo's prenatal eclipse (five months before his birth) on April 18, 1931, at 27°03' Aries, falling as it does in his 6th house of health, repeats the emphasis on 6th house matters (including service-oriented jobs) already noted by his 10th house Virgo stellium. This Aries eclipse squares his natal Pluto, opposes natal Mars (his 6th house ruler), and closely trines his Midheaven. Virgo, when unafflicted, tends to work well and industriously in a subordinate position, and individuals with this in their charts are often agile with their hands. To the women he silenced forever, he looked like such a harmless, helpful workman. Most of these women readily believed him when he claimed the landlord had sent him to repair their bathroom plumbing leaks or broken windows.

Police are aware that many long-time criminals gradually adopt an established mode of operation or "trademark." The Strangler was no exception. The distinctive bow he tied around his victim's throats became his "signature." Although of average height, he was physically strong and powerful, as suggested by his Scorpio Ascendant and Taurus Moon. (During his stay in the service, he won a middleweight U.S. boxing title.) After gaining entrance to a woman's home, his strength enabled him to overpower and strangle her as soon as her back was turned.

The Strangler's 10th house contains a stellium of four planets in the intercepted sign of Virgo—Sun, Mercury, Venus, and Neptune. His pose as a workman was flawless; during the day he really *was* a workman and manual laborer, so he knew how to gain access to women's apartments without raising their suspicions. Upon leaving, after raping and murdering them, he simply blended into the surrounding environment and quickly disappeared. Neptune, which is often associated with deception and disguises, is the highest, or focal, planet in his 10th house of occupation; it squares his Equatorial Ascendant at 02° Sagittarius, and semi-squares his 6th house ruler, Mars. His Venus/Neptune conjunction in Virgo, near the cusp of his 10th house, aspects all four of the planets that make up his Cardinal grand square, so his fantasies and delusions about women actually ruled his life, affecting his judgement and mentality (Mercury).

Murdered in prison on November 25, 1973, DeSalvo died of sixteen stab wounds inflicted by a fellow inmate.

Important Dates as Illustrated by Secondary Progressions and Transits to Albert DeSalvo's Natal Chart

By the time Albert was thirteen and his mother divorced his abusive father, Albert's progressed Midheaven at 10° Virgo had reached an exact conjunction with his natal Sun (representing the male parent), while Uranus, the planet of divorce and separation, opposed his progressed Equatorial Ascendant at 12° Sagittarius and exactly squared his natal Mercury. Progressed Mercury was conjunct progressed Neptune in his 10th house. His progressed Moon (representing the mother) at 24° Scorpio was conjunct his progressed Ascendant at 25° Scorpio and in sextile to progressed Venus at 25° Virgo, so the action taken was favorable for his mother, who remarried the following year, making a new life for herself.

Albert's enlistment in the army September 16, 1948, was an important event in his life, as indicated by the progressed Moon's square to his 4th house ruler, Uranus. This enlistment marked his first break from his family, and can be interpreted as his initial attempt to establish his own independence (Uranus) and individuality. At this time, transiting Pluto at 15° Leo squared his natal Scorpio Ascendant, and transiting Saturn at 29° Leo was just one degree past (or, separating from) a conjunction with his Midheaven.

At age twenty-two, while stationed in Germany, he met his wife-to-be, Irmgrad, and they were married on December 5, 1953. Secondary progressions to his chart are as follows: progressed Midheaven at 19° Virgo was inconjunct Uranus, and progressed Mercury (his Sun sign ruler) at 15° Virgo trined the cusp of his 7th house of marriage. Progressed Sun at 01° Libra sextiled his progressed Ascendant at 02° Sagittarius, and this progressed Ascendant was exactly conjunct his Equatorial Ascendant. On the date of his marriage, DeSalvo's progressed Moon at 22° Pisces made a favorable sextile to his natal Moon in Taurus in the 7th house of partnerships, and trined his Ascendant ruler, Pluto.

Two years later, on January 15, 1955, he committed his first sex offense, molesting a nine-year-old girl, but charges were dropped. At this time, the progressed Moon in the first decan of Aries was exactly conjunct his natal North Node at 05° Aries (a degree of rape) in his 5th house of children, in semisquare aspect to his natal Moon. The progressed Moon was also inconjunct his natal Neptune. Progressed Jupiter (denoting excessive self-indulgence) at 15° Leo was applying to a close square of his Scorpio Ascendant.

The transits for this event are as follows: transiting Mars at 29° Pisces was inconjunct his Midheaven and transiting Neptune at 28° Libra exactly sextiled his Midheaven. Transiting Pluto at 26° Leo was approaching an exact conjunction with his 28° Leo Midheaven, and Saturn at 19° Scorpio, then in his 1st house, had just passed an exact conjunction with his Ascendant degree of 16° Scorpio.

On February 15, 1956, after seven-and-a-half years of service, Albert was discharged from the army. By this time his progressed Moon had moved to 18° Aries, in conjunction with Uranus, his 4th house ruler of beginnings and endings. At the same time, his progressed Midheaven at 21° Virgo was exactly trine his natal Moon (ruling emotional and domestic matters) in his 7th house of marriage, indicating a new start as a civilian, with emphasis on his need to renew his relationships with his wife and children.

Transits for this event are as follows: Pluto (which rules adjustments and transformation) at 27° Leo and transiting Jupiter at 26° Leo were now both conjunct his Leo Midheaven, while the Sun at 25° Aquarius in his 4th house opposed both Pluto and the Midheaven. Saturn at 02° Sagittarius was exactly conjunct the Equatorial Ascendant. Mars at 20° Sagittarius trined natal Uranus. Despite the molestation charges filed against him a year earlier, in 1955, he received an honorable discharge because the mother of the child refused to press charges.

After four years of civilian life, working as a handyman and plumber to support his wife and two young children, DeSalvo was arrested and charged with breaking and entering. Let's examine the progressions for the date of this arrest, March 17, 1960, when he was twenty-eight years old. His progressed Moon at 07° Gemini, falling in his 7th house of partnership matters, directly opposed the progressed Ascendant at 07° Sagittarius, and squared his natal Venus at 08° Virgo.

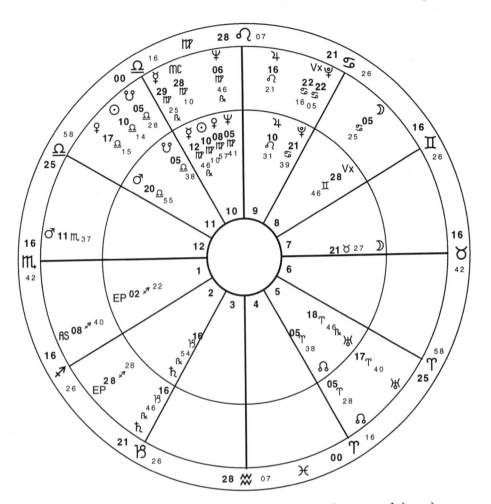

Comparison of Albert DeSalvo's natal (inner) and progressed (outer) charts at the time he committed his first murder

This event reportedly had a bad effect upon his marriage, as his wife was understandably upset by the fact that he would have to spend two years in prison. She agreed to take him back, but only on her own terms—he would have to prove that he had reformed. Her reaction angered him, and he brooded about it. Released from prison in April of 1962, he immediately went on a secret rampage which escalated into rape, theft, and, finally, the ultimate crime: murder.

The first murder was committed on June 14, 1962, when DeSalvo killed Anna Slesers, a fifty-five-year-old woman living alone in Boston. By this time,

DeSalvo's progressed Midheaven at 28° Virgo was conjunct his progressed Mercury, his Sun sign ruler, at 29° Virgo. The 29th degree signifies that by now it was probably too late to stop his self-destructive behavior. He had crossed a line. His marriage, which until then had offered him some solace and comfort, was steadily deteriorating, as indicated by an afflicted progressed Venus at 17° Libra (representing his wife) exactly opposing his natal Uranus and squaring natal Saturn—activating his explosive Cardinal grand square. His erratic behavior was becoming a source of stress and frustration for her, and she was no longer willing to compromise, having begun to suspect the worst.

During this interval, progressed Mars at 11° Scorpio (his Ascendant ruler) was making a favorable sextile to his natal Sun, but this only added fuel to the fire. His progressed Equatorial Ascendant at 28° Sagittarius, in square aspect to his progressed Midheaven, was exactly opposite his natal Vertex. Progressed Jupiter exactly squared his natal Ascendant, and his progressed Vertex at 22° Cancer exactly conjoined natal Pluto in his 9th house of law and order.

According to police reports, twelve more murders followed in quick succession, until the last, of nineteen-year-old Mary Sullivan, which occurred on January 4, 1964. From 1962 to 1964, while these murders occurred, transiting Uranus and Pluto occupied DeSalvo's 10th house, activating his natal Midheaven degree and later triggering his stellium of four natal planets within 05–12° Virgo. He was finally caught and convicted on January 18, 1968, when transiting Jupiter (representing justice) reached a conjunction with his Neptune-ruled 10th house, and Mars (representing police) opposed Neptune from his 4th house of endings.

Six years later, while in prison, DeSalvo was assaulted by a fellow inmate and died on November 25, 1973, of sixteen stab wounds. Progressions for his death show the progressed Midheaven at 09° Libra sextile natal Jupiter, and his progressed Sun at 21° Libra was exactly square Pluto and inconjunct his natal Moon. Progressed Mercury (which rules his 8th house of life and

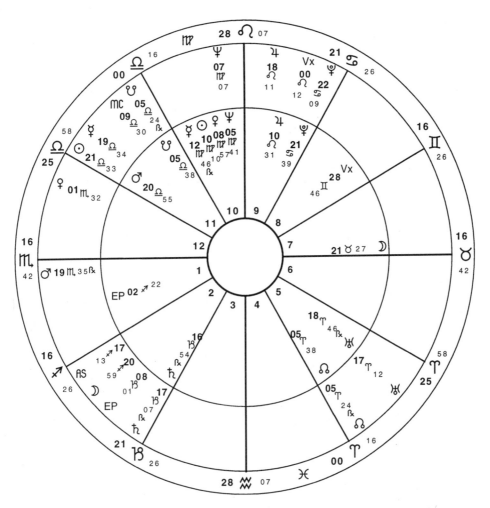

Comparison of Albert DeSalvo's natal (inner) and progressed (outer)
charts at the time of his death

death) at 19° Libra (the homicidal degree) was opposite Uranus, his 4th house ruler, and conjunct his natal Mars. His progressed Ascendant at 17° Sagittarius trined his 4th house ruler, Uranus, while the progressed Moon at 21° Sagittarius was exactly inconjunct natal Pluto (the planet of death) and inconjunct his natal Moon. The Equatorial Ascendant at 08° Capricorn exactly trined his natal Venus.

Transits for his death at age forty-two show that a recent New Moon at 02°24' Sagittarius had, about twenty-four hours earlier, formed an exact

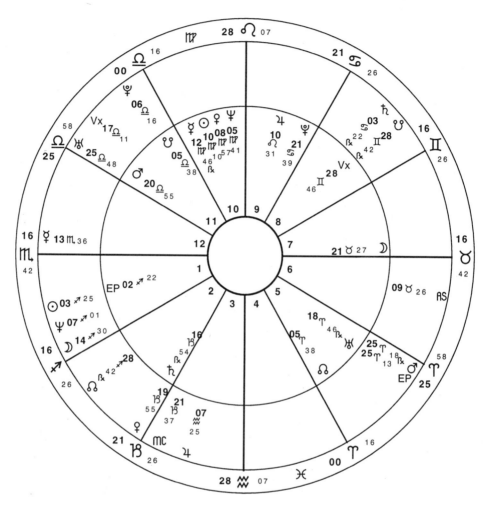

*Transits (outer circle) to Albert DeSalvo's natal chart (inner circle)
at the time of his death*

conjunction with his Equatorial Ascendant. The New Moon was also conjunct his natal Mars/Saturn midpoint of death at 03°55' Sagittarius.

Transiting Uranus, ruler of his 4th house of endings, at 25° Libra opposed transiting Mars (violence) at 25° Aries, activating and repeating the natal Mars/Uranus opposition within his 5th and 11th houses. Uranus had just recently passed its halfway cycle, or its opposition to his natal Uranus, at 18° Libra.

Other important transits for his violent death are as follows: transiting Pluto, co-ruler of his Scorpio Ascendant, at 06° Libra conjoined his natal South Node, was in exact sesquiquadrate aspect to his natal Moon, and squared transiting Saturn at 03° Cancer in his 8th house of death. Transiting Neptune at 07° Sagittarius within his 1st house squared his stellium of planets in Virgo, and almost exactly squared his natal Venus in that sign. Transiting Venus at 19° Capricorn conjoined his natal Saturn in that sign, squared his natal Mars, and opposed his natal Pluto in Cancer. A violent end to a violent character.

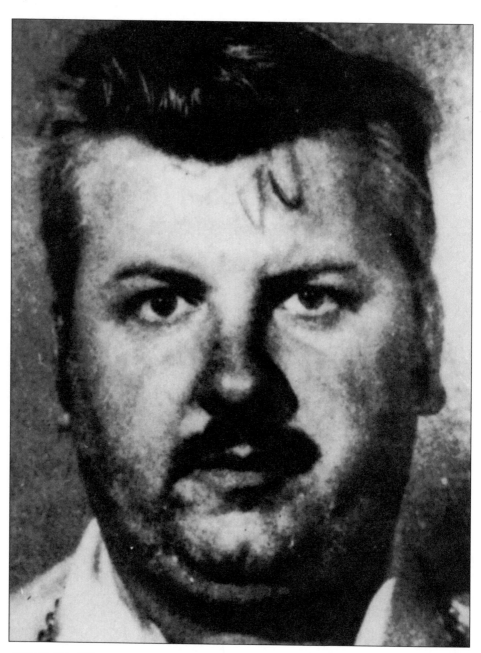

AP/Wide World Photos

Chapter Five

Chicago's Killer Clown

John Wayne Gacy—His Story

— Sandra Harrisson Young

T HE FAT MAN WITH THE BLOATED FACE

and watery blue eyes looked down at the terrified boy he'd hand-

cuffed to a board and smiled. It was a completely evil smile. For the

first time, the boy may have realized that being raped wasn't the worst

thing that could happen to him.

DESTINED FOR MURDER

John Wayne Gacy came into the world on March 17, 1942, St. Patrick's Day, the second of Marion and John Stanley Gacy's three children. It was a difficult and dangerous birth that nearly cost the life of the child who was to be their only son. But the baby John survived and grew into a man.

A man who would murder the sons of thirty-three other families.

Young John's parents couldn't have been more different from each other. Marion was a cheerful woman who liked to have fun and spend time with her friends. The man she chose to marry when she was thirty was dour and solitary and had a violent temper when he drank—which was often.

From the moment of his birth, the young John was a disappointment to his father. One can only imagine John Stanley's thoughts and feelings as he, a robust, masculine man, watched his son grow into a feminine, sickly, and ungainly boy.

Marion tried to offset her husband's behavior: the more abusive the older Gacy was toward their son, the more protective she became. This protectiveness extended beyond the walls of their home. Because the young John seemed to be in such fragile health, with a condition she called an "enlarged bottleneck heart"—which his doctors never heard of—she wouldn't let him roughhouse with the neighborhood boys. John did, in fact, begin having fainting spells at the age of five. He would be doing something any normal child would do and suddenly, for no obvious reason, drop to the ground unconscious. When the doctors couldn't find anything wrong with him, John Stanley assumed his son was faking and became more derisive than ever.

More than anything in the world, John Wayne Gacy wanted to be respected by his father, but it was a losing battle. John's basically feminine nature offended the older man and gave him lots of fuel for the verbal abuse he heaped on the boy, calling him a "he-she" and telling him he was going to grow up to be "queer."

John Stanley was a skilled machinist, a perfectionist in his work, but whenever the young John tried to work on a project with him, he invariably ended up bungling it. "You're dumb and stupid," were the words his father constantly threw at him. Every time he tried something and failed, he was "dumb and stupid."

Of course, he grew up to become a very good murderer. Someone who was truly "dumb and stupid" could never have covered up thirty-three murders for as long as Gacy did.

What turns a seemingly normal child into a monster? John Wayne Gacy, in recalling important events in his life, claims to have been molested by a mildly retarded neighborhood girl when he was four or five. He told his mother, who in turn told his father. A screaming match between the parents resulted, leaving John with the feeling that telling had been the wrong thing to do.

He decided that he wasn't going to make that mistake again, and when a contractor friend of his father's started taking the nine-year-old John for rides in his truck and, under the guise of wrestling, shoved John's face in his crotch, John didn't tell his parents.

When John was ten, his family moved to a new house closer to Chicago. It was larger than the old house and had a full basement that the older Gacy turned into a private retreat, locking everyone else out. He would come home from work and head straight downstairs to drink and listen to music—and do whatever else it was he did down there. When he finally emerged for dinner, he was usually drunk and ready to pick a fight.

The young John found his own dark and private place under the porch of the new house. Here he would store in a paper bag underwear he'd stolen from his mother's dresser. He would spend hours there, touching the underwear and watching others come and go, knowing they couldn't see him. When his mother found out what was happening to her missing underwear, she told her husband. He was furious and beat the boy viciously. The next time John's mother caught him with her underwear, she kept it to herself.

The one thing John did seem to inherit from his father was a willingness to work hard. Starting young, he did volunteer work at school, mowed lawns, delivered newspapers and groceries, and took some of the heavier household work off his mother's shoulders.

John wasn't particularly socially active in high school. He was fat and unattractive, and no more popular with the boys than he was with the girls. He was eighteen when he finally managed to find a girl willing to have sex with him, but couldn't follow through; he fainted before he could consummate the act. To hear John tell it, though, he was quite the lover.

His father knew better. Clearly, John Sr. thought his son was homosexual.

When John was nineteen, in his senior year of high school, he dropped out and left home without telling anyone where he was going. He ended up in Las Vegas, working at a mortuary. He was given a room next to where the bodies lay. While no one knows what went on between Gacy and the dead bodies, the owner would come in some mornings to find naked bodies that had been clothed the night before, with the clothing in a neatly-folded pile beside them. The owner reported this to the police, but Gacy quit his job before any kind of investigation could be pursued. Knowing what is now known about Gacy, one can only imagine what went on.

Back in Chicago, Gacy went to work for Nunn Bush Shoes as a management trainee and joined the Jaycees. Around this time he met Marlynn Myers, a fellow employee, and in September of 1964, they married.

As it turned out, this marriage was a good career move on John's part. Marlynn's father owned several Kentucky Fried Chicken franchises in Waterloo, Iowa. And while Fred Myers tried to talk his daughter out of marrying Gacy until the day of the wedding, afterward he made the best of things by offering Gacy a job managing three of his franchises in Waterloo, a $15,000 salary plus a percentage of the profits, and a house. John knew a good deal when he saw one.

Life in Waterloo was busy. In 1966, Marlynn gave birth to a son, Michael, and eighteen months later to a daughter, Christine. John was kept busy with his job and work with the Jaycees. He wanted to be president of the chapter, and knew that the best way to achieve it was to constantly volunteer. Against his father-in-law's wishes, he brought free buckets of chicken to Jaycee meetings and let people think he owned the franchises rather than that he simply managed them. He bragged and lied. He even stole under the guise of protecting local businesses.

John hired both boys and girls to work at his restaurants, but it was the boys he spent time with after hours. He opened his basement recreation room to them, providing them with alcohol and a pool table. He'd make bets with them: the loser had to give the winner a blow job. Or the winner could have sex with John's wife, but his payment for arranging things was a blow job.

John's "Waterloo," so to speak, came in the form of a blond, fifteen-year-old boy named Donald Voorhees, the son of a fellow Jaycee. John gave him a ride late one afternoon. Marlynn was out of town, so John brought the boy to his house and showed him a stag film. After that, John talked the boy—the child, really—into oral sex. They met several times after that. Each time, the boy asked for money and Gacy complied.

Everything was fine until Donald heard his father say that Gacy had asked him to be his campaign manager in his bid for the presidency of the local Jaycee chapter. The boy told his father what had happened, and the man went straight to the police. When police searched Gacy's house they found the films, just as Donald had said they would. Gacy was promptly arrested and charged with sodomy.

As investigators discovered, Donald Voorhees wasn't the only boy whose life Gacy had scarred. Edward Lynch testified before the grand jury that Gacy, who was his boss, had done the same thing to him, and that when he'd resisted Gacy's advances, Gacy had pulled a knife on him. A struggle had ensued and Lynch was cut. That seemed to bring Gacy to his senses, because he immediately apologized and got the boy a bandage.

That wasn't the end of Edward's ordeal, though. Gacy was somehow able to talk him into allowing his hands to be bound. Immediately the boy knew it was a mistake. When Gacy tried to sit on his lap, Edward managed to knock him off. Gacy slammed his face down on a narrow bed and started choking him. The boy was helpless. He could feel himself losing consciousness and still Gacy was choking him. It wasn't until he actually *did* lose consciousness that Gacy finally let up, apologized profusely, and took the boy home. A few days later, Lynch found himself unemployed.

Edward went to the police and the police went to Gacy—who, of course, denied everything and claimed it was simply an effort of his enemies to keep him from the presidency he sought. He volunteered to take two polygraphs and failed both of them, yet still managed to find some supporters among his Jaycee friends.

It was discovered that Gacy had hired someone to beat Donald Voorhees up to keep him from testifying. Voorhees didn't back down; after the attack he went straight to the police, and John found himself in more trouble than ever.

The police found themselves with all the witnesses they needed to put Gacy away. Boy after boy came forward with his own tale of coerced sex with Gacy. One admitted to having been seduced by Marlynn and "caught" in the act by Gacy, thereby "owing" Gacy a blow job.

In a surprise move, Gacy pleaded guilty to sodomy, obviously to get out of doing any jail time. He was surprised by the tough sentence handed down by a usually-lenient judge: ten years in the Iowa State Reformatory for Men at Anamosa. The day he was sentenced in 1968, Marlynn filed for divorce. He never saw his children again.

This episode, however, was not without merit. Gacy learned a valuable lesson: the next time there would be no witness.

Predictably, he did well in prison. As he had in his life on the outside, John worked his way up the social ladder, got himself a job in the kitchen and began peddling his influence, cooking fancy steak dinners and doing other favors in return for cigars and special privileges.

While John was in prison his father died. It was on Christmas Day, and John wasn't notified for several days, nor was he allowed to attend the funeral. He was left with a terrible hole in his life and a feeling of guilt that perhaps what he'd done had contributed to his father's death. He had humiliated and disgraced the man whose approval he'd craved more than anything else, and now he'd never be able to make it right.

Christmas became a bleak time of year for him after that.

Gacy got out of prison on June 18, 1970 (child molesters were—and still are—routinely under-punished), and went to Chicago to live with his mother. His first job after his release was as a cook at Bruno's Restaurant. It was while he worked at this restaurant that he met a policeman by the name of James Hanley. Gacy fictionalized James into "Jack Hanley," a man's man who was everything Gacy was not, and later blamed an alter ego named Jack Hanley for the bad things that John Wayne Gacy had done.

Gacy just couldn't stay away from boys. He knew what the consequences would be if he were caught, but even the threat of returning to prison didn't stop him.

In February of 1971, he picked a boy up at a bus station and assaulted him. He was caught and charged, but the charges were dropped when the boy failed to show up in court. Unpunished, Gacy went on as usual. He was released from parole in October of 1971.

In the meantime, Gacy got involved with a young male hustler named Mikel Ried. Unlike Gacy's other pickups, his affair with Ried lasted several months.

Gacy continued working as a cook while moonlighting in construction. He was most interested in the construction, though, and eventually started his own company, which he named "PDM," for painting, decorating, and maintenance. Gacy, his mother, Mikel Ried, and a cook at Bruno's moved into a home at 8213 West Summerdale Avenue in Norwood Park, Illinois, just outside of Chicago. Everything was going along well. Business was good. People were content.

And then, according to Ried, Gacy just snapped. Ried was working in the garage when Gacy attacked him from behind with a hammer. This was life and death, and as horrified as Ried was, he managed to defend himself and even land a blow of his own. It brought Gacy to his senses and he stopped the attack, apologizing profusely. Ried wasn't stupid, though. Gacy's apology notwithstanding, he packed his things and was gone the next day.

In 1971, Gacy started dating a woman named Carole Hoff. She was a family friend from long ago and had even once had a date with John in high school. Now she was a divorced mother of two who didn't like living alone.

Apparently Gacy treated her well; even his admission that he was bisexual didn't put her off. The two married in the summer of 1972. Carole and her two daughters moved into the house on West Summerdale and Marion Gacy moved out.

What Carole didn't know was that there was someone else in the house, buried in the crawlspace, the only evidence of his presence a strange musty smell that she attributed to dampness.

According to Gacy, his first murder took place on January 2, 1972, six months prior to his marriage—and it was an accident. He'd gotten drunk and gone cruising the streets looking for a boy. He eventually picked up Tom McCoy at the Greyhound bus station and brought him home. The two of them ate and had sex. Gacy claimed that in the morning he woke to find McCoy coming at him with a knife. In the ensuing struggle, the boy was stabbed and killed. Gacy shoved him into the crawlspace for later burial, so his mother wouldn't see the body when she got home from having spent the night at a relative's house. Gacy later discovered when he walked into the kitchen and saw eggs and bacon on the counter that the boy hadn't intended to stab him at all. He'd been fixing breakfast.

Something else had happened, however: as Gacy had stabbed the boy, he'd had the most powerful orgasm he'd ever experienced.

It was the beginning of the end for thirty-two more boys over the next seven years.

Gacy's marriage didn't fare well after the first year. The couple's sex life dwindled into nothingness as Gacy became more involved in his business and his liaisons with young boys. By 1975, sex between them completely stopped, and Carole had just about had it. (She first separated from and later divorced Gacy.)

As he had done in Iowa and then in prison, Gacy gained some minor prominence through sheer determination, volunteering his time and efforts, having large neighborhood picnics and becoming indirectly involved in politics. He was appointed secretary-treasurer of the Norwood Park Township Street Lighting District and joined the River Grove Moose Lodge. Gacy joined the Lodge's Jolly Jokers Club, a volunteer group that visited hospitals and marched in parades. It was for this club that Gacy created his now-famous "Pogo the Clown." As Pogo, he managed to get close enough to then-First Lady Rosalyn Carter to have his picture taken; a picture he hung with pride in his home office above the buried bodies of his victims.

As had been his custom with his ex-father-in-law's Kentucky Fried Chicken franchises, Gacy continued to hire young men to work for PDM Construction. Those he could seduce, he did.

Sometimes he had to resort to force.

His second victim, an eighteen-year-old named John Butkovich, had worked nearly a year for Gacy when he was murdered on July 31, 1975. Gacy had intended to bury the body in the crawlspace, but because of his wife's unexpected return, was forced to jam it into a three-by-one-foot area in the garage floor and then cover it with concrete.

The toll mounted: Darrell Sampson was last seen on April 6, 1976. Randall Reffett and Samuel Stapleton both disappeared on May 14, 1976, and were later found buried together. Michael Bonnin disappeared on June 3, 1976. William Carroll disappeared on June 13, 1976, and Rick Johnston dropped from sight on August 6, 1976. Gregory Godzik, a PDM employee for only two weeks, was murdered on December 12, 1976.

1977 was less than a month old when John Szyc, a hustler who tried to sell a car to Gacy, was murdered. Gacy then turned around and sold the car to an employee named Mike Rossi.

Gacy murdered nine boys in 1977 and buried them all beneath his house. Others were attacked but escaped death. Robert Donnelly, a nineteen-year-old who had lost his father and was under psychiatric care because of it at the time of his attack, lived to tell the police the disgusting and torturous things Gacy had done to him, but when Gacy claimed that the sex had been consensual, the police decided to take the contractor's word for it rather than the boy's, and no charges were filed.

The frightening thing about what happened to Robert Donnelly is that it could have happened to anyone's son. He was innocently walking to a bus stop when Gacy blocked his way with a car, pointed a gun at him and demanded identification, clearly implying that he was a policeman. He then handcuffed Robert and threw him into the car. When Gacy got the boy to the house on West Summerdale, he tried to get him to drink some whiskey, but when he wouldn't, forced his mouth open and poured it down the boy's throat. He then anally raped him, dragged him to the bathroom, and thrust his head into a tub of water over and over again until the boy lost consciousness.

It wasn't over yet for Robert. As soon as he came to, Gacy urinated on him, forced him to watch homosexual movies and made him play Russian roulette with his gun. The boy couldn't remember exactly how many times he'd had to pull the trigger, but thought it was somewhere between ten and fifteen. Each time Robert pulled the trigger he thought he was going to die.

Click...Click....Click.

When it finally did explode, it turned out to be a blank cartridge.

Robert's nightmare continued as Gacy once again bound, gagged, and raped him. And after all of that, he made the boy take a shower and dress. Putting him in his car, Gacy, his double chin hanging over his shirt collar, sweat glistening on his greasy forehead, smiled. "How does it feel to know you're going to die?"

Robert didn't die. For reasons even Gacy didn't understand, he let the boy go after delivering a final threat about what would happen to him if he went to the police.

No threat Gacy made, though, could be worse that what had already been done to him: Robert did go to the police and file a report. Unfortunately, though, he didn't come across as a credible witness. Not only was he under psychiatric care, but also had a severe stutter. And when the police interviewed Gacy, the businessman and active community member said that most of what Robert said had indeed happened, but that it had been consensual. The police chose to believe Gacy and didn't press any charges.

Gacy's next victim came along just three months later. He was Jeff Rignall, a twenty-six-year-old gay man. Though he voluntarily got into Gacy's car, Gacy turned around and drugged him with chloroform, burning the man's face and causing him permanent liver damage. When Gacy got him to the West Summerdale house, he stripped and tied him to a board that immobilized his arms and neck. He was raped over and over again with objects and by Gacy himself, and was forced to perform oral sex. When talking to police after the attack, Jeff claimed that another man had been present and also sodomized him, but that he hadn't seen who it was.

Jeff Rignall wasn't about to let John Wayne Gacy get away with what he'd done. When the police seemed disinclined to charge Gacy with anything, Rignall hired his own lawyer and sued in civil court. Gacy ended up settling out of court for $3,000.

And still Gacy's reputation in the community was unsullied. None of the dirt seemed to stick to him.

Though Robert Donnelly and Jeff Rignall survived, others didn't. William Kindred disappeared in January of 1978. Tim O'Rourke vanished that spring. Frank Landingin disappeared on November 4, and James Mazzara disappeared later that month.

Rob Piest, the victim who would put an end to Gacy's murderous rampage, disappeared the night of December 11, 1978. It was his mother's birthday.

Rob was the kind of son every parent hopes for. He was a good student, an athlete, and a hard worker. The night he vanished, he'd been working at Nisson's Pharmacy, his after-school job. John Wayne Gacy had come in that evening to talk to the owner about some work and spotted Rob stocking the shelves. As the murderer moved around the store with the owner, he'd stolen glances at his prey and made his plans. The obvious ploy for Gacy—and one that had worked time and time again—would be to offer Rob a job for a lot more money than he was making at the pharmacy.

Gacy bided his time. He didn't approach Rob on that first visit, but made sure to leave his appointment book behind so he'd have a reason to return to the pharmacy.

Mrs. Piest showed up at the pharmacy a little before nine o'clock to pick up her son. He wasn't quite ready, so she wandered around as she waited. Suddenly, an excited Rob grabbed his jacket from the girl at the front counter who'd been wearing it, and ran over to tell his mother that he was going to talk to a contractor about a job and would be back in a few minutes.

It was the last time Elizabeth Piest would see her son alive.

She waited until twenty minutes past nine, wondering and worrying. Leaving word at the pharmacy for Rob to call her the minute he got back, she drove home to see if perhaps the contractor had dropped him off there. As soon as she saw that Rob wasn't home she called the pharmacy, only to find out he still hadn't returned. She got the contractor's name from the pharmacist, but held onto it a few more minutes, hoping against hope to hear from her son. By ten o'clock, the entire Piest family was worried. Rob's father, Harold, made the pharmacist call Gacy's home, but he only got an answering machine.

The Piests had had enough. They went to the police for help, but didn't find any sympathetic ears. In their experience, runaway kids usually came home after a couple of days on their own—and no matter how hard the Piests tried, they couldn't convince the police that their son would never have run away. Nor could they convince them that John Wayne Gacy, a respectable businessman with friends in high places, had had something to do with their son's disappearance.

With the police unwilling—and, frankly, unable because of the tiny force's skeletal late shift—to do anything about finding Rob Piest that night, Rob's family started searching. They searched through the night, feeling more and more helpless and hopeless. Their Rob would never have just taken off. Something was wrong. Terribly, dreadfully, horribly wrong.

The next morning, after a sleepless night of searching, the Piest family showed up at the Des Plaines Police Department to demand action. This time the police were willing to listen, because they now knew about Gacy's 1968 felony conviction and the battery charges stemming from incidents in 1972 and 1978.

The night after Rob's disappearance, four detectives went to Gacy's house to question him. Gacy couldn't have been more cooperative, even going so far as to invite the detectives inside. He said he would come to the police station to make a statement, but that he first had to attend to some family matters. An uncle had just died, and there were some things Gacy needed to take care of.

The detectives checked out Gacy's story and discovered that, indeed, an uncle had died. But the things Gacy had to take care of had nothing to do with that uncle. They had to do with disposing of the body of Rob Piest, who lay dead in the attic over the detectives' heads.

As charming and helpful as Gacy was, the detectives still felt uneasy. Perhaps it was the musty odor of decay that pervaded the house. Perhaps Gacy was just a little too charming and helpful.

Whatever the reason, police delayed Gacy at the station for several hours the next day while the detectives got a search warrant for his house. When it finally came through, they went straight to West Summerdale and looked for evidence that Rob Piest had been there. They found some interesting items, such as a dildo, pornographic books, a homemade bondage board, various pieces of jewelry, including a high school ring with the initials "J.A.S."—and a film development receipt from Nisson's Pharmacy.

Nothing there tied Gacy to Rob Piest. At least nothing they were aware of at the time. A little over a week later they'd discover that the receipt had belonged to a clerk at Nisson's who'd slipped it into Rob's jacket pocket while wearing it the night he disappeared.

That night all they had to go on were their gut feelings that Rob had been at Gacy's house and that Gacy knew exactly what had happened to him. Based on that hunch, the Des Plaines police began twenty-four-hour surveillance of Gacy.

It was a real eye-opener for the men assigned. Gacy seemed to need little to no sleep. The reason, of course, was his constant pill-popping: pills to make him relax, pills to keep him awake. He drove the Chicago streets and expressways at speeds in excess of one hundred miles per hour, as though challenging the officers he knew were following to arrest him.

They didn't. Instead they kept pace with him as he puffed on marijuana and drank until the early hours of the morning. When he went home, they sat outside and waited for him to begin his seemingly endless round of daily appointments again.

Other detectives were interviewing Gacy's neighbors, employees, and ex-employees. As they compiled information, they were slowly drawn to the sickening conclusion that Rob Piest wasn't the only missing boy with a connection to Gacy.

Gacy was unpredictable. One minute he was filing lawsuits against the police department and the next he was inviting surveillance officers along for drinks and dinner at restaurants they'd followed him to.

Late one cold night, Gacy invited two of the surveillance officers into his house to warm up. The officers couldn't believe their luck. While one of them kept Gacy talking, the other, claiming to need to use the restroom, took a quick look around the house. Spotting a television he thought might belong to one of the missing young men, he quickly took down its serial numbers and then went to the restroom. As he dried his hands, the furnace kicked on, sending a blast of hot, pungent air into the little room. The detective sniffed, trying to figure out why the smell of the air was familiar.

It wasn't until some time later that he realized Gacy's house smelled like a morgue.

The discoveries kept coming. Mike Rossi, one of Gacy's former roommates and lovers, was driving John Szyc's car—and John Szyc was missing. The police also learned that Gacy had had some employees dig grave-size trenches in the crawlspace of his home. They'd been told they were for drainage tiles.

The constant surveillance was wearing Gacy down. He was getting frantic and making stupid mistakes. Late on the night of December 20, 1978, Gacy raced to his attorney's office. While Gacy drank and cried and talked to his lawyer until almost 3:30 a.m., the detectives waited outside. The lawyer, Sam Amirante, stayed in the office until Gacy fell asleep, then checked to make sure the detectives were still there, seemingly afraid now to be alone with his client.

When Gacy awoke, he took off again with the detectives right behind him. He stopped at a service station and slipped the young attendant, an acquaintance, a bag of marijuana. The detectives retrieved it moments later and continued to follow Gacy. He went home for his dog and dropped the animal off at a neighbor's house. Then he visited a friend and, distraught, told him that he'd "killed thirty people, give or take two or three." He said that they'd been blackmailing him and had deserved to die.

He went to see a couple of employees and told them some strange things about the mob and wanting to visit his father at the cemetery. One of the young men was frightened enough to talk to the pursuing detectives. They decided to arrest Gacy that day, on a drug charge based on the marijuana they'd confiscated from the service station attendant. It was December 21, 1978.

This time, when they returned to Gacy's house to search for evidence of missing boys, they had some idea of where to look—and what they'd find.

Nothing could have prepared them for the magnitude of Gacy's evil.

Gacy's house had been built on a reclaimed swamp. The crawlspace was continuously flooding. To keep the smell of decaying bodies to a minimum, and to enhance the process of decomposition, Gacy had spread hundreds of pounds of lime over the mud.

As the detectives entered the crawlspace, the smell of death was nearly overwhelming. When they carefully dug into the earth, noxious gases from the decaying bodies escaped, telling them exactly what was there.

On December 22, Gacy was charged with murder. In exchange for a visit to his father's grave, he agreed to return to his house on West Summerdale. He pointed out where John Butkovich had been buried in the garage, but wasn't much help that day in designating where the other bodies were. John, a neat-freak, was enraged at the mess police were making of his house and had to be taken away.

When evidence technicians wearing protective clothing were called in, the real digging began. Body after body, most unrecognizable and some no more than bones, was removed from the crawlspace. Some had been buried one on top of the other in obscene positions. Some had underwear jammed into their throats; some had the ropes they'd been strangled with still knotted around their necks.

The technicians and detectives had to be meticulous in their work to make sure that the remains of one body didn't mix with those of another. Identification promised to be difficult enough.

Days passed and more bodies were found. In an attempt to cooperate, Gacy drew a remarkably accurate map depicting the gravesites.

People gathered outside the house, standing for hours in the bitter Chicago cold. Some were relatives of missing boys, waiting to find out if their son or brother had been one of Gacy's victims.

The body of the boy who'd signaled the end of Gacy's rampage wasn't there—but his blue parka was, jammed under the floor of the utility room.

Of the twenty-nine bodies found on Gacy's property, all but six were identified. That wasn't even the final toll; quite simply, when he couldn't pack another corpse into the crawlspace, Gacy had started throwing bodies into the Des Plaines River. That was what had happened to Rob Piest and three others. It wasn't until spring that Rob's body finally surfaced and his devastated family was able to lay him to rest.

Gacy couldn't remember the specifics of his victims, such as names, ages, or even how many there were. Of one thing, however, he was certain: they'd all deserved exactly what they'd gotten.

Another thing he "knew" was that he hadn't actually murdered Rob Piest. He'd handcuffed the boy, knotted a rope around his neck, and was beginning to tighten the knot when he had to stop to take a business call. When he returned, the boy was dead. So actually, Gacy reasoned, Rob had killed himself by struggling to get free and causing the rope to tighten. Gacy was blameless.

Gacy went to trial on February 6, 1980. While his attorneys tried to depict him as crazy, the prosecutors presented him as a murderous, evil creature. The jury deliberated less than two hours and found him guilty of thirty-three counts of murder. On March 13th, they deliberated again and sentenced him to death.

His appeals devoured fourteen long years. Fourteen years in which he painted clown pictures, wrote a book, and even had a girlfriend who visited him regularly with her children. He was finally executed by lethal injection in 1994.

Thirty-three young men are still dead.

Important Dates in the Life of John Wayne Gacy

March 17, 1942: John Wayne Gacy was born in Chicago, Illinois, at 12:29 a.m. (CWT), according to Lois Rodden's *Astro Data II*. His parents were Marion and John Stanley Gacy.

Approximately 1947: John was molested by a neighborhood teenage girl, and began having fainting spells.

Approximately 1951: John was molested repeatedly by a contractor friend of his father's.

1952: The Gacy family moved from their suburban home to a house nearer Chicago.

1960: John attempted intercourse with a girl for the first time but fainted before the act was consummated.

1961: John dropped out of high school in his senior year, ran away from home, and worked for three months at a Las Vegas mortuary.

1964: John met and married Marlynn Meyers.

1966: Marlynn gave birth to a son and the family moved to Waterloo, Iowa, where Gacy began working for his father-in-law as the manager of three of his Kentucky Fried Chicken franchises.

1968: Marlynn gave birth to a daughter.

1968: John was sentenced to ten years' imprisonment at the Iowa State Reformatory for Men. Marlynn filed for divorce the same day, and Gacy never saw his children again.

December 25, 1969: John's father died.

June 18, 1970: Gacy was released from prison and paroled to Chicago, where he lived with his mother.

February 1971: Gacy assaulted a boy and was charged, but the charges were dropped when the boy failed to appear in court.

October 1971: Gacy was released from parole.

1971: Gacy began to date Carole Hoff.

January 2, 1972: Gacy murdered his first victim, Tom McCoy.

Summer 1972: Gacy married Carole Hoff.

1975: Gacy stopped having sex with his wife.

July 31, 1975: Gacy murdered John Butkovich and buried him in the garage.

April 6, 1976: Darrell Sampson disappeared.

May 14, 1976: Randall Reffett and Samuel Stapleton disappeared.

June 3, 1976: Michael Bonnin disappeared.

June 13, 1976: William Carroll vanished.

August 6, 1976: Rick Johnston disappeared.

December 12, 1976: Gacy murdered Gregory Godzik.

January 1977: John Szyc murdered.

1977: Robert Donnelly assaulted but not killed.

1977: Jeff Rignall assaulted but not killed.

January 1978: William Kindred disappeared.

Spring 1978: Tim O'Rourke vanished.

November 4, 1978: Frank Landingin disappeared.

November 1978: James Mazzara disappeared.

December 11, 1978: Rob Piest murdered.

May 10, 1994: John Wayne Gacy was executed by lethal injection.

Note: Investigators were unable to attatch names and dates of death to all the human remains discovered.

Astrological Blueprint for John Wayne Gacy

—Edna L. Rowland

John Wayne Gacy was born at Edgewater Hospital in Chicago, Illinois, on March 17, 1942. According to Lois Rodden's *Astro Data II*, his birth certificate records the birth time as 00:29 A.M. (CWT), near the "witching hour" of midnight.[1] A solar eclipse on March 16 at 25°44' Pisces preceded his birth by about six hours. The New Moon in Pisces falls in his 4th house of endings and closely opposes the dispositor, Neptune, indicating his hold on reality was precarious at best and that his judgement was poor. Both luminaries in adverse aspect to Neptune (which represents escapism) at 28° Virgo in detriment in the 10th house points to his self-indulgent attitude and abuse of alcohol and drugs. His reputation as a heavy drinker was well-known.

Jupiter-ruled Sagittarius is Gacy's Ascendant (signifying the self and physical appearance). Jupiter trines Venus, supplying him with a surface charm which he used to good advantage to seduce young boys and cover up his depraved nocturnal activities. Jupiter's square to the Nodes depicts his obesity and losing battle with weight problems. He was short, unattractive, and over-weight.

	☉	☽	☿	♀	♂	♃	♄	♅	♆	♇	MC	AS	IC	DS	☊
☉		27 ♓ 24	13 ♓ 08	04 ♓ 48	00 ♉ 55	04 ♉ 56	25 ♈ 03	26 ♈ 32	27 ♐ 17	29 ♉ 49	21 ♊ 53	28 ♑ 41	21 ♓ 53	28 ♈ 41	19 ♊ 40
☽	002 ☌ 49		14 ♓ 33	06 ♓ 12	02 ♉ 20	06 ♉ 21	26 ♈ 27	27 ♈ 57	28 ♊ 41	01 ♊ 14	23 ♊ 17	00 ♒ 05	23 ♓ 17	00 ♉ 05	21 ♊ 04
☿	025 42	028 ⚺ 31		21 ♒ 56	18 ♈ 04	22 ♈ 05	12 ♈ 12	13 ♈ 41	14 ♐ 26	16 ♉ 58	09 ♐ 02	15 ♑ 49	09 ♓ 02	15 ♈ 49	06 ♐ 48
♀	042 ∠ 23	045 ∠ 12	016 41		09 ♈ 43	13 ♈ 45	03 ♈ 51	05 ♈ 21	06 ♐ 05	08 ♉ 38	00 ♐ 41	07 ♑ 29	00 ♓ 41	07 ♈ 29	28 ♏ 28
♂	069 51	067 02	095 □ 33	112 △ 14		09 ♊ 52	29 ♉ 58	01 ♊ 28	02 ♌ 12	04 ♋ 45	26 ♋ 48	03 ♍ 36	26 ♈ 48	03 ♊ 36	24 ♋ 35
♃	077 54	075 05	103 36	120 △ 17	008 ☌ 03		04 ♊ 00	05 ♊ 29	06 ♌ 14	08 ♋ 46	00 ♌ 50	07 ♍ 38	00 ♉ 50	07 ♊ 38	28 ♋ 37
♄	058 ✶ 07	055 ✶ 17	083 □ 49	100 30	011 44	019 47		25 ♉ 36	26 ♋ 20	28 ♊ 53	20 ♋ 56	27 ♒ 44	20 ♈ 56	27 ♉ 44	18 ♋ 43
♅	061 ✶ 05	058 ✶ 16	086 □ 48	103 29	008 ☌ 45	016 48	002 ☌ 58		27 ♋ 50	00 ♋ 22	22 ♋ 26	29 ♒ 14	22 ♈ 26	29 ♉ 14	20 ♋ 13
♆	177 ☍ 24	179 ☍ 45	151 ⚻ 42	135 ⚼ 01	112 △ 43	104 40	124 △ 27	121 △ 29		01 ♍ 07	23 ♍ 10	29 ♎ 58	23 ♐ 10	29 ♋ 58	20 ♍ 57
♇	127 △ 40	124 △ 50	153 22	170 ☍ 03	057 ✶ 48	049 45	069 32	066 34	054 55		25 ♌ 43	02 ♎ 31	25 ♉ 43	02 ♋ 31	23 ♌ 30
MC	171 ☍ 47	168 ☍ 57	162 30	145 49	101 55	093 □ 52	113 △ 39	110 41	010 47	044 ∠ 07		24 ♎ 34	17 ♐ 46	24 ♋ 34	15 ♍ 33
AS	114 △ 37	117 △ 26	088 □ 55	072 Q 13	175 ☍ 31	167 28	172 ☍ 44	175 ☍ 43	062 ✶ 47	117 △ 42	073 35		24 ♑ 34	01 ♍ 22	22 ♎ 21
IC	008 ☌ 12	011 ☌ 02	017 29	034 10	078 04	086 □ 07	066 20	069 18	169 12	135 ⚼ 52	180 ☍ 00	106 24		24 ♈ 34	15 ♊ 33
DS	065 ✶ 22	062 ✶ 33	091 □ 04	107 46	004 ☌ 28	012 31	007 ☌ 15	004 ☌ 16	117 △ 12	062 ✶ 17	106 24	180 ☍ 00	073 35		22 ♋ 21
☊	167 20	164 31	166 56	150 ⚻ 15	097 □ 29	089 □ 26	109 13	106 14	015 14	039 40	004 ☌ 26	078 01	175 ☍ 33	101 58	

Midpoints and Aspects for John Wayne Gacy

Jupiter conjunct Mars in the 7th house or Descendant (the not-self, or other people) depicts the apparently affable, chubby, extroverted clown persona Gacy projected to the public during the day.

Was he the jolly good fellow he appeared to be?

Actually, this day-time persona was only a mask, for at night his dark side emerged, as he cruised the streets preying upon vulnerable, needy youths (Mercury), luring them to his house with promises of jobs, better wages, money, drugs, alcohol—whatever it took to cast his spell. No longer the generous businessman who operated a construction company in the neighborhood and volunteered his services to the local Jaycees, at night he turned into a "killer clown" who took what he wanted—a pedophile of

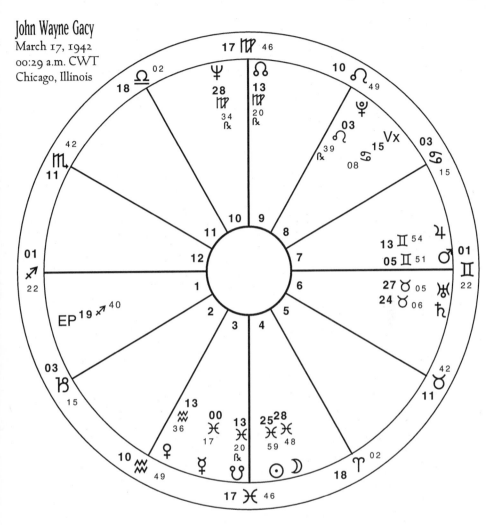

John Wayne Gacy
March 17, 1942
00:29 a.m. CWT
Chicago, Illinois

Birth chart for John Wayne Gacy

the worst kind, who slaughtered all thirty-three of his victims without a trace
of remorse.

Mars, Mercury, and the Ascendant form a Mutable T-square. The planetary focal point, Mercury (which rules adolescents and youths), is almost
exactly square his Ascendant at 01° Sagittarius and squares Mars (violence).
Mercury at 00°17′ Pisces in the 3rd house is also widely inconjunct natal
Pluto in his 8th house of death. Pluto at 03° Leo aspects both Ascendant and
Midheaven, and makes an out-of-sign trine to the natal Moon, as well as a
sextile to Mars.

Gacy's natal Mars/Saturn death midpoint at 00° Gemini falls almost directly on his Descendant or 7th house cusp. The Sun/Pluto and Moon/Pluto midpoints are conjunct Gacy's Ascendant. The Ascendant rules the physical body; the Descendant signifies the public and our attitudes toward other people.

No one is compelled to be a murderer, but might these potentially violent midpoints and Pluto aspects point to some type of secret death wish, falling as they do conjunct Gacy's 1st and 7th house cusps? (Midpoints and/or planets falling in angular houses have special significance or power.) Pluto rules Gacy's 12th house of secrets and hidden enemies, and is conjunct his Mars/Neptune midpoint, and Ebertin describes this planetary picture as follows: "The tendency to cause damage to others, brutally or of suffering likewise oneself from other people. (Dissolution, death.)"[2]

Gacy's Mars/Uranus midpoint at 01° Gemini conjoins his 7th house cusp and opposes his Ascendant, making him impulsive, accident-prone, and, according to Ebertin, inclined to commit acts of violence. The Mars/Pluto midpoint in Gacy's birth chart (called in Ebertin's *The Combination of Stellar Influences*, the "midpoint of murder") falls within a 01° orb of his 8th house cusp—the house which rules life and death, as well as what we expect from our sexual partners.[3]

Important Dates as Illustrated by Secondary Progressions and Transits to John Wayne Gacy's Natal Chart

We won't review every event in Gacy's life here, but will attempt to analyze events we believe may have had an important influence in molding or conditioning Gacy's environment and character, and the depraved lifestyle that he later adopted.

Astrology is not fatalistic. "The stars impel but do not compel." Whether we like it or not, we're all responsible for the choices we make along the way, and it's the choices we make, rather than the planets, that shape our lives. As an astrologer, I sincerely believe that how we react to events and the attitudes we adopt toward them are entirely within our control. Free will is what makes us individuals; it is our tool for developing and expanding consciousness.

When we ruthlessly exploit other people's weaknesses, however, we damage our own humanity and tend to regress rather than progress. The following astrological analysis is given in an effort to understand and comprehend—not to excuse, condone or rationalize—criminal behavior.

Let's begin with 1947. As early as age five, John began having fainting spells and was allegedly molested by a neighborhood teenage girl. In 1951, when he claims to have been repeatedly molested by a contractor friend of his father's, his progressed Ascendant was approaching an opposition to his natal Mars governing sexual activities.

This is not unusual, since most experts would agree that the great majority of mass murderers and serial killers experience sexual activity at a very early age, thereby forming their sexual-preference identities early on— probably much earlier than do the majority of children. In many cases the abused child grows up to retaliate and becomes an adult abuser.

When Gacy was eleven years old, he was hit on the head by a swing and began to experience severe blackouts (at which time his progressed Midheaven was conjunct Neptune in opposition to the natal Moon). In 1953, a blood clot on the brain was diagnosed and medically treated.

Later on he developed heart trouble. A sickly boy, he couldn't take part in the normal physical activities and sports his peers and schoolmates indulged in. As a result, his mother became more protective of him (natal Moon sextile Saturn), and he felt "different." Gacy's Jupiter/Uranus midpoint is occupied by Mars, a midpoint configuration Ebertin describes as denoting epilepsy or seizures.[4] These events and their astrological correlations tend to confirm the accuracy of Gacy's recorded birth time and Ascendant degree of 01°22' Sagittarius.

At age eighteen, he is said to have attempted intercourse with a girl for the first time, but to have fainted before completing the act. At this time, Gacy's progressed Ascendant had reached 14° Sagittarius, in opposition to his Ascendant ruler, Jupiter. Progressed Mercury at 28° Pisces was exactly conjunct his Moon, and this was when Gacy began to realize that his sexual relations with the opposite sex (represented by the Moon) were less than rewarding. As a teenager, he was probably beginning to recognize his preference for the energetic masculine activities (Mars conjunct Jupiter) of which he had been deprived in childhood, and gradually began moving toward a homosexual orientation.

During this formative period (1960–61), he became a high school dropout, left home, and began working for a mortuary. Throughout those two years, his progressed Midheaven (ruling one's occupation and reputation) at 05°06' Libra was in favorable trine aspect to natal Mars in 05° Gemini. However, when transiting Uranus moved into Virgo near the end of 1961 and squared his natal Mars, he was abruptly fired.

Despite what he probably knew about himself by now, in 1964 he decided to settle down, marry, and have a family. Transiting Saturn had just entered Pisces and was now conjunct natal Mercury and square the Ascendant, setting limits (Saturn) on his same-sex sexual activities.

With the dual sign Gemini on his 7th house cusp of marriage, he seemed destined to have two marriages (Venus is exactly trine Jupiter in Gemini). When he met his first wife in 1964, his 7th house ruler, Mercury, had progressed to 05° Aries and was sextile Mars, which occupied his 7th house. His marriage to Marlynn Meyers lasted about five years, during which time he fathered two children. That year (1969), when Gacy was twenty-seven years old, they divorced and his father died. At this time, transiting Pluto (death) at 27° Virgo was conjoined his natal Neptune and in opposition to both his natal Moon (representing females) and natal Sun (representing males) in Pisces (the sign of sorrows).

He had been convicted of sodomy the previous year, and sentenced to ten years in the Iowa State Reformatory. Transiting Neptune, his Sun sign ruler, hovering near his Ascendant, was making a trine aspect to his natal Moon, so he probably began drinking again. On June 18, 1969, Gacy was released from prison and paroled to Chicago to live with his mother. His progressed Moon (representing the mother) at 10° Aries was semisquare natal Saturn. Progressed Sun at 23° Aries was in favorable trine aspect to his progressed Ascendant at 22° Sagittarius. Shortly after assault charges against him were dropped the following year (February of 1971), he began to date Carole Hoff, who eventually became his second wife.

This was just the calm before the storm.

Not long afterwards, on January 2, 1972, Gacy murdered his first victim, Tom McCoy. At this time, transiting Neptune at 04° Sagittarius was conjunct his Ascendant and square Mercury. Transiting Uranus (rebellious urges) at 18° Libra (a homicidal degree) conjoined his progressed Midheaven at 17° Libra. Transiting Saturn at 00° Gemini was conjunct the Descendant, and directly opposed his Ascendant. Saturn and Neptune in opposition across these angles indicates he was depressed and gradually losing his grip on reality. Drugs and alcohol (Neptune-ruled) were becoming a daily (Saturn) habit. On the date of this first murder, transiting Mars at 04° Aries in Gacy's angular 4th house of endings was opposite transiting Pluto at 02° Libra in his 10th house. Both planets were aspecting his natal Mars and Pluto, as well—and these are the two most potentially violent planets in the zodiac.

In the summer of 1972, Gacy married Carole Hoff, but by 1975 they were no longer having sex. They divorced on May 2, 1976, when his 7th house ruler, Mercury, formed a critical conjunction with progressed Sun at 29° Aries; then these progressed planets made an inconjunct aspect to his natal Neptune. When the marriage broke up, Gacy's Ascendant had progressed to 27° Sagittarius and was square natal Neptune (ruler of his 4th house of endings), and square his Sun/Moon conjunction in 26–28° Pisces.

The murders and mysterious disappearances (Neptune) continued for six years, from 1972 to 1978—some even throughout his second marriage—until he was finally arrested and charged with assault and murder on December 22, 1978. Most of the thirty-three male victims had been strangled, and some had been choked with ropes—predictable, with Gacy's natal Saturn/Uranus conjunction in 24–27° Taurus. These degrees of Taurus are occupied by two so-called "malefic" fixed stars (Caput Algol and the Pleiades), denoting violent death and fatal injury to the neck or throat if heavily afflicted.

This modus operandi was also typical of Richard Speck, a mass murderer who brutally strangled eight student nurses in 1966. Speck, a Sagittarian born on December 6, 1941—just three months before Gacy—had natal Saturn at 23° Taurus (the sign ruling the throat and neck) in his 8th house. Speck also

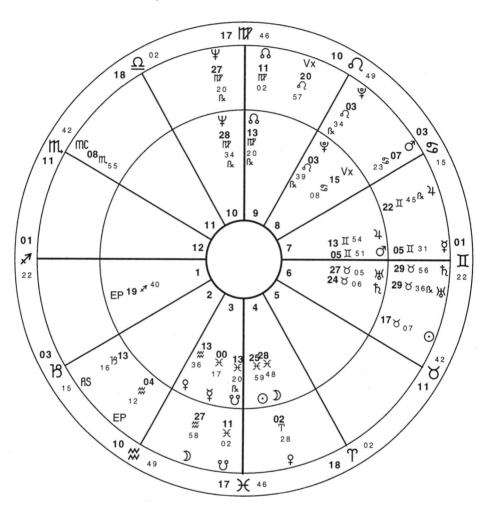

*Comparison of Gacy's natal (inner wheel) and progressed (outer wheel)
charts at the time of his execution*

had a Saturn/Uranus conjunction trine Neptune in almost the same degrees
as Gacy, but their charts are reversed, as Gacy has a Virgo Midheaven with
Neptune in the 10th house, while Speck has a 29° Virgo Ascendant with
Neptune conjunct his Ascendant. Both men were alcoholics and drug abusers,
as denoted by Neptune accented and afflicted in angular houses.

On death row for the last thirteen years, Gacy was scheduled to be
executed by lethal injection in January, 1994, but a successful appeal delayed

his execution. Gacy was finally executed by lethal injection on May 10, 1994, after an unsuccessful appeal. His secondary progressions for the date of his death were as follows: Progressed Sun at 17° Taurus conjoined a transiting New Moon at 19° Taurus, falling in his 6th natal house. The progressed Sun was almost exactly sextile Gacy's 4th house cusp. His progressed Moon at 27°58' Aquarius was exactly square his natal Uranus and inconjunct both natal and progressed Neptune—a chillingly appropriate configuration for a quick death by injection of lethal drugs. Transiting Pluto at 26° Scorpio in his 12th house of prisons was also square his progressed Moon, opposite his natal Uranus, and sextile his elevated natal Neptune. Progressed Neptune, his 4th house ruler, was opposite his natal Moon, his 8th house ruler. Transiting Jupiter, his Ascendant ruler, was exactly conjunct his progressed Midheaven at 8° Scorpio. Gacy's progressed Equatorial Ascendant at 4° Aquarius was opposite natal Pluto in his 8th house of death, and progressed Venus at 2° Aries was trine his natal Pluto.

Tony Crossley © Camera Press/Retna Ltd.

Chapter Six

Britain's Fatal Friend

Dennis Nilsen—His Story

– Sandra Harrisson Young

FEBRUARY 3, 1983. AT 23 CRANLEY GARDENS, a six-tenant flat in London, England, Dennis Nilsen, a thirty-seven-year-old civil servant, filled a large soup pot with water and put it on two burners so it would heat quickly. Walking to the plastic sheet he had on the floor, he picked up the head he'd just severed from the young man's

DESTINED FOR MURDER

body and carefully dropped it into the water. He waited until it came to a boil before turning the burner down to simmer. Looking at the corpse again, he knew he needed to finish dismembering it and store it someplace out-of-the-way. He also knew from experience what a big job that was. And tonight he just wasn't in the mood.

Leaving the body lying in the middle of his living room floor, Dennis called his dog, Bleep, and the two of them went for a walk.

D ennis was born on November 23, 1945, in Fraserburgh, Scotland. His mother, Betty, was a Scot; his father, Olav, a Norwegian soldier Betty had met and married during the war. The community he grew up in was isolated by the violence of the North Sea, and the people there tended to keep to themselves. They trusted only each other—if that. The result of such a climate and inclination was a certain amount of inbreeding among the populace over the centuries. Along with this inbreeding came strains of insanity—some virulent, some mere eccentricities.

Olav remained a soldier and only made rare visits to Fraserburgh to see his wife, but three children resulted: Olav, Dennis, and Sylvia. Betty and the children lived with her parents in their tiny home.

Dennis, a loner almost from birth, grew up without any real connection to his mother. It wasn't that she didn't try. It was more that Dennis was an odd, unapproachable child. He had no memory of his father at all—his mother divorced his father when Dennis was three years old—and didn't get along particularly well with either his brother or sister.

His one connection to the world of humanity was his grandfather, Andrew Whyte. Dennis didn't just love his grandfather, he obsessively adored him. Andrew, a fisherman, was his grandson's only friend, and in the world they shared, the boy's adoration was returned completely. The two of them would go for long walks and talk to each other about things they'd tell no one else. For Dennis, his grandfather was everything, the center of his universe.

And then his universe collapsed. One day, just before Dennis turned six, his grandfather went out on one of the fishing boats, and the next day he was declared dead from a heart attack. Andrew Whyte's body was brought home and lay in a casket in the small house. Although Dennis was carried out to look in the casket, he was never told that his grandfather had died. The boy didn't understand death. He only knew that his grandfather had to be very, very ill to be lying so still.

Then his grandfather was gone, his body taken away for burial. Dennis was left thinking the man had gone away to get well and would soon be home again. So Dennis waited for his grandfather and his friend—the only person in the world the boy loved—to come back.

He didn't, of course. And with the realization that his grandfather wasn't coming back, a part of Dennis died too. "Nature makes no provision for emotional death," he said after his arrest for murder.

Not long after his grandfather's death, Dennis moved with his mother and siblings to a new home. Betty Nilsen worked hard to provide her children with the necessities and a few little luxuries, the occasional ice cream cone or movie. But Betty, for all that she loved her children, couldn't figure Dennis out. She wanted to hug him, but something about the child compelled her to keep her distance.

Dennis was still young when his mother married for the second time. Adam Scott took on the three Nilsen children, and Betty gave birth to one child a year for the first four years of their marriage.

Dennis didn't like his new stepfather at first. He was jealous of the man's relationship with his mother. His behavior became even more remote, and he began to get into trouble with the police for petty crimes.

Any positive feelings he was able to muster were lavished on animals: pigeons, rabbits, gulls. But he wasn't allowed to keep any animals in the house. His mother wouldn't have them. There were times when, because they had to be kept outside even in the harshest weather, the animals died. It broke his heart.

When he was ten, the family moved to Strichen, a few miles outside of Fraserburgh. Dennis managed to make some friends, but still preferred his own company. He developed an intellectual relationship with a man named Robert

Ritchie, his Aunt Lily's husband. Ritchie introduced Dennis to socialism, radical thought, and classical music, all of which had profound influences on the adult Dennis.

In school, his performance was mediocre and, though he had some friends, he wasn't particularly close to anyone. He also had a dawning recognition that he was attracted to boys rather than girls. It was a secret he kept to himself. There were boys on whom he developed crushes—in one case he had a crush on a picture of a boy in a textbook—but he never acted on his feelings. In fact, he went through his entire school life without any sexual experiences at all.

When Dennis was fifteen, he went from school and work in a fish cannery to the Army Catering Corps, where he had to work with other males and conform to military discipline. He later described these years as the happiest of his life. He got along with everyone and learned how to speak his mind and focus outward a little more. Within three years he'd completed his training and was sent to Osnabruck, Germany, to serve as a private with the First Battalion of the Royal Fusiliers. It was here that Dennis started drinking on a daily basis. His homosexual urges grew stronger, but he completely suppressed them. Not one of the men with whom he worked knew about Dennis's sexual inclinations.

In 1967, Dennis was sent to work at Al Mansoura Prison in Aden, South Yemen, where Arab terrorists were detained. It was here that Dennis got his first real sight of blood and mutilated bodies—there was so much, in fact, that it soon became commonplace to him. It was also here that Nilsen claims he killed for the first time. There was nothing sexual about it at all; on the contrary, it was completely a matter of self-defense against an attack by an Arab man. He never told anyone about the incident until his arrest for multiple murders many years later.

In the summer of 1967, Nilsen was transferred to work in the Persian Gulf. For the first time ever, he had his own room. It was here that he had his first sexual experience with another person—a boy whose age he didn't know. This was also where he came up with the idea of placing a mirror so that he could see himself reclining. Pretending the reflection was someone else, he would let his sexual fantasies play themselves out. Gradually, over time, he began to allow the reflection to represent himself, but kept his body motionless so it would appear dead.

Dennis was transferred again in 1969, this time to Berlin, where he had his first sexual experience with a woman. He was able to perform adequately, but didn't find it particularly worthwhile.

In 1971, Nilsen took up his last post in the Shetland Islands. He loved it there, and felt comfortable with the people and the land. Over the years, he'd become an avid home-movie maker and brought this interest with him to the Shetlands. There he met a young private with whom he became emotionally entangled.(The young man was not gay—they did not become lovers.) They shared an interest in filmmaking and worked on movies together. The private was only eighteen and very homesick. Nilsen fell deeply in love, and took reels of film of his companion. He claimed later that he would masturbate as he watched the footage of his friend reclining; shades of watching himself in the mirror; shades of death.

After more than eleven years in the army, Dennis decided not to re-enlist. The authoritarian attitudes were beginning to rub him the wrong way. As soon as his time was up, he decided, he would move on. First, though, he had to put an end to certain facets of his military life. He and the young man who had been such a close friend ceremoniously burned all the film he had so painstakingly and lovingly shot—15,000 feet of it. It was part of the past, never to be seen again. Dennis didn't mind the loss of the film; it was the end of his relationship with the young man (who chose to remain in the army) he mourned for more than two years.

He went from the Shetlands to visit his family in Strichen while deciding what to do next with his life. During this visit, he met with his brother, Olav, and Olav's wife. As the visit progressed, the brothers got into a terrible fight over homosexuality. His brother had guessed that Dennis was homosexual and told others of his suspicions. Olav beat Dennis badly, and Dennis never forgave him. The two brothers never spoke again.

Dennis had to get away. It was clear to him that he didn't fit in at home any more now than he had before joining the army. In an effort to find his place in life, he became a police constable. But the same leftward leanings that had disenchanted him with army life bothered him in this career. After only a year on the job, he resigned and found himself out in the world without much of anything.

He was unemployed for several months, but eventually found work at Jobcentre, on Denmark Street in London. He liked his new job, placing people in positions for which they were suited. He was aggressive in his work, and while that aggressiveness alienated some of his fellow workers, that was all right with him. He was doing it the way he wanted.

As happy as he was at work, though, Dennis was becoming increasingly dissatisfied with his personal life. He went from pub to pub, anonymous encounter to anonymous encounter. He was completely promiscuous—although never in public—and completely unhappy. "Sex in its natural place," he said, "is like the signature at the end of a letter. Written on its own, it is less than nothing. Signatures are easy to sign, good letters far more difficult."

He began to use the mirror again, looking at himself—loving himself. The "dead" Dennis.

He was becoming more confused about his identity. Was he the living Dennis or the dead Dennis? When he received news that his biological father had died and left him one thousand pounds, he discovered that Olav Nilsen hadn't even been a Nilsen. His father's real name had been Olav Magnus Moksheim. Dennis wasn't a Nilsen at all, but a Moksheim. His already-unstable mind took another hit.

He accepted the money and used it to get himself a larger, ground-floor flat with a private garden at 195 Melrose Avenue. He moved into this flat with a young man named David Gallichan, whom he'd known for only one day. Together they created a home, with a dog named Bleep, a cat named D.D., and a bird.

Though the relationship between the men lasted for two years, it never became a very warm or fulfilling one for Dennis. When the still-promiscuous Gallichan finally moved out, Nilsen felt more relief than loss. Without Gallichan, Nilsen devoted himself to his dog, his job, and politics.

Dennis had never learned moderation in expressing his views. Rather than mellowing, he was, if anything, becoming more strident with age, and frequently alienated even those who agreed with him. It was this alienation that prevented him from getting the promotions he felt should have been his. It certainly wasn't his work, which was good and very thorough. He worked at Jobcentre for eight years before being promoted to the position of executive officer and transferred to the Kentish Town Jobcentre.

Over the years, Nilsen got burned in personal relationships and turned more inward. He began putting talc on his face and smearing charcoal under his eyes to make himself look dead. He tore what looked like bullet holes in a tee-shirt and dripped a blood-like substance on the holes. His costume complete, he would lie in front of his ever-present mirror and look at himself, pretending to be dead.

And he would drink. Too much and too often.

In December of 1978, Nilsen brought a young man home with him. They drank, talked, and slept together, but didn't have sex. In the morning, Nilsen gazed at the sleeping youth and thought about how beautiful he was—and that he would probably leave when he awoke. He explored the young man's body and found himself aroused.

He hadn't really planned to kill; it happened quite suddenly. One moment he saw a tie lying on the floor and the next he had it around the sleeping young man's neck.

The youth instantly awoke and bucked, trying to get Nilsen off him. They fell to the floor and the young man scooted across it with Nilsen on top of him, pulling the tie tighter and tighter until he lost consciousness.

At first Nilsen thought the man was dead. He removed the tie, but then realized he was still breathing. Thinking fast, Nilsen filled a bucket with water and drowned him. Exhausted, he took a brief rest, then carried the body into the bathroom. He bathed it and himself, and then lay in bed beside the corpse, exploring it. He was aroused, and attempted unsuccessfully to have sex with the body, but gave up when he couldn't maintain his erection.

He ended up putting it under the floorboards where it would stay cold. He left the body there for a week before bringing it out again, washing and examining it to see what effect being dead had had upon the body. The young man was still quite lovely, very pale. He masturbated onto the youth's stomach, cleaned him up, and then suspended him by the ankles, where he swung gently all night, his fingertips brushing the floor. The next morning Nilsen masturbated on him again, and then replaced him under the floorboards, where he remained for more than half a year.

It was August 11, 1979, when Nilsen brought him out again, carrying him into the garden and burning him to ashes in a bonfire, obliterating the smell of burning flesh by tossing rubber into the flames. When the body was completely cremated, he raked the remains into the garden.

It was as though the young man had never existed. In fact, there has never been any proof that he did. Nilsen never even knew his name, and no one came looking for him. There were no consequences. He could just put the incident out of his mind and go on with his life.

Altogether, twelve men died at the Melrose Avenue flat. Eight of the twelve remain unidentified.

His second victim was Kenneth Ockendon, a Canadian visiting London and due to return home on December 4, 1979. The two men met quite by chance on December 3 and spent the day together drinking, talking, and listening to music.

As had happened with the first victim, Dennis couldn't bear the thought of Ken leaving for Canada the next day. Before he knew it, he'd strangled the man with a stereo headphone cord. After a day spent in a cupboard while Nilsen was at work, Ockendon's body was taken out, washed, and put in bed with Nilsen before being lowered under the floorboards. Nilsen brought him out several times over the next couple of weeks, taking care to clean the body, dress, and then arrange it on the bed or in a chair, as though it were a guest, even speaking to it as if the man were still alive.

His third victim was a displaced, unstable teenager. Martyn Duffey had had a small run-in with police and left home in May of 1980, only to meet up with Dennis Nilsen. The course of his death followed almost exactly that of the first victim, including being drowned.

In the twelve months between the Septembers of 1980 and 1981, Nilsen murdered seven men whose identities are still unknown.

Billy Sutherland was twenty-seven when he met Nilsen. Sutherland was a thief who'd been to prison and had no qualms about sleeping with men for money. Nilsen doesn't remember much about the murder, only that it happened.

Another victim was Malcolm Barlow, a twenty-four-year-old misfit whom nobody really liked—including Nilsen. Barlow was killed more or less because Nilsen didn't want him around.

Yet Nilsen said later that he hadn't really hated any of the men he had killed. He didn't even really understand why he had killed them at all. It had just happened.

Disposing of the bodies grew to be a problem. Some ended up in pieces, stuffed into suitcases which were then left in his unlocked garden shed. Others were put in cupboards. Hands and arms that didn't fit into suitcases were shoved under bushes outside. Eventually he ended up with the parts of six bodies he had to get rid of. In December of 1980 he built one last bonfire, secreting the suitcases with their grisly contents and bags of heads in the center of the fire where they couldn't be seen. He lit it early in the morning and it burned all day long. When the fire finally died out, Nilsen crushed the remaining bony evidence into powder and spread it throughout the garden.

No one guessed what he was doing. No one called the police.

As the killing continued at the Melrose Avenue house, bodies once again began to stack up under the floorboards. The day before Nilsen moved into his new flat at 23 Cranley Gardens, he built another bonfire and the same scene ensued.

Nilsen's move was a death knell for his last three victims. The first of these was John Howlett, a real loser who had accomplished little in his life beyond giving others grief. His crime against Dennis Nilsen was that he was very much an unwanted guest. When Nilsen told him to leave, the sleepy Howlett refused. Nilsen first strangled and then drowned him. It was the most difficult of the murders; Howlett was strong and very nearly succeeded in fighting Nilsen off. In the end, though, he wasn't strong enough.

Then there was Graham Allen, who was apparently murdered while eating an omelet Nilsen had cooked for him.

Stephen Sinclair, twenty, was the last of Nilsen's victims, and the one that would be Nilsen's undoing. Sinclair was a troubled man with a drug problem. Although he'd known Sinclair only a day, Nilsen felt protective toward him. In Nilsen's own mind, he killed Sinclair as a way of giving the man some kind of peace. It was January 26, 1983.

The problem that now plagued him was his inability to dispose of the victims. There was no private garden and there could be no more bonfires. His solution was to cut the bodies into small pieces and gradually rinse and flush them into the sewage system. Of course, there were some parts he couldn't do that with. Shoulder blades went over a fence into a dump. Other large bones were treated with salt, put in a tea chest, and left in a corner of his apartment.

The beginning of the end came for Dennis on February 3, 1983, when the plumbing clogged. The apartment building's toilets had been unusable for an entire day. Now they were not only unusable, but had backed up and had the entire ground floor smelling like a sewer. The tenants were angry and wanted the problem fixed. Dennis claimed to have no trouble at all with his own plumbing when approached by his enquiring neighbors, but, in fact, he did—along with the uneasy feeling he knew what was causing it.

When the regular plumber arrived the next day, it quickly became clear to him that the problem required a specialist. So the tenants spent the remainder of the weekend unable to use their toilet facilities.

Dennis had another problem. Stephen Sinclair's decapitated body still lay in the middle of his living room floor. He really wasn't in the mood—in fact, it was the last thing he wanted to do—but he began the tedious and familiar process of cutting the body into sections and bagging and storing them in his wardrobe, along with the boiled head.

When the plumbing specialist finally arrived four days later, it was dark. Despite a stench that nearly overwhelmed him, he climbed down into the sewer while a tenant shone a flashlight. What he saw was a pool of rotting flesh with pieces of bone floating in it. It neither looked nor smelled like normal sewage, and he had a very bad feeling about it.

With the tenants of the house (including Nilsen) listening, he called his supervisor and told him what he'd found and what he suspected it was. He was ordered to leave it until the next morning.

Dennis spent a restless evening debating what he could do to cover himself. Unaware that his neighbors could hear his movements, he left his flat and climbed into the sewer himself. With his bare hands, he pulled out the rotting flesh handful by handful, dropping it into a plastic trash bag. When the bag held as much as it could bear without breaking, he disposed of it behind a hedge and went back to his flat, his mind still working. He thought of buying some chicken from a fast-food outlet, chopping it up and tossing it into the sewer to replace what he'd removed.

For some reason he didn't.

He thought of committing suicide.

For some reason he didn't.

Instead he went to bed and slept. In the morning he left for work as though everything was fine. While there, though, in addition to his regular duties he tidied his desk, suspecting it would be his last day.

It was obvious to the workman when he returned that the contents of the sewer had been tampered with. He climbed down to investigate and discovered that some rotting flesh and bone slivers still remained in the drain leading from the house.

His supervisor looked at what he'd found and a decision was made to call the police. In a matter of hours, police confirmed what the workman had suspected all along: the debris was human. And the only one who had tampered with it was Dennis Nilsen.

They were waiting for him when he got home from work that night. With only a slight hesitation, he let them into his flat.

Despite the wide-open windows, the air reeked of decaying flesh. There was no need to ask Nilsen anything except where the body was. "In two plastic bags in the wardrobe," he told them.

The next question was whether it was one body or two.

"Fifteen or sixteen," came his shocking answer.

The policemen were speechless.

But Nilsen was relieved. He couldn't have stopped the killing himself; now it was being done for him.

In fact, once he started talking about what he'd done, he couldn't seem to stop. And not only did he talk, but he filled pages and pages in his journals with his thoughts and feelings. As shocking as his crimes had been, almost more shocking still was his ability to articulate himself with such clarity. A man who had murdered as many men as he had, and who had mutilated his victims as grotesquely as he had, must have been insane.

Was he? Is he?

A court said he wasn't. In the end, Dennis Nilsen was convicted of six counts of homicide and two of attempted homicide. He now resides at Brixton Prison, and though he'll be eligible for consideration of parole beginning November 4, 2008, it's unlikely he'll ever see the light of day outside prison walls.

Important Dates in the Life of Dennis Nilsen

November 23, 1945: Dennis Andrew Nilsen was born at 4:00 a.m. (GMT) in Fraserburgh, Scotland.

1948: Dennis Nilsen's parents divorced.

October 31, 1951: Dennis' grandfather, Andrew Whyte, died.

1955: Dennis moved with his family and stepfather to Strichen, a neighboring town.

1961: Dennis joined the Army Catering Corps.

1964: Nilsen took his army passing out parade after successfully completing every area of study and testing. On a short visit home, he had an accident on a motorscooter and suffered a hard knock to the head. Later, Nilsen was posted as private to the First Battalion of the Royal Fusiliers at Osnabruck, Germany.

1967: Nilsen was sent to Aden, South Yemen, to guard Arab terrorist detainees at Al Mansoura Prison. He later claimed to have killed an Arab there in self-defense.

Summer 1967: Nilsen was transferred to the Persian Gulf, where he had his first sexual experience with another person.

1969: Nilsen was posted to Berlin.

1971: Nilsen was posted to the Shetland Islands.

1972: Dennis left the army and returned home for a visit. While there, he had a falling-out with his brother, Olav, and severed their relationship completely.

December 1972: Dennis joined the Metropolitan Police Training School.

December 1973: Dennis quit the police force.

May 1974: Nilsen found work at a London Jobcentre.

1975: Dennis' father, Olav, died and left him one thousand pounds. With the money, Dennis and his new lover, David, moved to 195 Melrose Avenue in London.

Summer 1977: Nilsen's lover moved out of their Melrose Avenue home.

December 1978: Nilsen killed his first victim.

August 11, 1979: Nilsen burned his first victim's remains and spread the ashes in his garden.

December 3, 1979: Nilsen killed his second victim, a Canadian named Kenneth Ockendon.

May 1980: Nilsen killed his third victim, Martyn Duffey.

September 1980–September 1981: Nilsen killed Billy Sutherland, Malcolm Barlow, and seven men whose identities are still unknown.

October 3, 1981: Nilsen moved to 23 Cranley Gardens.

1981–2: Nilsen murdered John Howlett.

1981–2: Nilsen murdered Graham Allen.

January 26, 1983: Nilsen murdered his last victim, Stephen Sinclair.

February 8, 1983: Human flesh was discovered in the plumbing of Nilsen's building.

February 11, 1983: Nilsen was charged with murder.

Astrological Blueprint for Dennis Nilsen

—Edna L. Rowland

The large pot Dennis Nilsen used to boil hacked-up pieces of human flesh has become an exhibit at Scotland Yard's Black Museum. Before he was arrested on February 9, 1981, Nilsen had murdered fifteen young men—all of them drug addicts or drunkards he found in the London pubs he visited regularly.[1]

According to Lois Rodden's *Profiles of Crime*, Dennis Andrew Nilsen was born in Fraserburgh, Scotland, on November 23, 1945, at 4:00 a.m. (GMT).[2] The time is from his birth certificate.

On the date of birth the Sun is just entering the sign of Sagittarius (00° Sagittarius). The Moon occupies 18° Cancer and the 19th degree of Libra is rising on the Ascendant. Nilsen's ruling planet, Venus, in detriment at 13° Scorpio, occupies the 1st house and is opposite the Vertex. Nilsen was tall and good-looking, befitting a Venus-ruled Ascendant. Jupiter, his Sun sign ruler, although technically in the 12th house, is on the cusp of his 1st house at 18° Libra. The Ascendant and Jupiter are both in homicidal degrees (18–19° Libra).

Since the Sun is in the 2nd house at birth, this is a nighttime (predawn) birth. The Midheaven degree is 27° Cancer, but the signs Leo and Aquarius are intercepted in the 4th and 10th house angles. Mars, Saturn, the Moon, Jupiter, and Neptune are in Gauquelin plus sectors.

On July 9, 1945, just four months before Nilsen's birth, there was a solar eclipse at 16°27' Cancer in Nilsen's 9th house, in close conjunction with his natal Moon. At home in the sign of Cancer, the Moon is decreasing in light and conjunct Saturn—an aspect indicating extreme introversion and moodiness. Although Saturn is technically in the 9th house, it is within orb of a conjunction to the Midheaven. Saturn aspecting the Midheaven or within the 10th house is sometimes called by astrologers "the Napoleon aspect." Saturn here indicates someone who is inordinately proud, and often indicates a "fall from grace" or sudden loss of status. (For example, President Nixon, a Capricorn, had his ruler, Saturn, in the 10th house at birth, according to Marc Penfield's *An Astrological Who's Who*.)[3]

Jupiter, Nilsen's Sun sign ruler, at 18° Libra is closely conjunct his Ascendant degree, but exactly square the natal Moon, symbolic of an extremely self-indulgent, pleasure-loving attitude. Incidentally, Neptune is dignified in the 12th house, but makes only one aspect, a sextile to Pluto, indicating a craving for drugs. Neptune in the 12th house is often seen in the charts of secret drinkers or alcoholics.

Pluto at 11° Leo occupies the degree of Neptune's North Node; it is culminating in Nilsen's 10th house, and conjunct the other occupant of the 10th house—Mars, Pluto's lower-octave planet. The co-rulers of the sign Scorpio, Mars and Pluto are the two most violent planets in the zodiac. In Nilsen's chart, Pluto (which rules death, change, and transformation) is exalted by sign and house position.

	☉	☽	☿	♀	♂	♃	♄	♅	♆	♇	MC	AS	IC	DS	☊
☉		24 ♍ 43	11 ♐ 08	22 ♏ 03	01 ♎ 25	09 ♏ 38	27 ♍ 34	08 ♍ 16	04 ♏ 14	06 ♎ 08	29 ♍ 05	09 ♏ 51	29 ♐ 05	09 ♒ 51	15 ♍ 20
☽	131 33		05 ♎ 21	16 ♍ 16	25 ♋ 38	03 ♍ 51	21 ♋ 47	02 ♋ 29	28 ♌ 27	00 ♌ 22	23 ♋ 19	04 ♍ 04	23 ♈ 19	04 ♊ 04	09 ♋ 33
☿	021 16	152 ⚻ 49		02 ♐ 41	12 ♎ 03	20 ♏ 16	08 ♎ 12	18 ♓ 54	14 ♏ 52	16 ♎ 46	09 ♎ 43	20 ♏ 29	09 ♑ 43	20 ♒ 29	25 ♍ 58
♀	016 53	114 △ 39	038 10		22 ♍ 58	01 ♏ 11	19 ♍ 07	29 ♌ 49	25 ♎ 47	27 ♍ 41	20 ♍ 38	01 ♏ 24	20 ♐ 38	01 ♒ 24	06 ♍ 53
♂	118 △ 10	013 23	139 26	101 16		10 ♍ 32	28 ♋ 29	09 ♋ 11	05 ♍ 09	07 ♌ 03	00 ♌ 00	10 ♍ 46	00 ♏ 00	10 ♊ 46	16 ♋ 15
♃	041 44	089 □ 48	063 ⚹ 00	024 50	076 25		06 ♍ 42	17 ♌ 24	13 ♎ 22	15 ♍ 16	08 ♍ 13	18 ♎ 58	08 ♐ 13	18 ♋ 58	24 ♌ 28
♄	125 △ 51	005 ☌ 41	147 07	108 57	007 ☌ 41	084 □ 06		05 ♋ 20	01 ♍ 18	03 ♌ 12	26 ♋ 09	06 ♍ 55	26 ♈ 09	06 ♊ 55	12 ♋ 24
♅	164 28	032 ⚺ 54	174 ☍ 15	147 34	046 ∠ 17	122 △ 43	038 36		12 ♌ 00	13 ♋ 54	06 ♋ 51	17 ♌ 37	06 ♈ 51	17 ♉ 37	23 ♊ 06
♆	052 31	079 02	073 47	035 37	065 38	010 46	073 20	111 56		09 ♍ 53	02 ♍ 50	13 ♎ 35	02 ♐ 50	13 ♋ 35	19 ♌ 04
♇	108 43	022 50	129 59	091 □ 49	009 ☌ 26	066 58	017 08	055 44	056 ⚹ 11		04 ♌ 44	15 ♍ 29	04 ♏ 44	15 ♊ 29	20 ♋ 59
MC	122 △ 49	008 ☌ 44	144 05	105 55	004 ☌ 39	081 04	003 ☌ 02	041 38	070 17	014 05		08 ♍ 26	27 ♎ 41	08 ♊ 26	13 ♋ 56
AS	041 18	090 □ 15	062 ⚹ 34	024 24	076 51	000 ☌ 26	084 □ 33	123 △ 09	011 13	067 24	081 30		08 ♐ 26	19 ♋ 12	24 ♌ 41
IC	057 ⚹ 10	171 ☍ 15	035 54	074 04	175 ☍ 20	098 55	176 ☍ 57	138 21	109 42	165 54	180 ☍ 00	098 29		08 ♓ 26	13 ♈ 56
DS	138 41	089 □ 44	117 △ 25	155 35	103 08	179 ☍ 33	095 □ 26	056 ⚹ 50	168 46	112 △ 35	098 29	180 ☍ 00	081 30		24 ♉ 41
☊	150 ⚻ 19	018 46	171 ☍ 35	133 ⚼ 25	032 09	108 34	024 27	014 08	097 □ 48	041 36	027 30	109 01	152 29	070 58	

Midpoints and Aspects for Dennis Nilsen

Because Nilsen's Sun is actually on the cusp of Scorpio/Sagittarius, his basic personality and individuality partakes of both the Pluto-ruled Scorpio sign and the Jupiter-ruled Sagittarius sign. His Equatorial Ascendant is at 01° Scorpio, and his Ascendant ruler, Venus, resides in Scorpio as well. A Libra Ascendant usually seeks some type of companionship and is rarely a loner, but his ruler, Venus, in close square to Pluto, tends towards relationships that are obsessive, compulsive, or based upon shared addictions.

Nilsen's Midheaven degree at 27° Cancer is another important indication of the ongoing violence in his life, since it occupies the Mars/Saturn (28°29' Cancer), or death, midpoint. Reinhold Ebertin, a cosmobiologist, describes this midpoint in his book

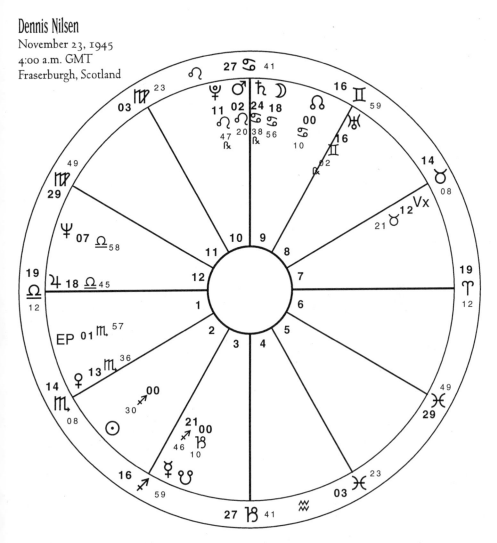

Dennis Nilsen
November 23, 1945
4:00 a.m. GMT
Fraserburgh, Scotland

Birth chart for Dennis Nilsen

Astrological Healing: The History and Practice of Astromedicine as follows: "Disease, grief, preoccupation with death."[4] Certainly, an apt description of a serial killer bent on self-destruction! Progressed Mars (which turned retrograde when Nilsen was eleven years old) occupied this 28° Cancer Mars/Saturn midpoint when Nilsen killed his first and second victims.[5] When David Gallichan, his young lover, left him in the summer of 1977, Dennis' rage knew no bounds, and the rampage of murders began. The defense psychiatrist at

Nilsen's court trial, Dr. James MacKeith, stated that "Nilsen suffered from a severe personality disorder, due to a lack of a father, the death of his grandfather, and loneliness."[6]

A little about Nilsen's childhood might be appropriate here. Nilsen's parents divorced when he was only three years old, and this had a depressing effect upon his childhood, as indicated by the close conjunction of Moon and Saturn in his 9th house—the Moon and Saturn being the rulers of his 4th and 10th houses, the parental angles. Dennis grew up in his grandparents' home. His grandfather's death at Dennis' first Saturn square further deprived his childhood. This had been an affectionate and close tie, and the grandfather had apparently served as a father substitute for the little boy.

Important Dates as Illustrated by Secondary Progressions and Transits to Dennis Nilsen's Natal Chart

When Dennis Nilsen's parents divorced in 1948, transiting Saturn was conjunct his natal Neptune in the 12th house of secret sorrows. Transiting Pluto was trine his Mercury, and Neptune at 19° Libra was conjunct his natal Jupiter and exactly conjunct his Ascendant degree. A few years later, on October 31, 1951, when Dennis was six years old, his grandfather, Andrew Whyte, died. The progressed Midheaven at 03° Leo was conjunct both natal and progressed Mars. His progressed Ascendant at 23° Libra was square natal Saturn, ruler of his 4th house of endings.

In 1955, at age ten, Dennis moved with his family and stepfather to a new home in Strichen (his mother had remarried the previous year). At this time, his progressed Midheaven was at 07° Leo, in conjunction with his natal Mars/Pluto midpoint. His progressed Sun at 10° Sagittarius was approaching a trine to his natal Pluto in the 10th house, indicating that major adjustments (Pluto) to a new school and new living conditions would be necessary.

In August of 1961, at age sixteen, Dennis joined the Army Catering Corps. He seemed to like the discipline of the army—and the uniform. His progressed Sun at 16° Sagittarius had now reached an exact opposition to his natal Uranus, which meant breaking away from family ties and leaving home for the first time. When he joined the army, his progressed Midheaven at 13° Leo was square his Ascendant ruler, Venus, and his progressed Mercury (travel) retrograde at 12° Sagittarius was trine natal Pluto. His Sun sign ruler, Jupiter, was retrograde, transiting his 4th house. Progressed Jupiter at 21° Libra in his 1st house was sextile natal Mercury, his 9th house ruler of long-distance (overseas) travel.

By 1964, Nilsen had successfully completed every area of study and testing in the army. On his way home for a short visit, he suffered a hard knock to his head from a motorscooter accident. Progressed Mercury was inconjunct his Mars/Uranus accident point at 09° Cancer at this time. Shortly thereafter, he was posted as a private to the First Battalion at Osnabruck, Germany. At this time, progressed Sun at 19° Sagittarius was making a favorable sextile aspect to his Ascendant, and his progressed Midheaven at 16° Leo was sextile natal Uranus.

In 1967, Nilsen allegedly killed an Arab terrorist in self-defense at Al Mansoura Prison. That summer, he was transferred to the Persian Gulf where he had his first sexual experience as transiting Pluto in Virgo squared his progressed Sun at 22° Sagittarius.

In 1969, when his progressed Sun at 24° Sagittarius had reached an exact inconjunct aspect to his natal Saturn in the 9th house of long journeys and overseas travel, Dennis was posted to Berlin, Germany. A year later he was posted to the Shetland Islands.

In 1972, he finally left the army, after eleven years of service. At this time, transiting Uranus (representing sudden changes) was approaching a conjunction with both his Ascendant and Jupiter. After leaving the army at age twenty-seven, he returned to his family for a visit. During this visit he had a falling-out with his older brother, Olav, and severed their relationship completely. His brother is represented by Nilsen's 3rd house ruler, Jupiter, and by natal Mercury within his 3rd house of siblings. Uranus is often present or afflicted when a long-standing relationship or friendship is severed or circumstances beyond one's control cause sudden, unexpected separations.

On December 23, 1972, Nilsen joined the Metropolitan Police Training School. His progressed Sun at 28° Sagittarius was inconjunct his natal

Midheaven, and he wasn't able to make the required adjustment to the restrictive lifestyle of a policeman. At age twenty-seven, his progressed Moon was making its first return to its natal position, making this an important year in his life. One year later, in December of 1973, Nilsen quit the police force—just as his progressed Moon at 27° Cancer reached an exact conjunction with his Midheaven, and transiting Uranus at 26° Libra squared his progressed Moon and his Midheaven. He found another job as a personnel director at the London Jobcentre the following year, when his progressed Moon reached a conjunction with his natal Mars in his 10th house (which rules occupations and professions).

In 1975, when his father died and left him an inheritance of one thousand pounds, progressed Venus (ruler of his 8th house of inheritances) was exactly conjunct his natal Mercury, and his progressed Sun had just recently changed signs by moving into Capricorn, in conjunction with his South Node. With this inheritance he purchased a home on London's Melrose Avenue, which he shared with his lover, David.

In the summer of 1977, David moved out, leaving Dennis alone, angry and depressed. During this time, Dennis' progressed Sun at 02° Capricorn was making an inconjunct aspect to his natal Mars. Transiting Neptune at 14–15° Sagittarius was opposite his natal Uranus, and transiting Saturn at 10–11° Leo was conjunct his natal Pluto. His progressed Moon was square natal Uranus, indicating a separation.

The following year, in December of 1978, Nilsen killed his first victim, as his progressed Midheaven moved into Virgo in square aspect to his natal Sun. His progressed Ascendant was now at 10° Scorpio square natal Pluto. The violent planet Pluto at 18° Libra (a homicidal degree) was also transiting his natal Jupiter and natal Ascendant degree. Transiting Neptune at 17° Sagittarius opposed his natal Uranus, and the progressed Moon at 03° Libra in December of 1978 was sextile his natal Mars. During 1978 and 1979, Nilsen's rage finally erupted and he killed his first two victims. These two undetected murders were followed by thirteen others between 1978 and 1983.

The last victim, Stephen Sinclair, was murdered on January 26, 1983, after Nilsen moved into an apartment at 23 Cranley Gardens. On this date, transiting Pluto at 29° Libra was squaring Nilsen's Midheaven, and progressed Mars at 28° Cancer was retrograding back and forth, activating his natal Midheaven degree and the fatal Mars/Saturn (death) midpoint. This Mars-square-Pluto aspect can be indicative of murder. Progressed Venus at 00° Capricorn was exactly conjunct his South Node. Progressed Mercury, ruler of his 12th house of self-undoing, was exactly opposite his natal Uranus. Human flesh was found in the plumbing of Nilsen's apartment building on February 8, 1983, and the police charged him with murder on February 11, 1983.

On the date he was charged with Sinclair's murder (and confessed to all the others), his progressed Midheaven at 05° Virgo was semisquare his natal Ascendant, and his progressed Ascendant at 13° Scorpio was exactly conjunct Venus, his ruling planet. His progressed Sun at 08° Capricorn was separating from an exact square to Neptune, and the progressed Moon at 22° Scorpio was making a semisquare aspect to natal Neptune in his 12th house of incarceration and confinement.

When he flushed parts of his victim's bodies down the toilet, it apparently clogged the plumbing, and the other apartment tenants filed a complaint. On November 4, 1983, Nilsen was convicted of all charges by a jury vote of ten to two, and sentenced to life imprisonment.

A Study of Serial Killers

Astrological Observations

—Edna L. Rowland

I N 1966, RANDOM HOUSE PUBLISHED

Truman Capote's book, *In Cold Blood*, about the murder of the

Clutter family in Kansas. It is said to have been the first novelization

of a true-crime story; this was long before bookstores had a separate

category for the true-crime genre.

Around that time, I received a check for one hundred dollars from *Dell's Horoscope Magazine* for my first published article about Richard Speck, the brutal mass murderer who killed eight student nurses in their Chicago dormitory. That check launched my career as a freelance writer. Since then, I've written many articles for *Dell's Horoscope* and *American Astrology*, and crime-writing has become one of my specialties. I've written about John Lennon's assassination, the Green Beret murders, and the serial killer Ted Bundy, to name just a few.

This book is unique in my experience in that it's divided into two parts—the first is a portrait of a well-known murderer by Sandra Harrisson Young, the author of over twenty-seven novels, and the other an astrological analysis of the killer by myself, an experienced freelance author and professional astrologer. The co-authors of the book are also unique, in that we belong to two opposite Sun signs—polarities that complement each other.

Sandra is a communicative Gemini, whereas I am a philosophical Sagittarian. Some of our views may occasionally diverge, since we approach our subjects from different points of view as writers, but our conclusions are often similar. At the same time, we're always clearly following our own unique Sun sign paths. This is not a book on astrological counseling or how to erect charts. As authors, we assumed that our readers were already familiar with basic astrological concepts.

Now we'd like to pose a question to our readers: can a serial killer be spotted by examining his or her astrological birth chart?

In my opinion, an experienced, professional astrologer should be able to pick out from a total of ten or twelve random charts at least three having the most potential for violence or instability. Is this the same thing as predicting murder? No, it isn't, because astrology is not fatalistic. Astrology deals with probabilities—although many people wish it *could* be more specific.

Then, too, there is a distinct difference between mundane (event-oriented or predictive) astrology and natal astrology, which deals with birth charts. People have choices, but events don't. To put it another way: events don't have the potential for change, but people do.

As Sandra, my co-author, clearly mentions in the preface to this book, many other people are born on the same dates as murderers. What makes the murderers different? Choices. I agree with her on this one hundred percent.

Another difference that we often overlook is gender. In our society, boys and girls are raised and conditioned in drastically different ways. According to current statistics in the United States, men are three times more likely to be murder victims than women. Most murders are committed by males under the age of thirty-five; less than one-tenth are over fifty.

Mass murderers usually have a unique mode of operation which distinguishes them from other types of murderers. They may go berserk, killing several people at one time (Richard Speck, for example, killed eight student nurses in one night), while serial killers such as Ted Bundy and Jack the Ripper usually kill one person at a time over an extended period.

Serial killers and mass murderers are similar in that they both usually kill strangers or acquaintances rather than members of their own family, and that, as a rule, they tend to be older than other types of killers. Statistics show that while forty-five percent of homicide arrestees are under twenty-five, only fifteen percent of mass murderers or serial killers are under twenty-five.

No astrologer can say for sure that this or that person will end up a murderer, because no one is born fated to become a murderer, rapist, criminal—or even a doctor or lawyer, for that matter. Murder, however, when it occurs in the continual pattern many serial killers and mass murderers display, can become (like any other habitual behavior or lifestyle) an occupation.

When we think of a professional killer, we usually think of someone paid to kill—but doesn't the pattern of continuous killing reveal that the killer is receiving some form of satisfaction or reward, whether it be money, a feeling of power and control, sexual gratification, or sadistic pleasure?

Although we all have inborn potentials which tend to move us in certain directions, I believe we're also endowed with the gift of free will, enabling us to choose our vocation or lifestyle.

In this respect, a dysfunctional childhood environment is certainly a liability, but it doesn't necessarily destine us to a life of crime. We're responsible for the choices we make and attitudes we adopt.

Is there a pre-existing bias if an astrologer/writer is presented with the chart of a known and convicted murderer, and a crime has already been committed? Shouldn't an ethical astrologer abstain from making any comments, for fear of taking on the role of a prophet—in this case, a prophet of doom?

I'm more than willing to admit that the counseling branch of astrology offers more opportunity for positive thoughts and happy endings to interviews. After all, how many good things can be said about someone who has committed numerous violent and despicable crimes? Not many true-crime books have happy endings, unless you consider the capture and eventual punishment of the criminal a joyful event. There is usually a certain sadness to contemplating evil deeds.

We're not attempting the counsel or rehabilitation of prison inmates here, though—that falls into the natural province of accredited psychiatrists and psychologists. I'd like to clear up any confusion on this point that may remain: in writing about true crime as an astrologer, I'm not acting in the role of counselor. Instead, I'm collecting, recording, and interpreting facts and events which have already occurred. There's little room here for either counsel or prophecy. Instead, I'm taking on the role of a researcher from an astrological perspective.

Admittedly, as a true-crime writer I'm primarily interested in the psychological motivation behind a crime. Any events that seem to lead up to the crime or precipitate it also interest me, since they may provide clues as to motivation.

As an astrological researcher, I use the astrological chart as a tool to examine the trouble spots, weaknesses, or possible instability of the criminal personality. In this respect, certain houses take on special importance. The angular houses (1st, 4th, 7th, and 10th) are always important. I'm especially interested in pointing out afflictions to the parental angles (4th and 10th houses), since these often denote early childhood experiences, child abuse, or a family heritage which may have contributed to a criminal's having chosen the wrong path in life. I'm also interested in mapping secondary progressions and transits to the natal chart in order to interpret important events that occurred beforehand and may have led to an act of murder.

This is hardly the same as predicting that a man or woman is destined to break the first commandment, "thou shall not kill." In our society, when a confirmed criminal becomes a danger to our way of life, we prefer to distance ourselves from him or her by moving them to a prison, where we can safely contemplate their sins against society. On second thought, should we even attempt to analyze the motivations behind violent crimes such as murder and rape? Is the art of astrology capable of this?

Maybe not, but the only other choice is to ignore the increasing violence in our society, turn our heads and try to forget that, for the most part, psychopaths are very much like the rest of us. They walk among us, and we don't recognize them. There are important differences, but as a rule, they tend to blend into society very well.

The "bogeyman" may be real to children, but he's actually only a projection of our own fears. Isn't it about time we realized that we truly live in a violent society where atrocious crimes are committed every day (especially in America), sometimes right under our noses?

Jeffrey Dahmer, for instance, the Milwaukee serial killer described in the second chapter, committed seventeen murders before he was arrested. Doesn't that tell us something? Ed Gein, who lived in the small town of Plainfield, Wisconsin, was long considered just a good neighbor who did odd jobs and occasional baby-sitting, before his crimes of murder and grave-robbing were discovered. When he was first arrested, no one in town could believe he was guilty. He seemed so harmless. And then there was the Russian serial killer, Andrei Chikatilo, born in Yablochnoye, Ukraine, who killed fifty-two people before he was finally captured and brought to justice.

Two other broad categories of murderers are recognized by criminologists: the disorganized serial killer, who tends to be careless or sloppy in committing crimes, and the highly organized killer, who plans everything in advance, often following a precise ritual repeated over and over again. Jeffrey Dahmer is an example of an organized murderer. John Wayne Gacy and Dennis Nilsen also tend to fall into this category. Killers may further be analyzed according to the

DESTINED FOR MURDER

type of victims they choose—whether these be predominantly homosexuals, prostitutes, children, adolescents, or of one gender.

What are some of the danger signals that tell us we may have a potential serial killer in our midst? The following is a checklist which should be used only as a guide. Many persons who are not and never will become murderers may also have experienced some of these unfortunate circumstances in their lives.

Criminologists and psychiatrists generally agree that some of the following traits or circumstances have been found in most psychopaths' and serial killers' backgrounds:

1. A dysfunctional family where divorce or separation has occurred, resulting in the total breakup of the family.

2. Early sexual abuse.

3. Battering of a parent, usually the mother, which the child witnesses and/or is helpless to prevent. Usually accompanied by drunkenness or drug abuse on the part of one or both parents.

4. Deliberate cruelty to animals or insects.

5. Bed-wetting. This is sometimes a sign of unusual or prolonged stress in children, especially if it continues for a long time.

6. Setting of fires. This may develop into arson.

7. Head injuries, falls, or other signs of neglect or lack of close supervision by parents, which often results in irreparable brain damage.

8. Placement in a juvenile home or other punitive institution at an early age.

9. Feeling of being unwanted due to illegitimacy or being orphaned. This may cause later problems with self-esteem.

10. Withdrawal from society and/or creation of imaginary playmates to compensate for an inability to make or keep friends. (This only applies if these traits are carried into adolescence, when the child naturally tends to become more gregarious and aware of his or her sexual orientation. We should also make a distinction between this and the natural tendencies of introversion and extroversion, which are not considered abnormalities unless either becomes excessive.)

A chart's parental angles should always be examined carefully, because negative or afflicted planets in either the 4th or 10th houses may point, or give us a clue to, possible child abuse. For example, Neptune afflicted in the 4th or 10th house may indicate an irresponsible parent who is either alcoholic or on drugs. Uranus in these houses may represent separation or divorce. Mars or Pluto heavily afflicted in one of these angles may indicate more serious physical and/or violent sexual abuse on the part of parents. A badly afflicted Saturn in the 4th house may indicate extreme deprivation of the necessities of life, poverty, neglect, or indifference on the part of parents or caretakers.

Again, we must exercise caution in interpreting these trends, since not everyone with planets in these houses will experience such unfortunate experiences or circumstances in early childhood. No one has perfect parents, and nowadays, the support exists to help many of us survive dysfunctional families. If more than one of the outer planets occupies parental angles, though, it's worth examining the rest of the chart for confirmation.

Planetary aspects and placements, and the rulers of the following houses, should also be examined carefully: the 8th house (which rules death *and* sexual preferences); the 4th house (which rules our family heritage and endings, including the end of life);[1] and the 12th house. (The 12th house rules imprisonment or incarceration in any institution where we may be deprived of our freedom. This is sometimes referred to as "the house of self-undoing.")

Angular house placements are always important in any chart. The 1st house or Ascendant is particularly significant, since it rules the self, the physical body, and, to some extent, the outer personality. Planets in angular houses (the 1st, 4th, 7th, and 10th houses) will have strong effects, and we are also beginning to realize the importance of planets occupying the Gauquelin plus sectors. (A brief explanation of these sectors is included in the Glossary.) Each chart is individual, however, and must be examined as an entity or whole.

In the examination of charts of criminals or mass murderers such as those described in this book, we can't overlook the importance of midpoints. Although all midpoints are vitally important, the following can be classified as key in cases of murder or crime: the Mars/Saturn midpoint (death); Mars/Pluto (murder); Saturn/Pluto (cruelty or violent assault); and the Mars/Uranus midpoint (accident proneness). The Sun/Pluto or Mars midpoints are equally important in indicating the potential for violence, and the Moon/Saturn midpoint should be also noted, since it often indicates an unnatural dependency on one of the parents beginning in early childhood. Occupied midpoints should be given special attention, as well as those aspecting chart angles or the cusps of angular houses.

Natal charts for the murderers described in this book have been interpreted and erected for the geocentric tropical (seasonal) zodiac, and the Placidian house system has been utilized.

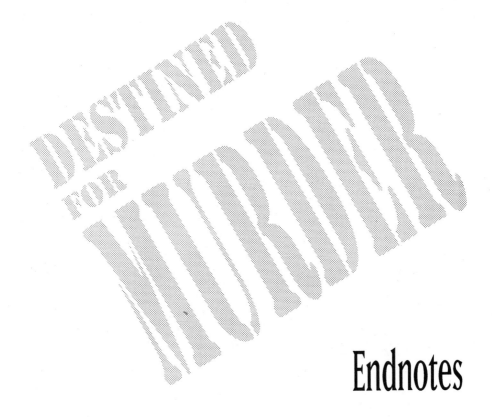

Endnotes

Chapter 1: The Cannibal Grave-Robber—Edward Gein

1. Harold Schechter, *Deviant: The Shocking True Story of the Original "Psycho."* Pocket Books, a division of Simon & Schuster, New York, NY, 1989.
2. Lois Rodden, *Profiles of Crime.* Hollywood: Data News Press, 1991. Birth data for Ed Gein as stated in "Astro Data V" on p. 63.

Chapter 2: The Milwaukee Wolf Man—Jeffrey Dahmer

1. Lois Rodden, *Profiles of Crime.* Ibid. Birth data for Jeffrey Dahmer as stated in "Astro Data II" on p. 37.

2. Ann E. Parker, *Astrology and Alcoholism*. York Beach, Me.: Samuel Weiser, 1982.

3. Reinhold Ebertin, *The Combination of Stellar Influences*. Aalen, Germany: Ebertin-Verlag, 1960, p. 197.

4. Ed Baumann, *Step Into My Parlor: The Chilling Story of Serial Killer Jeffrey Dahmer*. Chicago: Bonus Books, 1991.

5. Ted George and Barbara Parker, *The Fixed Stars—Health and Behavioral Imbalances*. Jacksonville, Fl.: Arthur Publications, 1985.

6. Annette Rubin, LMAFA, "The Astrological Common Denominator in the Diagnosed Schizophrenic," *The Astrological Review*, Summer, 1969. pp. 16–22; transcript of talk given at Guild meeting, June, 1969.

7. Reinhold Ebertin, *The Combination of Stellar Influences*. Ibid., p. 93.

Chapter 3: The Hillside Stranglers—Kenneth Bianchi and Angelo Buono

1. Lois Rodden, *Profiles of Crime*. Ibid. Birth data for Kenneth Bianchi as stated in "Astro Data V."

2. Lois Rodden, *Profiles of Crime*. Ibid. Birth data for Angelo Buono as stated in "Astro Data V." This given time is taken from official birth records supplied to Rodden by Victoria Shaw.

3. They may have also shared a *folie a deux*—a psychiatric condition in which two persons (usually but not necessarily related by blood) share the same delusions and act out the same psychosis.

4. Traditionally, Mars represents physical and/or masculine energy, which need not be expended negatively.

5. Reinhold Ebertin, *The Combination of Stellar Influences*. Ibid.

Chapter 4: The Boston Strangler—Alberto DeSalvo

1. Police called him "The Green Man" because he often wore green work trousers.

2. Gerold, Frank. *The Boston Strangler*. New York, New York: Signet Books, 1966.

3. For this 1960 offense, he was sentenced to two years' imprisonment, and was released in 1962.

4. Lois Rodden, *Profiles of Crime*. Ibid. Birth data for Alberto DeSalvo as stated in "Astro Data V."
5. Reinhold Ebertin, *The Combination of Stellar Influences*. Ibid.

Chapter 5: Chicago's Killer Clown—John Wayne Gacy

1. Lois Rodden, *Astro Data II*. San Diego: Astro Computing Services, 1980. Birth data for John Wayne Gacy. (Rodden later corrected this birth time for Gacy to 00:29 a.m. in her quarterly newsletter, *Data News*.)
2. Reinhold Ebertin, *The Combination of Stellar Influences*. Ibid., p. 151.
3. Reinhold Ebertin, *The Combination of Stellar Influences*. Ibid., p. 152.
4. Reinhold Ebertin, *The Combination of Stellar Influences*. Ibid., pp. 162–163.

Chapter 6: Britain's Fatal Friend—Dennis Nilsen

1. Colin Wilson and Donald Seaman, *The Encyclopedia of Modern Murder*. New York: Arlington House, 1988, p. 179.
2. Lois Rodden, *Profiles of Crime*. Ibid.
3. Marc Penfield, *An Astrological Who's Who*. York Harbor, Me.: Arcane Publications, p. 355.
4. Reinhold Ebertin, *Astrological Healing: The History and Practice of Astromedicine*. York Beach: Samuel Weiser, 1989, p. 363.
5. Reinhold Ebertin, *The Combination of Stellar Influences*. Ibid., pp. 178-179.
6. Colin Wilson and Donald Seaman, *The Encyclopedia of Modern Murder*. Ibid., p. 180.

A Study of Serial Killers: Astrological Observations

1. Both the 4th and 8th houses rule death; however, the 8th house is a *public* house whereas the 4th house is a *private* house. In addition, the 8th house rules sexuality whereas the 4th house, in and of itself, has no sexual significance. A 4th house ending has horary significance.

Glossary

— Edna L. Rowland

activate
To move to activity.

adverse aspect
See "hard" under "aspect, modifying terms for."

afflict, afflicted, afflictions
Difficult or unfavorably aspected planets or houses. Usually refers to "hard" aspects such as the square, semisquare, inconjunct (mildly adverse), or sesquiquadrate, etc. May also refer to a planet or house with difficult, stressful aspects and little or no beneficial aspects to counteract the negativity.

Air signs
A triplicity of three signs: Gemini, Libra, and Aquarius.

angles

See "angular."

angular

The 1st, 4th, 7th, and 10th houses and planets therein. Sometimes called *angles*, since these cusps divide the four quadrants of the birth chart. Planets on or close to these cusps or angles are thought to strongly affect an individual.

applying

When a planet is approaching or going toward an exact degree or aspect with another planet, or house cusp, it is applying; the opposite of separating.

Aquarius

See "signs."

Aries

See "signs."

Ascendant

The zodiacal degree and sign on the eastern horizon (on the left-hand side of the chart) at the time of birth; sometimes called the *rising sign*.

aspect

The longitudinal distance between two planets, such as the square (90°), or the trine (120°), etc.

conjunct: 0°.
inconjunct:: 150°.
opposition: 180°.

semisextile: 30°.
semisquare: 150°.
sesquiquadrate: 135°.
sextile: 30°.
square: 90°.
trine: 120°.

aspect, modifying terms for

hard: Stressful or unfavorable aspects such as the square (90°), semisquare (45°), sesquiquadrate (135°), and inconjunct (150°) which is mildly adverse.

soft: Favorable aspects such as the trine (120°), sextile (60°), and semisextile (30°). The conjunction (0°) may or may not be considered beneficial depending upon the planets involved.

astrology, types of

horary: A branch of astrology which has its own set of rules, and concentrates on casting a chart for the moment a question is asked, or an event occurs.

mundane: Also called judicial or political astrology, as it is devoted to the study of planetary cycles or patterns that affect world events or politics, and forecasting future events.

natal: Genethliacal astrology, devoted to the study of the birth charts of individuals and their life and character.

"at home"

See "home sign."

Balsamic Moon

A phase of the Moon or personality type as defined by astrologer Dane Rudhyar, classifying all persons born with the Moon less than 45° behind the Sun, or three-and-a-half days before the New Moon. Moon semisquare the Sun.

benefic

Usually refers to the beneficial planets Venus and/or Jupiter, if not afflicted.

birth chart

See "chart."

birth data

The month, date, year, birthplace (longitude and latitude), and hour of birth—the data necessary to erect an exactly timed natal birth chart.

Cancer

See "signs."

Capricorn

See "signs."

Cardinal

Refers to the common leadership qualities or characteristics of the signs Aries, Cancer, Libra, and Capricorn.

challenging aspect

See "hard" under "aspect, modifying terms for." The negativity of this type of aspect is often difficult for the individual to overcome.

chart

In natal astrology also called a horoscope, radix, nativity, or birth chart, and usually refers to a chart erected for an individual based on the month, date, year, birthplace, and birth time. May also refer to a progressed or transit chart for a timed event.

close aspect

Another way of saying that an aspect is nearly or almost exact. See "exact aspect."

conjunct, conjoined, conjunction

Within the same sign and degree of longitude. See "aspects."

co-ruling, co-ruler

Refers to a planet which shares rulership of a sign with another planet.

cosmobiologist

A member of the German cosmobiology movement, an empirical school of astrology founded by Reinhold Ebertin. A cosmobiologist is an astrologer who focuses mainly on the angularity and midpoints between two planets.

crossing

Passing over another planet or house cusp.

culminating

A planet above the horizon, usually in or near the 10th house cusp; also called an *elevated* planet.

cusp

The line dividing any two houses of the horoscope. For example, the line of the Ascendant marks the 1st house cusp, the next line marks the 2nd house cusp, etc.

cusp ruler

The planet ruling the sign on the cusp of the house.

cycle, Moon

In reference to secondary progressions, the twenty-seven-year cycle of the Moon refers to the Moon's return to its own natal sign and degree position.

cycle, Uranus

In reference to the transits of Uranus, the 42–47-year cycle refers to its half-way point, or opposition, to natal Uranus. (This occurs between ages 42–47, depending upon the natal position of Uranus and other factors.) Uranus completes its cycle in 84 years.

decan, decanate

Each thirty-degree sign contains three decans of ten degrees each.

degree

One-360th of any circle. Some astrologers have assigned specific meanings to certain degrees, such as 18–19° Aries/Libra (a homicidal degree) or 8–9° Taurus (an alcoholic degree). In horary and natal astrology the 29th degree is regarded as a "critical degree" regardless of what sign it occupies.

depressing aspect

See "hard" under "aspect, modifying terms for."

Descendant

The opposite point or angle from the Ascendant; the 7th house cusp.

detriment

A planet in the opposite sign to the sign that it rules. For example, Venus rules Taurus, so Venus in Scorpio is considered to be in detriment.

dignify

A somewhat antiquated term used to describe the condition of a planet that is strengthened by either sign position (essential dignity) or house position (accidental dignity).

dispositor

Ruler of the sign another planet is located in. For example, if Mercury is in Taurus, Venus (which rules Taurus) is said to be Mercury's dispositor.

diurnal

The apparent diurnal (daily) motion of the planets resulting from the axial rotation of the Earth.

dual sign

Refers to a "double-bodied" sign such as Gemini, Sagittarius, or Pisces.

Earth Signs

A triplicity of three signs: Taurus, Virgo, and Capricorn.

eastern horizon

The left-hand side of the chart.

East Point

See "Equatorial Ascendant."

eclipse

An astronomical phenomena involving the Sun, Moon, and Earth. There are two kinds of eclipses that interest astrologers—solar and lunar.

ecliptic

The apparent, or elliptical, path of the sun, where eclipses occur.

elements

The four elemental substances—Fire, Earth, Air, and Water.

elevated

A planet above the horizon, usually in or near the 10th house cusp; also called a *culminating* planet.

ephemeris

An astrologer's almanac containing the computed positions of the Sun, Moon, and planets for each day of the year.

Equatorial Ascendant

The East Point (EP), sometimes called the second Ascendant, since it's calculated from the equator rather than from the ecliptic. It is the point where the eastern horizon intersects the prime vertical and the celestial equator.

exact aspect

An aspect with no orb. Used loosely to refer to an aspect within a one-degree-or-less orb.

exaltation, exalted

A traditional classification of a planet that is said to be more favorable for a planet than even the sign it rules.

falls on

Loosely used to mean conjoin or conjunct.

favorable aspect

See "soft" under "aspect, modifying terms for."

Fire signs

A triplicity of three signs: Aries, Leo, and Sagittarius.

Fixed

Refers to the common steadfast qualities or characteristics of the signs Taurus, Leo, Scorpio, and Aquarius.

fixed star

A self-luminous celestial body, as distinguished from a planet which shines by reflected light.

focal planet

A planet which either by transit or progression enters an empty space created by a T-square.

Full Moon

The monthly or progressed phase of the Moon where the Sun and the Moon are in exact opposition (180° apart).

Gauquelin plus sector

Michel and Francoise Gauquelin's research defined certain areas of the diurnal chart as "Gauquelin plus sectors," attributing greater importance to planets in these plus sectors. Roughly, these are planets that are either rising or culminating, just past the eastern horizon (Ascendant) or upper meridian, but actually it is much more complicated. With statistical tests conducted from 1959–65, the Gauquelins found a planetary effect in the areas of heredity, choice of profession, and personality. Gauquelin named this study "neo-astrology."

Gemini

See "signs."

geocentric

Earth-centered, in contrast to heliocentric, which is Sun-centered.

grand cross

See "grand square."

grand square

A challenging, stressful configuration composed of four planets, each one making squares, and an opposition to the other three planets.

Cardinal grand square: A grand square composed of Cardinal planets.

Fixed grand square: A grand square composed of Fixed planets.

Mutable grand square: A grand square composed of Mutable planets.

grand trine

A configuration of three planets, each 120° from the other, forming a triangle.

Fire grand trine: A grand trine composed of Fire planets.

Earth grand trine: A grand trine composed of Earth planets.

Air grand trine: A grand trine composed of Air planets.

Water grand trine: A grand trine composed of Water planets.

hard aspect

See "aspect, modifying terms for."

harmonious aspect

See "soft" under "aspect, modifying terms for."

higher octave planet

Uranus is the higher octave of Mercury, and Neptune is the higher octave of Venus.

highest planet

At the top of the chart. See "culminating."

home sign, "at home in"

A planet residing in a sign that it rules.

horary astrology

See "astrology, types of."

horizon

The horizontal line dividing the chart or circle into two sectors—above and below.

horoscope

See "chart."

house

There are twelve houses, roughly dividing the twenty-four-hour diurnal circle into approximately two hours for each house; they are numbered counterclockwise from the Ascendant. Each house has a distinct meaning. Houses may be equal or unequal in size depending upon the house system or method used to compute them. The following keywords are associated with the various houses. (See an astrology textbook for additional meanings.)

1st: Self, outer personality, physical characteristics.

2nd: Monetary gains, possessions. Value systems.

3rd: Siblings. Elementary school. Short trips.

4th: Home, childhood conditioning. Parents and heritage. End of life.

5th: Romantic love, children, and creative pursuits.

6th: Service to others, jobs, health.

7th: Marriage, partnerships of all types, public enemies.

8th: Death, inheritance. Sexual preferences. Joint finances.

9th: Religious beliefs or philosophy. Legal matters. Foreign travel.

10th: Reputation. Profession and fame or publicity. Parents.

11th: Friendships, hopes, and wishes. Step-children or adopted children.

12th: Prisons or hospitals. Self-undoing. Hidden enemies. Secrets.

house ruler

The planet which rules the sign on the cusp of the house, or a planet ruling an intercepted house. (However, planets within houses are also considered influential and may modify delineations accordingly.)

IC

Abbreviation for Imum Coeli. The point opposite the Midheaven or meridian; the fourth house cusp. (Not to be confused with the Nadir.)

inconjunct

See "aspect."

inharmonious aspect

See "hard" under "aspect, modifying terms for."

inner planets

Mercury, Venus, Mars, and Jupiter.

intercepted

Refers to more than one sign occupying a house, resulting in two successive houses with the *same* signs on their house cusps. Most house systems, with the exception of the equal house system, utilize houses of various sizes.

Jupiter

See "planets."

Leo

See "signs."

Libra

See "signs."

lifecycle midpoint

The half-way point (or age) between the dates of life and death.

lower octave planet

The opposite of higher octave. See "higher octave."

luminaries

The Sun and Moon which illuminate the day and night. For convenience, astrologers may sometimes refer to the Sun and Moon as planets but the difference is clearly understood.

lunar Nodes

The Moon's Nodes—a point (not a planet) where the Moon passes the ecliptic, sometimes referred to as the Dragon's Head (North Node) and Dragon's Tail (South Node).

malefic

An antiquated term that applies to certain planets deemed to have a harmful or unfavorable influence, usually Mars and Saturn; but may also be loosely applied to an afflicted planet, or a conjunction with a malefic.

Mars

See "planets."

Mars/Pluto midpoint

See "midpoint."

Mars/Saturn midpoint

See "midpoint."

Mars/Uranus midpoint

See "midpoint."

Midheaven

Medium Coeli (MC); the 10th house cusp; the meridian of the birthplace.

midpoint

Halfway point between two planets, calculated by adding both planets' longitude, then dividing this sum in half. *Note:* The significance of any of these midpoints can be modified by a planet or planets occupying (located upon, or conjoined) the midpoint.

Mars/Pluto midpoint: Murder. Rage and/or revenge. Ruthless aggression. Sexual drive. Power struggles.

Mars/Saturn midpoint: Death. Depression. Frustration or impotence.

Mars/Uranus midpoint: Accident-proneness. Risk-taking. Rebellion.

Moon/Saturn midpoint: Co-dependency—usually, but not always, parental. Maternal deprivation.

Saturn/Pluto midpoint: Cruelty or violent assault. Sadism. Inner compulsions or obsessions.

Sun/Pluto midpoint: Rape and/or homicide. Urge to control. Manipulation.

Sun/Mars midpoint: Violence. Masculine aggression and virility. Assertive, likely to take action.

minor aspect

See "aspect."

Moon/Saturn midpoint

See "midpoint."

Moon

See "planets."

Mutable

Refers to the common flexible qualities or characteristics of the signs Gemini, Virgo, Sagittarius, and Pisces.

mutual reception

A helpful relationship between two planets, each of which occupies the other's sign of rulership or exaltation.

Nadir

The lowest point—the opposite of the Zenith. (Not to be confused with the IC.)

natal

Birth, as in natal chart.

native

Refers to the individual who owns the nativity, or birth chart.

natural cusp ruler

The planet which rules the corresponding sign that would be on the cusp if 0° Aries was the 1st house cusp (Ascendant). For example, Mercury is the *natural ruler* of the 3rd house because Mercury rules the 3rd sign, Gemini.

negative aspect

See "hard" under "aspect, modifying terms for."

Neptune

See "planets."

New Moon

A phase of the Moon; when the Sun and Moon are in conjunction (an aspect of

0° orb), occupying the same sign and degree. It may refer to either a transit or progression, as well as a natal configuration.

Nodes

See "lunar Nodes." There are other planetary nodes besides those of the Moon, but they are referred to rarely.

North Node

See "lunar Nodes."

occupied midpoint

See "midpoint." When planets occupy the empty space on either side of the midpoint it is sometimes called a *tree* or *planetary picture* by cosmobiologists.

opposed, opposing, opposition

See "aspect."

orb

The area of effective influence for an aspect. Progressions require smaller orbs—usually one degree on either side of an exact aspect. The orb for transits and natal planets varies depending on the type of aspect.

outer planets

Uranus, Neptune, and Pluto. Saturn may be thought of as an outer planet by some astrologers, but I consider it a "bridge" planet dividing the inner and outer planets.

parental angle

In natal astrology *parental angle* refers to the 4th and 10th house cusps and all planets occupying or ruling these two angular houses (which describe the parents).

Placidian house system

One of several house systems used to erect charts. The Placidus house system is used for charts consistently throughout this book.

planets

Sun: In astrology, the Sun may stand for the ego or self, and also symbolizes the father and significant males in the life.

Moon: The luminary which astrologically represents the emotional body, feelings, the nurturing or maternal instinct, early childhood, the home, the mother, and important females in the life.

Mercury: This planet represents the mental capacity or mind and travel. In horary astrology, it refers to young people or adolescents.

Venus: In astrology, Venus stands for the social urge, the pleasure principle, love, affection, and beauty. Negatively, it can indicate laziness, and/or lack of will.

Mars: The planet representing the principle of physical force and energy. In a male chart, it represents passion, lust, and/or masculine assertion; negative aspects or afflictions can denote excessive force, aggression, or violence. In horary astrology, Mars refers to stabbing and cutting instruments, gunshots, police, etc. A violent planet when afflicted.

Jupiter: The planet which represents the religious principle. Optimism, expansion, and growth. Negatively, it can indicate greed, self-indulgence, and irresponsibility.

Saturn: Astrologically, Saturn is the "bridge" between the inner and outer planets, and is associated with necessary limitations or frustration due to lack. It can also indicate selfishness, restriction, fears, and anxiety. Death and karma. On the positive side, it stands for discipline and responsibility. It symbolizes the father in natal astrology. In horary astrology, it refers to older or more mature persons.

Uranus: The planet that rules astrology. Associated with sudden events and impulses, freedom, independence, changes, separation, and unconventional or platonic friendships.

Neptune: In natal astrology, the planet associated with idealism, compassion, sympathy, and sacrifice. Negatively it stands for pity, feelings of persecution, deception, and a tendency to escape from reality by using drugs or alcohol. Rules disappearances.

Pluto: Represents transition from one plane to another, death, transformation. Negatively, it represents large gangs or groups, gangsters, and rape. Phobias and obsessions. A violent planet when afflicted.

Pluto
See "planets."

prenatal eclipse (PE)
A solar eclipse occurring just before birth as marked in the natal chart.

progressed
Only *secondary* progressions are used in this book, and they are calculated on the formula that each day after birth is equal to one year of life. See "secondary progressions."

public houses
The six houses above the horizon, from the 7th house to the 12th house consecutively, and the 7th and 10th houses in particular.

qualities
Refers to the division of the twelve signs of the zodiac into three groups (of four signs each) which share common characteristics, or "qualities."

radix
Birth, or *radix*, in reference to a chart.

retrograde
When a planet is apparently traveling backward along the plane of the ecliptic. This apparent motion is only from our viewpoint upon Earth.

rising
Refers to a sign (the Ascendant) or a planet which is rising on or near the eastern horizon, or crossing it. See "eastern horizon."

ruler
In natal astrology, *ruler* usually refers to the planet ruling the Ascendant (and thus is the ruler of the native's chart), but it can also refer to sign or house rulerships. The planet ruling the sign on the house cusp is the ruler of that house, but planets within the house are also influential and may modify interpretations.

Sagittarius
See "signs."

Saturn
See "planets."

Saturn/Pluto midpoint
See "midpoint."

Scorpio
See "signs."

secondary progressions
Aspects formed by planets after birth, based upon a chart calculated for the same time as the natal chart but the *date* changing by one day per year of life. Used by astrologers to predict or track events after birth.

separating aspect
An aspect past the point of being exact. See "exact aspect."

semisextile
See "aspect."

semisquare
See "aspect."

sesquisquare
See "aspect."

sextile
See "aspect."

sign
One of the twelve thirty-degree divisions of the tropical zodiac. The signs follow each other thus: Aries, Taurus, Gemini, Cancer, Leo, Virgo, Libra, Scorpio, Sagittarius, Capricorn, Aquarius, Pisces. A planet is modified by the sign as well as the house it occupies. Each sign has its own distinct meaning—refer to an astrology textbook for an in-depth explanation of each sign.

soft aspect
See "aspect, modifying terms for."

solar eclipse
The phenomenon that occurs only at the time of a New Moon, when the Sun and Moon form a conjunction near one of the Moon's Nodes.

South Node
See "lunar Nodes."

square
See "aspect."

stellium
Three or more planets located in one sign or house, accenting it and thus making it more important.

Sun
See "planets."

Sun/Mars midpoint
See "midpoint."

Sun/Pluto midpoint
See "midpoint."

sunrise chart
A chart calculated for the exact time of the Sun's rising at a certain location, and

usually substituted for a natal chart when the true birthtime is unknown. Unlike a solar chart, it can be progressed.

synastry

Comparison of two or more individual's charts to promote further insight into their relationship, their compatibility, or lack of it. In chart comparison, the astrologer examines the exchange of planetary aspects between two charts, as well as their planetary sign and house positions.

T-square

A dynamic configuration or pattern of two planets in opposition squaring a third planet which forms the base of a "T." Sometimes called a *T-cross*.

Taurus

See "signs."

tight aspect

See "close aspect" and "exact aspect."

time abbreviations

    CDT: Central Daylight Time
    CST: Central Standard Time
    CWT: Central War Time
    EDT: Eastern Daylight Time
    EST: Eastern Standard Time
    GMT: Greenwich Mean Time

transit, transiting

The current position of a planet in comparison to a planet, angle, midpoint, etc. at a different time.

trine

See "aspect."

tropical zodiac

The seasonal or *moving* zodiac beginning with 0° Aries (the point of the Vernal Equinox), in contrast to the sidereal or fixed zodiac of constellations.

Uranian astrology

Sometimes loosely, but erroneously, used to refer to cosmobiology. (See "cosmobiologist.") Uranian astrology is the Hamburg school of astrology founded (1878–1943) by Alfred Witte and Friedrich Sieggrün with an accent on delineations of midpoints. (Witte invented the 90° dial.) Witte observed that hard aspects have more significance than soft aspects. In the 1930s another German astrologer, Reinhold Ebertin, adopted and refined this older system to what is now known as cosmobiology.

Uranus

See "planets."

Venus

See "planets."

Vertex

Abbreviated as "Vx" in the chart. The point in the chart where the prime vertical intersects the ecliptic in the west. The antivertex is the corresponding point exactly opposite in the east. The point where the vertex falls in the chart is supposed to be the most "fated" part of the horoscope.

Violent signs

Aries, Libra, Scorpio, Capricorn, and Aquarius.

Virgo

See "signs."

Water signs

A triplicity of three signs: Cancer, Scorpio, and Pisces.

wide aspect

An aspect having a very wide orb, larger than usual. May also refer to a planet that normally might be out of orb or aspect to another planet, but is part of a T-square, grand trine, or grand square pattern, and therefore is included as part of that configuration.

Zenith

The point in the sky directly overhead which is always exactly ninety degrees in longitude from the Ascendant. It is the opposite point to the Nadir.

zodiac

A distinction should be made between the moving or tropical zodiac which is oriented in relation to the equinoxes, and the sidereal or fixed zodiac which is oriented in relation to the stars or constellations.

The tropical zodiac is divided into a 360-degree circle of twelve thirty-degree divisions of the ecliptic called signs which are used to measure the position of the planets and is the basis of the seasonal calendar. This seasonal zodiac begins with the point of the Vernal Equinox—zero degrees of the first sign, Aries—and when the Sun reaches this point on March 21 every year, it is the beginning of spring.

Bibliography

Bailey, F. Lee, and Harvey Aronson. *The Defense Never Rests*. New York, New York: Stein & Day, 1971.

Baumann, Ed. *Step Into My Parlor: The Chilling Story of Serial Killer Jeffrey Dahmer*. Chicago, Il.: Bonus Books, 1991.

Crockett, Art, ed. *Serial Murderers*. New York: Windsor Publishing Corp., Pinnacle Books, 1990.

Davis, Don. *The Milwaukee Murders — Nightmare in Apartment 213: The True Story*. New York: St. Martin's Press, 1991.

Ebertin, Reinhold. *Astrological Healing: The History and Practice of Astromedicine*. York Beach, Me.: Samuel Weiser, 1989.

_____ *The Combination of Stellar Influences*. Aalen, Germany: Ebertin-Verlag, 1960.

Ellroy, James. *Murder and Mayhem*. Lincolnwood, Il.: Publications International, Signet Books, 1991.

George, Ted, and Barbara Parker. *The Fixed Stars — Health and Behavior Imbalances.* Jacksonville, Fl.: Arthur Publications, 1985.

Gerold, Frank. *The Boston Strangler.* New York, New York: Signet Books, 1966.

Gollmar, Robert H. *Edward Gein.* Chas. Hallberg & Co., Pinnacle Pocket Books, 1981.

Gauquelin, Michel. *Neo-Astrology: A Copernican Revolution.* New York, New York: The Penguin Group/Penguin Books USA, Inc., 1991.

_____ *Birthtimes: A Scientific Investrigation of the Secrets of Astrology.* New York, New York: Straus and Girous/a division of Hill and Wang, 1983.

Lineman, Rose. *Your Prenatal Eclipse.* Tempe, Arizona; American Federation of Astrologers, 1992.

Lisners, John. *House of Horrors.* London: Corgi, 1983.

Lunde, Donald T. *Murder and Madness.* New York: W.W. Norton, 1979.

Masters, Brian. *Killing for Company.* Great Britain: Coronet Books.

Nash, Jay Robert. *Bloodletters and Badmen: A Narrative Encyclopedia of American Criminals.* New York: Evans and Company, 1973.

Parker, Ann E. *Astrology and Alcoholism.* York Beach, Me.: Samuel Weiser, 1982.

Penfield, Marc. *An Astrological Who's Who.* York Harbor, Me.: Arcane Publications.

Rodden, Lois. *Astro Data II.* San Diego, Ca.: Astro Computing Services, 1980.

Rodden, Lois. *Profiles of Crime.* Hollywood, Ca.: Data News Press, 1991.

Rubin, Annette. "The Astrological Common Denominator in the Diagnosed Schizophrenic." *The Astrological Review,* Summer 1969.

Rudhyar, Dane. *The Lunation Cycle.* St. Paul, Minnesota: Llewellyn Publications, 1967.

Schwarz, Ted. *The Hillside Stranglers: A Murderer's Mind.* New York, New York: Signet Books, New American Library, 1982.

Sullivan, Terry, and Peter T. Maiken. *Killer Clown.* Windsor, N.Y.: Paperback, 1991.

Wilson, Colin and Donald Seaman. *The Encyclopedia of Modern Murder.* New York: Arlington House, Crown Publishers, 1988.

On the following pages you will find listed, with their current prices, some of the books now available on related subjects. Your book dealer stocks most of these and will stock new titles in the Llewellyn series as they become available. We urge your patronage.

To Get a Free Catalog

You are invited to write for our bi-monthly news magazine/catalog, *Llewellyn's New Worlds of Mind and Spirit*. A sample copy is free, and it will continue coming to you at no cost as long as you are an active mail customer. Or you may subscribe for just $10 in the United States and Canada ($20 overseas, first class mail). Many bookstores also have *New Worlds* available to their customers. Ask for it.

In *New Worlds* you will find news and features about new books, tapes and services; announcements of meetings and seminars; helpful articles; author interviews; and much more. Write to:

Llewellyn's New Worlds of Mind and Spirit
P.O. Box 64383-K832, St. Paul, MN 55164-0383, U.S.A.

To Order Books and Tapes

If your bookstore does not carry the titles described on the following pages, you may order them directly from Llewellyn by sending the full price in U.S. funds, plus postage and handling (see below).

Credit Card Orders: VISA, MasterCard, American Express are accepted. Call us toll-free within the United States and Canada at 1-800-THE-MOON.

Special Group Discount: Because there is a great deal of interest in group discussion and study of the subject matter of this book, we offer a 20% quantity discount to group leaders or agents. Our Special Quantity Price for a minimum order of five copies of *Destined for Murder* is $51.80 cash-with-order. Include postage and handling charges noted below.

Postage and Handling: Include $4 postage and handling for orders $15 and under; $5 for orders over $15. There are no postage and handling charges for orders over $100. Postage and handling rates are subject to change. We ship UPS whenever possible within the continental United States; delivery is guaranteed. Please provide your street address, as UPS does not deliver to P.O. boxes. Orders shipped to Alaska, Hawaii, Canada, Mexico and Puerto Rico will be sent via first class mail. Allow 4-6 weeks for delivery. **International Orders:** Airmail—add retail price of each book and $5 for each non-book item (audiotapes, etc.); surface mail—add $1 per item.

Minnesota residents add 7% sales tax.

Mail orders to:
Llewellyn Worldwide
P.O. Box 64383-K832, St. Paul, MN 55164-0383, U.S.A.
For customer service, call (612) 291-1970.

The Instant Horoscope Reader
Planets by Sign, House and Aspect
by Julia Lupton Skalka

Find out what was written in the planets at your birth! Almost everyone enjoys reading the popular Sun sign horoscopes in newspapers and magazines; however, there is much more to astrology than knowing what your Sun sign is. How do you interpret your natal chart so that you know what it means to have Gemini on your 8th house cusp? What does astrology say about someone whose Sun is conjoined with natal Jupiter?

   The Instant Horoscope Reader was written to answer such questions and to give beginners a fresh, thorough overview of the natal chart. Here you will find the meaning of the placement of the Sun, the Moon and each planet in the horoscope, including aspects between the natal planets, the meaning of the houses in the horoscope and house rulerships. Even if you have not had your chart cast, this book includes simple tables that enable you to locate the approximate planetary and house placements and figure the planetary aspects for your birthdate to give you unique perspectives about yourself and others.

ISBN: 1-56718-669-6, 6 x 9, 272 pp., illus. **$14.95**

Time & Money
The Astrology of Wealth—How You Can Anticipate the Changing Times and Turn Them to Financial Advantage
by Barbara Koval

This book is about using a 2,000-year-old accumulation of knowledge to understand money, what it does, where it's heading, and how to make it work for you. *Time & Money* is based on the premise that astrology and its symbols form a theoretical model that contains almost everything you need to know about economic principles and trends. Using astrology, *Time & Money* demonstrates patterns of economic activity that enable the average person to dig through the hysteria that is seeping into our consciousness due to bank failures, national debt, and unemployment.

   Time & Money is for everyone. Students of astrology will gain an understanding of financial and economic analysis as well as mundane astrology. Investors, market analysts, and students of cycles will find much to apply to their own knowledge of fundamental and technical analyses of the financial markets—timings that can be enhanced by simple references to ephemerides and astrological charts.

0-87542-364-7, 352 pgs., 6 x 9, softcover **$12.95**